DOWN & DIRTY: DAWG

Dirty Angels MC, Book 7

JEANNE ST. JAMES

———

Editor: Proofreading by the Page
Cover Art: Susan Garwood of Wicked Women Designs
Beta Readers: Author Whitley Cox, Krisztina Hollo, Andi Babcock and Nessa Kreyling

———

www.jeannestjames.com

Sign up for my newsletter for insider information, author news, and new releases:
www.jeannestjames.com/newslettersignup

❀ Created with Vellum

Warning: This book contains sexually explicit scenes and adult language and may be considered offensive to some readers. This book is for sale to adults ONLY, as defined by the laws of the country in which you made your purchase. Please store your files wisely, where they cannot be accessed by under-aged readers.

————

DISCLAIMER: Please do not try any new sexual practice (BDSM or otherwise) without the guidance of an experienced practitioner. The author will not be responsible for any loss, harm, injury or death resulting from use of the information contained in this book.

————

Keep an eye on her website at http://www.jeannestjames.com/or sign up for her newsletter to learn about her upcoming releases: http://www.jeannestjames.com/newslettersignup

Down & Dirty 'til Dead

AUTHOR'S NOTE

It's hard to believe that Dawg's story is the eighth book in the DAMC series. There was something about the big, bad, bearded biker that hit me right in the feelz. Dawg quickly burrowed himself into my heart. And I have a feeling he'll remain there for quite a while.

Dear reader, I hope that Dawg's story hits you right in the feelz as well. While reading, if you have to use a tissue or two... #sorrynotsorry

CHAPTER ONE

"For fuck's sake," Dawg muttered. He glanced at the digital clock that was hidden behind the bar for the tenth time.

The bitch was late.

She'd begged him for an audition, even though his stable was full.

Her soft, husky voice over the phone finally convinced him to say yes. Against his better judgement, of course. Because when he asked her if she was experienced, she beat around the fucking bush.

Which meant she wasn't. And he had no patience for amateurs or novices.

None what-so-fucking-ever.

Scrubbing a hand over his beard, he shot a glance at the front entrance, then at the clock once more.

He grabbed a cold Iron City beer from the cooler behind the bar, popped the tab on the can and lifted it to his lips.

He was done.

No bitch was worth the wait.

None.

He'd been stood up. Almost like a bad date. Though it had

been a long time since he'd been on anything that was even remotely similar to one.

Well, unless fucking some random snatch until she came all over him was considered a date. Most likely it wasn't. An actual date probably included flowers, a movie and even dinner.

Or at least a shot of whiskey and a little fingering, before busting a nut.

"Fuck you, bitch. Dawg waits for no one," he muttered to the sweating beer can in his hand, then took another swallow of the ice-cold brew.

But, fuck him, if he didn't stand there and wait even longer. Again, it was that smooth as warm honey voice that made him keep his ass planted right where he was. He'd give her until he finished his beer. Then he'd head back up to his apartment, knock a quick one out with his own palm, and catch some more zzz's.

He slammed the can onto the bar, causing it to splash over his fist. With another curse, he wiped his dripping hand along his jeans.

Then he heard the door open down the front corridor and a sliver of *ass-crack-of-dawn* sunlight reflected off the wall. Suddenly a woman was standing at the end of the hall, pale as shit and eyes wide. Like a skittish doe about to be plowed down by a Mack truck.

Raking his gaze over her from top to toe, the first thing that hit him was she had sweet fucking tits. If they were real, she already had a leg up on this audition. The second was...

She was wearing a fucking high-neck blouse.

Who the fuck wore a boring beige top that covered her as much as a turtleneck to a stripper audition?

Her waist was narrow, her hips curvy, and...

She wore a skirt all the way to her fucking ankles.

And she wasn't even wearing heels!

"What the fuck," he muttered.

Maybe she was confused and was looking for a church nearby.

While there were a lot of "Oh Gods!" being said in his establishment, they were usually during private lap dances.

"Are you Dawson?"

A muscle ticked in his jaw as his teeth clenched. Dawson? He hadn't heard that name spoken out loud in a long damn time.

"Dawg," he grunted.

She blinked, but remained at the end of the corridor. He wanted to see what color those eyes of hers were and if they matched the husky tone of her voice.

"Dog? Like the woof-woof kind of dog?"

"What the fuck," he muttered once more. "No, like *Dawg*... D-A-W-G."

She tilted her head and studied him. There was another thing wrong with her... Her hair was pulled up high and tight. His customers liked his girls' hair long and loose. So they could swing it when they danced. So the men could imagine fisting it while they fantasized about one of his girls sucking them off. Or picture pulling it like the reins of a pony while fucking one of them doggy-style and slapping their ass.

Which never happened on his watch. Fuck no. His girls weren't whores. They were "exotic entertainers." They didn't put out for money. If they did, and he found out about it, they were outside looking in faster than they could say "G-string." He ran a respectable joint and certainly didn't need Shadow Valley PD breathing down his goddamn neck.

Though some of them did give it up to his brothers in the Dirty Angels MC, that was their choice and not for money. None were forced to do it. It had to be a mutual agreement between the brother and the girl.

A little reciprocal pleasure.

As he stared at the woman still hovering by the nearest escape route, he doubted this woman would give it up to any biker. She seemed way too uptight for that.

"I-I think I made a mistake."

That was an understatement. "I'd fuckin' say so."

Dawg finished off his beer, crumpled the can in his hand and whipped it into the recycle bin under the counter, then rounded the end of the bar.

Her eyes widened once again when he approached her. Which kind of, sort of, bothered him.

Yeah, he knew he could be a little intimidating. He was a big dude. He had a beard. He had a bunch of tats. He wore bulky silver rings on his thick fingers and a cut proclaiming that he was DAMC and damn proud of it. But he wasn't a man who hurt women.

Fuck no. When they screamed it was because he was licking their pussy so good that...

Fuck. Now he had half a fucking hard-on. And if he yanked on it to adjust it to a more comfortable position, she might just pee her panties. Or bloomers. Or whatever the fuck she wore under that awful shit-brown skirt.

"Don't know what you're lookin' for, but it ain't here."

He couldn't miss how hard she swallowed before taking a tentative step forward. "I called you about an audition."

Dawg eyeballed her up and down in slow motion on purpose, so she'd realize this place wasn't for her. When color flooded her cheeks, it cemented his opinion.

"What fuckin' stripper wears a goddamn shirt that don't show any cleavage an' a skirt—" he lifted a ringed finger, "—not short and leather, fuck no. One that covers her down to her ankles?"

She glanced down at herself for a second, then looked back up at him and shrugged slightly. "A kindergarten teacher."

Dawg's head jerked back. "A fuckin' what?"

She cleared her throat and pulled her shoulders back. *Which* he just happened to notice emphasized those big-ass tits. "A kindergarten teacher."

He blinked and let what she said sink in. "You wanna role play when you strip? My clientele might like that. Kinda like a sexy librarian. Or a sexy teacher who knows how to use a wooden ruler in a good way, but you gotta drop the 'kindergarten' shit. That might be a turnoff."

She shook her head and bravely took another step forward. Now she was only a few feet from him, causing his nostrils to flare when he caught a whiff of her scent. Flowers. Or something light. Nothing heavy and clingy like his girls wore.

And from where he stood, he didn't think she had a stitch of makeup on.

"No. I'm a real teacher. I teach kindergarten. You know, with children?"

He frowned. If she was a teacher, what the fuck was she doing in his club? Dawg waved his arm around Heaven's Angels Gentlemen's Club. "Does this look like a fuckin' kiddie school to you?"

Her head lifted slightly higher when she answered, "No."

He studied her for a second and decided he needed a better look. "Step under the light so I can see you better," he ordered. In no way was this woman here for any kind of audition. He pointed to the recessed light in the ceiling that was closest to him.

After a slight hesitation she did it. She bit her bottom lip and held it between her teeth as he checked her out once more. The lip thing was pushing the blood into his dick at an alarming rate. Which was surprising since the way she was dressed did nothing for him.

He took a step closer and her body wavered slightly, but she didn't back up even though she barely came up to his chin.

"Look up," he demanded. And when she did, he finally saw how blue her big eyes were.

Even though she held his gaze, she was nervous, and he could see the determination in her. She had a fire in her belly. He liked that. The woman was here for a reason and that reason was important, whatever it was.

Her blonde hair looked like her real color. Not all bleached out like some of his girls. He hated that shit and yelled at them all the time for it. He wanted his girls to look as natural as possible, but it was a losing battle.

But all that blonde hair was pulled back tight at the back of her head in a bun or whatever they were called. Similar to how Bella wore her hair when she was working in the bakery to keep it out of the cupcakes and icing and shit.

Her face was, just as he thought, clean of any makeup, naturally pretty, even wholesome looking. A perfect example of the *girl-next-door*.

But something about her was definitely not *girl-next-door* if she was here for a job.

"If you're a kindergarten teacher, you already got a job," he murmured, fighting to keep from reaching out and running a knuckle along her cheek to test how soft her flawless ivory skin felt.

"I need the money," she whispered back, not breaking his gaze. A spark had flared in her eyes when she admitted that.

Being a stripper wasn't one of her career goals. Fuck no. Probably wasn't even on her bucket list. She needed cold, hard cash. That was the real reason she was standing before him, trying desperately to hide her fear of him. She thought that flashing her tits would be a windfall, would get her out of whatever financial jam she was in.

"For what?"

She dropped her gaze and shook her head. "That's personal."

This woman was here for the wrong reasons.

Suddenly, he was feeling generous. "Look, if you need some scratch... a loan..."

Her eyes flicked back up to him. "No, no loan. I'm already in debt because of..."

"'Cause of what?"

She swallowed hard. "Nothing."

"Ain't nothin'."

She sucked in a breath. "Just forget it. I'm sure there are other clubs in the area who will give me a chance."

Though he needed fresh faces and fresh bodies to bring in new clientele, and to keep the regulars coming back, he didn't need any right now and he was sure he would regret his next decision.

When she turned to leave, he grabbed her wrist. "Hold up."

She stared at where he held her, her wrist looking tiny in his hand. He loosened his grip slightly since he didn't want the bulky rings on his fingers to bruise her, but not enough where she could slip away.

"What's your name?"

"What?"

"Your name. What's your name?" Dawg barked.

"E-Emma."

He already knew her real name; she had told him it on the phone. "No. Your stage name."

The confusion on her face was another telling sign that she didn't belong in his club, or even on a stage. And certainly not naked in front of a crowd of men, for fuck's sake.

"Em..." She hesitated. Then with a look of understanding, she began again, "Em... Ember!"

Ember. Fitting for that flame inside her. "Better. Can't have a kiddie-garden teacher named Emma on my fuckin' stage."

Her eyes widened in surprise. "You're going to give me a shot?"

Fuck. His big dumb ass was going to regret this. "Gonna give you an audition. Nothin' more 'til I see what you can do."

Relief crossed her face, and it made him shake his head.

He was such a fucking sucker.

He released her wrist. "Got an outfit you need to change into?" He jerked his chin toward the back of the club. "Dressin' room's in the back."

She glanced down at what she was wearing *again*. As if she didn't find anything wrong with that shit she covered herself up with from neck to toe. She could be going door to door, preaching religious shit and handing out pamphlets, dressed like that.

"I'm wearing it."

His lips twitched. Sure she was. "Got you. Wearin' it underneath that getup."

Her mouth opened, then it snapped shut. *Right*.

"I-I have to dance for my audition?"

His eyebrows shot up his forehead. "No, you're gonna hand me your fuckin' resume an' I'm gonna look it over... Of fuckin' course you gotta dance. Jesus fuckin' Christ." He turned on his heels and ducked behind the bar.

Normally on busy nights he had a DJ playing. During the day and on slow nights, he just used the high-tech sound system that was wired throughout the club. Each VIP room had their own smaller system, so the girls could pick whatever music they wanted for private dances. Then there was also a room off the main stage area for private parties, VIPs and special traveling entertainment troupes. It was a smaller version of the main club area, with its own stage and a bar.

He had to admit that his club was the shit and the nicest in the greater Pittsburgh area, if he said so himself.

He glanced at the woman who remained frozen in place near the entrance. "What music?"

"What do you mean?"

"What do you wanna dance to?"

She blinked at him.

"Ah, fuck. You don't have a routine ready an' a song picked out?" Of course not. All the red flags in his head were whipping in the wind.

"Should I have?"

This whole thing was going to be a disaster. He should just chase her out of there and stop wasting both of their time.

But he couldn't. He was dying to see what was underneath that virgin-like outfit of hers. If she had potential, he could get one of his seasoned dancers to give her a few pointers.

Yep, that's what he told himself. Had nothing to do with him wanting to check her out for himself. Fuck no. She didn't make him curious at all.

"Rock? Country? R&B? What?" he prodded.

When she didn't answer, he scrolled through his music and found a song that worked well to get his girls moving on stage. He set up the track and, grabbing the remote, headed down the long, narrow stage that was dead center in the main club area. It had a pole, from stage to ceiling, on each end and the bar was attached to the end closest to the entrance.

He settled his bulk into one of the low, vinyl club chairs that sat directly in front of one of the poles. He wanted a good seat and a very clear view.

He glanced her way. "Need help gettin' up on stage?" He jerked his chin toward the steps. "Stairs are down on this end."

She unfroze herself, shook her head and moved toward the back of the club where the three steps led to the lighted stage.

"Might wanna take those things off your fuckin' feet first," he suggested. He wasn't sure what they were called, but they were the most unsexy shoes he'd ever seen on a woman. Besides Crocs. Those gave him limp dick. Her shoes were a close second. Some kind of brown pleather shit.

She got to the end of the stage, bent over to unstrap her shoes, then kicked them off. Straightening her spine, she blew out a breath and climbed onto the stage.

Dawg leaned back in his chair and crossed his arms over his chest. "Lemme know when you're ready, *Ember*. I'll hit the music."

She nodded and eyeballed the pole.

"Poles are clean," he reassured her. "Cleaning crew just left 'bout an hour ago."

With a little nod, she wrapped a hand around it. He really wanted her to fist that hot little hand around his dick instead.

He sighed. "Gotta plan, right?"

Her gaze dropped to him. "Yes. Get naked."

Well, damn. "Normally gotta keep your bottoms on. Ain't legal to take 'em off when we're open to the public. But since the club's closed, leavin' that up to you. Sometimes I give private parties for my VIPs an' the girls go totally naked. They really rake in the tips those nights."

"I'll keep that in mind."

"You do that," Dawg said and then snorted, shaking his head.

"Okay," she said softly, staring up at the pole.

He cocked an eyebrow at her. "Okay, what?"

"I'm ready."

Dawg pinned his lips together. "Sure?"

She nodded, a determined look on her face.

Dawg shrugged and hit *play* on the remote. Ginuwine's *Pony* began to blast through the hidden speakers.

Her body jerked at the sound. "What's this?"

"Music. Just go with it."

She bit her bottom lip again, and that went straight to his dick. Then she began to move...

He was hoping he'd been wrong, and she was a secret little slut with hot moves that would make him want to bust a nut. But fuck no, she wasn't. Her hips moved in a wooden circular motion as she held a death grip onto the pole with one hand.

Dawg groaned. This was going to be worse than he thought. As she tried to match the rhythm of the song, she threw her head back and closed her eyes, letting the music move through her.

Dawg sat forward in his chair. Maybe this wouldn't be so bad...

She reached up to pull her hair clip out, and her golden hair cascaded down around her.

Holy fuck.

All that blonde hair and her natural looks...

He lost his breath as she continued to shift around awkwardly but reached for the top button of her blouse. Which was promising...

With visibly shaking hands, she worked the buttons out of their holes one by one, and as the fabric gaped, he caught glimpses of a black bra underneath.

He attempted to swallow the lump in his throat and he willed her fingers to move faster.

The little he saw was no grandma panty set. Fuck no, it wasn't. He swore he got a glimpse of see-through lace.

She stopped unbuttoning when she got to her waist and reached around to the back of her skirt. Suddenly it shifted when it became loose and she caught his gaze as she began to push it down her hips.

The "suggestive" wink she gave him looked more like an eye twitch.

Even though this woman had the seduction skills of an eighty-year-old virgin, Dawg's breath caught.

She stopped moving around the stage as she rolled the long skirt down her thighs. But he couldn't see shit since her baggy blouse covered the V of her legs. He wouldn't be surprised if the woman had a huge untrimmed bush trying to escape her panties.

Finally, the skirt dropped to her feet and she stepped out of it, almost tripping herself. He jerked forward as if he could catch her, but she caught her own balance and then stood there unsure, wearing just her blouse partially unbuttoned.

His eyes slid from her face down to her legs. What the fuck?

She was wearing thigh-high stockings!

Maybe she wasn't lying about wearing an "outfit" under her conservative clothing.

But she just stood there, staring at him!

"You done?"

She shook her head. And, fuck him, she bit that bottom lip of hers again. That was going to be her signature move. She could do some sort of naughty teacher routine, and bite her bottom lip, while giving his customers an *I-need-to-be-fucked* look.

They'd be throwing twenties at her. Fuck, maybe even fifties.

She had no idea just how dick-hardening sexy she appeared with all that blonde hair loose, wearing thigh-highs and that half-open blouse. Like her brains had just been fucked out, and she was in a sex coma.

Jesus. He needed to see the rest of her. But not up on that stage. That was too impersonal, and he wanted to get so much more personal.

"Maybe that big stage's makin' you nervous. How 'bout makin' this dance a little more personal."

Her brows furrowed. "How?"

"Gotta show me somethin'. Some kinda skill. Right now, you ain't showin' me nothin' I wanna see."

For the most part anyway. Nothing a strip club manager would
want to see. Dawg, the man? Fuck yeah. That was different.

He pushed to his feet and came around to the steps, holding
out his hand. She stayed where she was on the stage, her skirt
pooled at her feet, her blouse hanging crooked. She stared at his
hand as if it was going to bite her.

"All my girls gotta do private dances... you know, lap dances.
Get up close an' personal with my customers. Makes both of us
some extra scratch. Better than the tips you'll make on stage. The
stage is just used to entice these fuckers into the VIP rooms. Got
me? It's the tease. Gotta get 'em droolin' for you, get 'em rock
hard. Make 'em think they got a shot with you. They pay big
money for that personal time. That's where you make most of your
scratch. You act like they're special to you, not just any regular Joe,
an' they'll become regulars. The regulars are the best. They'll even
ask you out. You always say no, got me? No datin' the customers.
No fuckin' 'em, either."

"Am I hired?" she asked, surprise clearly in her voice.

No shit. He was just as surprised that he was wasting time on
this woman who had no fucking clue what she was getting herself
into.

"Nope. Ain't hirin' you yet. Gotta convince me to. Just like you
gotta convince the customers to throw those dollar bills on that
stage. Right now, you've only convinced me that you're lost."

"What do you mean?"

"That you don't belong here. This ain't for you."

She nodded. "You're right. That's exactly what I am. I'm lost."

Well, damn. He hadn't expected for her to agree.

Dawg dragged a hand through his hair that needed a damn cut
and shook his head. "Woman, you're crazy for bein' here. This ain't
you. Anyone can see it."

"No. I'm not crazy. I'm... I'm desperate. I need this... this job."

"Strippin' ain't a job, it's a career." One that could be lucrative
for the right woman. Only she wasn't the right woman.

"What do I need to do to get this job?"

The desperation in her voice, in her eyes, killed him, twisted his gut.

"Like I said. Money's in the lap dance. Gotta sell yourself. Right now, you ain't sellin' nothin' 'cept that you're an uptight teacher up there. C'mon down." He held out his hand again. She grabbed her skirt and approached the end of the stage, but avoided his assistance. She took two steps down until her gaze was level with his.

"I need this," she whispered.

He wanted to close his eyes and savor that honeyed voice of hers. But he didn't. He had to remind himself that this was business. "Why?"

"I-I have to make a lot of money and make it fast." The desperation was thick in her voice. And that bugged him.

"Why?"

Instead of answering him, she shook her head.

"Girls ain't got no secrets from me."

"So you think."

Damn. She was probably right. But when they were down on their luck, and they needed help, he was always there for them. He took care of his girls, made sure they didn't want for anything, and in turn, they took care of him. They came to work with a good attitude, and that spilled out on stage.

Happy strippers made the club money, ones with problems didn't. It was difficult to shake off a bad attitude when you were in the spotlight swinging around a pole only wearing a thong. There was nothing to hide up there.

He knew it. The clientele knew it. So he kept his girls happy.

"I'm going to ask again. What do I need to do to get this job?"

CHAPTER TWO

Dawg sat in a wood chair at the center of one of the private VIP rooms. Though the room had a couch—that he had cleaned on a regular basis—he preferred the chair. Why? Because the dancer had three-sixty access to him.

In a VIP room, the dancer could touch her customer. She could take it as far as she wanted to go, except for accepting payment for sex. Again, he wasn't putting up with that bullshit, because if the club got shut down, the MC would lose a huge portion of their income. And he had to do his part in keeping the DAMC coffers full.

He had taken Emma to the Red room, rightly named since everything in it was the color of blood and his was certainly pumping right now. His pulse was also thumping in his neck and his dick throbbing.

Emma stood in front of him, her fingers unfastening the rest of the buttons on her blouse, her hips swaying to another Ginuwine song that he had turned on when they first entered the room.

She seemed a little more comfortable in here, but not by much. He figured the large stage had been a bit too intimidating for this woman, who so clearly lost her fucking way.

"Woman, gotta act like I just paid you a Benjamin for two songs. You better make it worth my hard-earned money."

She glanced up from fiddling with her buttons. "Okay," she said softly, tossing her head to get her long, loose hair out of her face.

Fuck. He needed to just stop all this right here and now. He needed for her to pull that long, ugly skirt back on and then he needed to push her back out of the front door and lock it behind her.

That's what he needed to do.

He was just about to tell her all that when the last button popped free and her blouse gaped open. Then she started to move.

Suddenly she was channeling her inner Demi Moore from the movie *Striptease*. But not nearly as good.

She walked around him, attempting to strut, and placed a hand on his shoulder, then moved around behind him to push her chest against him.

What the fuck?

Her warm breath and her husky voice was suddenly in his ear. "You mean like this?"

Fuck yeah, like that.

He'd seen a lot of fucking lap dances, and hell, he'd done hundreds of auditions, so he'd received them himself. They were simply a part of the job. On a rare occasion, his body would react. But his reaction to this woman...

Fuck.

Like nothing he ever had before during a simple audition. And she wasn't even good at it. That was the fucked up part. She completely bombed when it came to doing a lap dance. Just like she had done on the big stage.

When she finished circling him, her blouse was hanging off her shoulders, but she was holding the fabric up to her tits, fucking hiding them.

That wouldn't do at all.

When he opened his mouth to tell her that, she slipped the blouse lower, and the black lace of her bra became visible.

His head jerked back.

When she dropped the blouse to her feet, and he saw her panties, he just about shot out of the chair.

Those were just as lacy. He was right; this was no lingerie set from a discount bargain barn that grandma shopped at.

Fuck no.

He not only lost all the oxygen in his lungs, but the remaining blood in his brain was now pooled in his dick.

The woman was hiding a hot little body on her under those ugly-ass clothes.

Fuck. And those tits...

"Wasn't expectin' that," he murmured before he could stop himself.

She gave him a small smile. "I might be a kindergarten teacher, but I'm not dead."

Fuck. His dick wasn't dead, either. Nope, it was fucking telling him just how alive he was.

When she reached back to unhook her bra, he jumped up from his chair and barked, "No!"

She jerked back at his shout and dropped her hands.

"No, that's enough. Fuck!" He raked his hand through his hair and dropped his gaze to his boots as he tried to slow his racing heart.

There was nothing he wanted more than to sit back on that chair, pull her into his lap and have her ride him until his nuts were completely empty.

But he couldn't do that.

She needed to get the fuck out of his club.

"Did I do something wrong?"

"Yeah, you came to the wrong place." He shook his head, trying to clear his lecherous thoughts. She'd probably run screaming if she knew just how much he was struggling to keep his hands off her. "You gotta go. Get your shit an' get the fuck out."

Her sweet, little mouth gaped open. "Why? What did I do?"

Scrambled my brain and made my dick harder than steel. "Nothin'. You didn't do nothin'. You gotta go."

"Mr. Dawson."

"Dawg!" he corrected her, louder than necessary.

"Mr. Dawg..."

"Just Dawg! Fuckin' goddamn it."

"Dawg. I really need this. *Please.*"

He shook his head, avoiding her pleading eyes. "No. No. Fuck no."

"I promise to get better. I'll work on my moves. I'll—"

He shook his head even harder. "No."

"Please!"

She dropped to her knees at his feet and grabbed his thighs, scaring the shit out of him. He jumped back. What the fuck was she doing?

She turned her face up, her light blue eyes brimming with tears, her ivory skin now sheet white. "Please," she begged again. "Please. I'll do whatever you want. I just... I—"

He grabbed her elbows and hauled her to her feet. "What the fuck you doin'? You offerin' me sex for this job?"

Her eyes widened. "No! No! I didn't mean to—" A tear rolled unchecked down her cheek. "I'm sorry. I—"

He grabbed her upper arms and gave her a little shake. "You gotta be straight with me. What the fuck's goin' on?"

"N-nothing."

He released her and stepped back. "Get the fuck outta my club."

"I'm sorry, I—"

"You're hidin' somethin' an' I don't wanna be a part of that shit. Get your clothes on an' get out."

———

E mma sat in her car in the empty parking lot. She could barely read the large sign she was parked next to, the tears in her eyes making her surroundings blurry. Heaven's Angels Gentlemen's Club.

This was what she'd been reduced to. Throwing herself at some big, tattooed biker and begging him to let her strip, for Christ's sake.

Strip. *Her.* Emma Jackson. Kindergarten teacher.

She was so desperate for money, she was willing to take her clothes off on a stage and let men toss dollar bills at her. To take strange men into a private room and *touch* them.

She dropped her head down until her forehead pressed against the steering wheel. She didn't know what else to do. She had no one to go to.

She only needed to do it long enough to get the money together for a retainer. Problem was, she needed to get the best. And she couldn't afford the best.

Hell, she couldn't afford the worst, either.

A kindergarten teacher's salary was crap. She lived paycheck to paycheck as it was, even living modestly. She never splurged on anything for herself. Not anymore.

She ran her fingers over her second-hand skirt. She couldn't even afford to buy new clothes. She was forced to shop at consignment shops just to get a decent wardrobe for work.

And now she didn't even have that job.

She grabbed the plastic hair clip in her lap and, gathering her hair in her hands, she twisted it into a knot and secured it to the back of her head.

She couldn't give up. She could *never* give up. She would do whatever she needed to do, or she would die first.

Because if she was forced to live life without her daughter she might as well be dead.

———

D awg squeezed his eyes shut as hard as his fist squeezed his dick. Even with his eyes closed, he couldn't get the picture of Emma out of his head. Her image was burned into the back of his eyelids.

How could a woman who dressed so damn awful turn him the fuck on so much?

It wasn't just her voice. Even under those Plain Jane clothes, it was the way she carried herself, even when she'd been nervous. The way she faced her fears head-on. The way she was determined to get him to hire her.

But no fucking way was that happening. First of all, she sucked at dancing. Second, even if she was good at it, he wasn't sure if he could sit there night after night and watch her shake her tits at other men.

He tilted his head back on his pillow and imagined what those tits would have looked like if he'd let her continue to remove that surprisingly sexy bra. Perfect ivory skin, pink hard-tipped nipples. Fuck, he wanted to bury his face in between them. Or his dick. Whatever.

He opened his eyes, spit on his palm and then went back to his fantasy. His hips lifted off the bed with each downward stroke, then dropped back to the mattress on the upstroke.

"Fuck!" he bellowed to the ceiling. His palm sucked. It was nothing like the real thing.

He needed some warm, tight, wet pussy hugging his dick, riding him hard. Tits bouncing and slapping together as she rode him like he was a wild pony. *She.* No, not just any she.

Emma.

It wasn't even a sexy name. It matched her kindergarten teacher job.

She'd only be a fantasy. Only be jerk-off material. Because a woman like her didn't do bikers like him.

He'd learned that lesson the hard way. Never again. That's why he liked it the easy way now.

He wasn't looking for another headache. He had enough headaches keeping his girls in line. He didn't need another one.

Even if she had sweet tits, a *bangin'* body, and hair he wanted to wrap around his fist when she was on her knees...

Fuck. Like when she was on her knees begging him for a job.

"For fuck's sake!" he bellowed again and sat up, giving up on jerking off.

The woman needed help, and he wanted to know why. How could an innocent-looking teacher be so damn desperate? What the fuck did she do to get herself in a jam like that?

Maybe innocent Emma wasn't so innocent after all. Maybe she was a dirty girl...

He frowned. *What the fuck?*

He sighed. He needed to get laid. Dropping his legs over the edge of the bed, he glanced at the clock radio on his nightstand. Ten-thirty. Moose should be downstairs by now to unlock the back door for the daylight girls to come in and get ready for an eleven AM opening.

He scratched his balls and yawned. He needed more sleep. He'd probably be up until after closing and Emma's little audition early this morning had cut into that time.

Who the fuck was he kidding? He wasn't going to get another wink of fucking sleep until he took the edge off. There were possible two ways to do that. Booze or knocking one out.

Rubbing a hand over his eyes, he moved over to the kitchenette in his apartment and opened a cabinet. He grabbed a bottle of Jack, unscrewed the cap and tipped it to his lips.

Dawg held his breath as the liquor filled his empty stomach then he slammed the bottle onto the counter, wincing through the burn.

Maybe that would help.

Dawg peered down at his still-hard dick. Maybe not.

CHAPTER THREE

Emma shut her car off and took a slow, deep breath. She glanced down at her outfit one more time. She made sure to pick something out of her closet this time that might not reflect her day job.

Or what used to be her day job. Before she had been "let go." Like those words softened the blow.

They didn't.

She needed this job at Heaven's Angels. The school year was over, and no one was hiring teachers anywhere at the moment. And even if they were, the salary wouldn't be enough for her needs.

So, she had dragged out her oldest snug jeans with a ripped-out knee, her tightest blouse—leaving enough buttons undone to give him a good eye full of her cleavage—and yanked on an old pair of heels she found at the back of her closet. Unfortunately, her feet were already killing her and all she did was walk in them out to her car.

She also had given the club manager plenty of time to cool down while she went home, got on the internet and did some research. Who knew that YouTube was a wealth of information on how to strip?

After dragging out her full-length mirror, she'd set her laptop up where she could see it and practiced for the past few hours. Until she was pretty sure she had a routine down pat.

When she came back more determined than ever to show this strip club manager how serious she was, she found the front door to the club locked. Not willing to give up that easily, she drove around back hoping she'd find another entrance. Like an employee entrance. A way to get back inside and beg for a second chance.

As she was preparing herself mentally in what she could assume was the employee parking lot, another car pulled up next to her and a female got out.

Emma scrambled from her car and called out to her. "Hi!" She added a little wave to be extra friendly, to show she was harmless and not some stripper stalker.

The woman wrestled a huge purse out of the car and slammed the door shut, before turning and giving Emma a suspicious look. "Yeah?"

"I... uh... I'm looking for Dawson."

The platinum blonde gave Emma the side-eye and a frown. "Dawson?"

What the hell was his nickname? Doug? Dog? *Ah...* "Dawg."

A knowing look crossed the other woman's face. "It's early yet. He's probably up in his place." She lifted her chin toward the back steps of the building.

"His place?"

The blonde pursed her bright red lips and studied Emma for a second. Probably wondering if she was some psycho bitch ready to take down her boss. "Yeah, he lives above the club. In the apartment there."

Emma glanced up and saw a light on in one of the windows. When she dropped her gaze, the dancer was gone and the back door with the sign "Employees Only" was shutting.

"Hey!" *Damn it.* She was hoping the woman would be willing to give her some pointers.

She sighed, then wobbled in her heels over to the metal steps to stare up them.

She was about to put herself in a position she knew better than to put herself in., but she had no choice. A minimum wage job just wouldn't cut it. She needed cash, and she needed a lot of it as soon as possible. And the banks refused to loan it to her. She had no assets, no income, nothing.

Not even family to beg, borrow or steal from.

She was desperate, and she was not leaving until she had this job.

She would do whatever she had to do to get her daughter back.

The first step was the most difficult and once she took that, Emma hurried up the rest of the stairs until she was staring at the plain steel door to this Dawg's apartment.

Taking a bolstering breath, she raised her fist and rapped on the door.

She waited.

Nothing.

She knocked again.

Nothing.

The third time she thumped as loud as she could. She got an answering shout but had no idea of what it consisted of.

As *who-she-assumed-was-Dawg* approached the front door, she heard a muffled grumble and a curse.

Crap, he was still in a bad mood. That didn't bode well for her.

The deadbolt clicked, and the door was thrown open.

Emma's jaw dropped, and she stepped back so quickly she teetered precariously in her heels. Before she could catch her balance, two large hands grabbed her arms and she was yanked upright hard enough to cause whiplash.

"What the fuck?" he bellowed, making her wince. "What the fuck you doin' here?"

His gaze raked her from head to toe and Emma struggled to hide the shiver that skittered down her spine.

That shiver wasn't from fear because, *goodness gracious*, she couldn't help but do the same to him. He was a big guy, that was for sure. And this time, he was practically naked. Maybe not *quite* naked. But close enough, since he only had a pair of unfastened jeans hanging off his hips like they had been pulled on in haste.

His dark blond hair was mussed, his narrowed emerald green eyes dark, and he wore no shirt.

None at all.

Holy moly.

Never in her life had she seen a human being with so many tattoos.

So. Many. Tattoos.

Down his sculpted arms, over his muscular chest and belly, and she could even see one peeking from the opening in his jeans. And he clearly wore no underwear because she noticed there was no end to the dark line of hair that went from his belly button all the way south.

Her gaze traced the line of an erection that was hard to miss under his denim. Heat flooded her cheeks, and she dropped her eyes quickly, only to have it land on his bare feet.

Lord, he had good looking feet.

She shook herself mentally at that thought and her gaze shot back up, but not before hesitating for a split second on that V where his jeans hung open. She silently scolded herself, then met his eyes.

He was grinning. Even with that thick beard that was darker than his hair covering his face, he was a good-looking man.

"Like what you see?"

"I... uh..." *Yes!* "No!"

His smile widened. "Bullshit. Whataya here for?"

She peeked over his shoulder into the dimly lit apartment. "Umm... Can I come in?"

He blinked. "For what?"

"I need to talk to you."

One of his eyebrows cocked. "Got nothin' to talk about."

"I beg to differ."

"Begged earlier. Didn't work. Ain't gonna work now."

She bit her bottom lip but released it as soon as his eyes focused on that and his smile disappeared.

Without warning, he reached out and brushed his thumb gently over her bottom lip which caused her heart to thump wildly.

He murmured, "That right there, baby girl…" His hand suddenly dropped, and he stepped back, his voice becoming colder. "That right there's enough to get me in trouble. What do you want?"

"A second chance."

A muscle in his jaw ticked as he studied her. "You failed—"

"I know. I know! I didn't realize that—"

"Strippin's an art? Not everyone's got the skill to do it?"

"I can do it, I swear!"

His hands settled on his hips as his head dropped back and he stared up at the door frame above him. He blew out a noisy breath.

She was pushing his patience. She knew that. But she wasn't leaving. Not until she did what she came to do. "Please… Let me audition again… or give you another lap dance. I… I practiced."

His head dropped forward to stare down at her. "You practiced."

"Yes!"

"You watch a lap dance how-to video?"

Emma grimaced. "No."

His lips twitched. "Don't even know you an' can tell you're lyin'."

What? How was that possible? "Okay, I watched a couple."

He snorted and tilted his head, his green eyes pinning her in place. "Just a couple?"

She hesitated and then thought maybe being honest with him might get her in the door. "Okay, more than a couple."

His gaze dropped to where the open buttons of her blouse ended right before the top of her bra. He jerked his chin at her. "Where'd you get those clothes?"

"My closet."

"When's the last time you wore 'em?"

"I don't know."

He ran his gaze slowly down her body and back up, then took a step back and lifted a hand to invite her in. "Shouldn't be doin' this up here. Should be doin' it downstairs where I ain't gonna get accused of nothin'." He turned and took a few steps deeper into his apartment. "Musta lost my damn mind. Hurry up before all the A/C escapes."

Emma rushed inside before Dawg changed his "damn mind" and she closed the door behind her. "Thank you. You don't know how much this means to me."

"Would if you actually told me what the fuck's goin' on an' why you're so desperate."

Her problem was on a need-to-know basis. And there was no reason for this strip club manager to know. "You just need to know I'm serious about this."

"Apparently. Comin' up to a stranger's apartment to strip an' do a lap dance. Think you lost your damn mind, too."

She definitely lost something, and she was determined to get it back.

She followed him farther inside, then he veered to the left and into the kitchenette, his jeans balancing precariously on his hips.

Was it wrong that she wanted them to slip just a little more, so she could see his ass? She swore she saw a couple dimples right above...

Yes. Yes, it was. She was here for an important reason.

He turned suddenly, leaned that ass back against the counter and crossed his arms over his chest, the flex of his heavily tattooed biceps drawing her eye. "Go."

She blinked. "Go?"

"Dance. Show me what you got. This is your last shot."

"Right here?" She glanced around the apartment. It looked like it almost took up the whole second floor of the club. She was standing in a large space that seemed to be a living room area, and it was open to the kitchenette where he stood. Then, from what she could see, there was a hallway with doors. Probably leading to at least one bedroom and a bathroom.

"Yep," Dawg answered, drawing her attention back to him.

And his naked chest. And his open jeans. And those beautiful feet of his. She winced at her thoughts. "Music?"

"Nope. Want music, shoulda brought your own." He pointed to an open area between the living room and kitchenette. "Dance. Now. 'Fore I kick your ass out again."

Emma licked her lips, drew in a breath and moved to the spot he indicated, almost twisting her ankle on the carpet in the process.

"How you goin' to wear platform heels when you can't even walk in what you got on?"

She lifted a hand as she moved into place. "I got this." She turned to face him when he grunted. "Just watch."

He snorted. "I'm watchin', baby girl. Ain't seein' shit."

She needed music. She really did. She pulled her cell phone out of her back pocket.

"You callin' the pigs?"

She glanced up, surprised. "What? No. Why would I do that?"

"Dunno. Thought maybe you're tryin' to set me up or somethin'. Cry rape, get me thrown in the slammer for not hirin' you earlier."

She frowned. Why would he think that? Did he have a reason to be paranoid? "No, I need music."

Hitting her music app, she scrolled through, found a song she practiced to a couple of times, turned the volume high, pressed play and tossed it on the nearby couch.

As soon as *Gorilla* from Bruno Mars started, she closed her eyes and began to move with the music. She followed the rhythm of the song and swung her hips, rocked her shoulders and tossed her head before reaching for the buttons on her blouse. She unfastened a couple but before he could see anything she turned her back on him, continuing to sway and unbutton.

She had to remember to tease, not just get naked. It was the show that men wanted, not just the final result. Or at least that's what the instructional videos stated.

Sway, sway, circle, circle, flirt, wink, purse your lips, touch yourself.

She tried to remember everything that the videos demonstrated.

She let the music flow through her and take over. When her blouse hung open, she dropped it just slightly down her back and turned her head to look over her shoulder at Dawg.

She pursed her lips and... jerked in surprise when she saw his expression. His eyes were so dark and his jaw tight as he watched her, but he hadn't moved an inch. In fact, he looked frozen in place. But from where she stood, she could see his chest rising and falling more rapidly than what was normal.

She ignored his reaction, hoping it was good, and turned in place once more, this time facing him when she reached for the top button on her jeans. Once they were loose, she began to tease him by tugging the waistband down one hip to show a little skin, then pulling it back up. She did the same to the other side. Tucking her thumbs into the top of her jeans, she wiggled them down until the top of the sexiest and most expensive Victoria's Secret panties she owned showed. She circled her hips to the music, then toed her heels off. Taking her time, she revealed her legs little by little until she was bent over, and her jeans pooled at her feet.

Rising slowly, she dragged her hands up her legs as she did so, then, when she was standing straight up, she punted her jeans away. They went flying and struck him smack dab in the center of his bare chest. With a grunt, he caught them and twisted the denim in his fist.

She continued to sway and roll her hips as she pushed her blouse off her shoulders. She shook and shimmied until it dropped to the floor, then suddenly feeling much braver—even though she shouldn't because she was now standing in front of this big biker in just her bra and panties—she decided to up the ante.

She rocked her hips with exaggeration as she approached him, biting her lip to draw his attention there. And, boy, did it!

He was staring at her mouth as she stepped toe to toe with him. Being that close reminded her how much smaller she was than him, especially since she was now barefoot. She spun around and backed up until her ass was pressed into his crotch and then she ground it in circles as she bent over to grab her ankles.

There was no mistaking that she was affecting him and not in a bad way. That hard line in his jeans couldn't be anything other than what she should expect from a customer during a personal lap dance, so she had to get used to it.

As she continued to work her ass against him, she reached back and unclipped her bra and let it fall to the floor. When she swung back up as she tossed her hair—she hoped in a sexy fashion—the top of her head cracked him right in the chin.

He grunted and jerked. She winced at the pain, grabbing her head and crying out, "Ow!"

His arm snaked around her waist as he held her up. "Fuck. You okay?"

She tried to turn to face him and put a little distance between them since her ass was still smashed against his searing hot erection, but he wouldn't loosen his hold.

"I... I think so. You have a hard chin."

"You gotta hard head, woman."

She glanced up over her shoulder at him. "Can you let me go?" The heat of his bare chest against the naked skin of her back made a tingle happen in places that have lied dormant for a long time.

"No, ain't lettin' you go. Not 'til I'm ready."

Something about his words made her think there was more behind their meaning than what was at the surface.

"Aren't you going to let me finish?"

"What's to finish? You're standin' in just your panties. You gonna pull them off, too?"

"If I have to."

"Woman," he said, the impatience thick in his voice. "This ain't you."

"But I did a good job, right? I can feel how well I did." She sure could. He was no small man. *Everywhere.*

"Got the same thing when you were wearin' those fuckin' ugly clothes this mornin'."

He did? "Is that normal?"

He grunted. "Yeah, I get hard."

"No, I mean over your dancers."

"No. Not over my girls."

"Am I one of your girls?" she whispered, optimism rushing through her.

"Nope."

All the air fled her as did her last thread of hope. "What did I do wrong this time?"

"Nothin'. Just ain't for you."

She jerked against the arm that was holding her like a vice against him. "Let me go."

She jerked again and when he released her without warning, she stumbled forward. He captured her wrist and pulled her upright before she fell to the floor. Pushing the hair out of her face, she glared up at him. "That's not your decision."

"Sure is."

"No, I mean whether this is for me or not. That isn't your decision."

"Yeah. It is."

Her mouth gaped open at his sheer bossiness. She snapped it shut. "No! I mean... I'll find somewhere else... another club."

"No, you won't."

She yanked at her wrist. "Why not?"

He pushed off the counter and pulled her to him. "'Cause other clubs don't give a shit about their girls like I do."

"Right."

"Listen, baby girl, this ain't for you."

"So you keep saying."

"I'm right. Been doin' this a long damn time. You're clearly outta your element."

"And you're wrong."

He sighed. Then before she could stop him—like she *could* stop him—he was pulling her over to the living room. He didn't release her until after he sank onto the couch. As she stood in between his parted knees, she stared at him in confusion.

"Show me," he demanded.

"Show you what?"

"Just plunked down five big ones for you to get me off. Gotta get me off without having sex with me. Can you do it?"

Huh? This wasn't on any of the videos! "What?"

"You heard me."

"I thought..."

"Need money so bad... this is what ya gotta do. Big spenders don't wanna just see you shake your tits an' ass. They wanna get somethin' out of it. Can't get paid for sex, though. Gotta ride that fine line if you know what I mean."

Oh Lord, she knew what he meant. She not only had to turn a customer on but appease him in ways that wasn't illegal if she wanted to bank a lot of money and do it quickly.

She closed her eyes and sucked a deep breath through her nostrils to calm her racing heart.

She could do this. She had to do this. She had no choice but to do this.

Right?

"So I can't touch you?"

"Can fuckin' touch me as much as you like, baby girl, but not in a way that could be seen as sexual contact. Means no suckin', no fuckin', an' no jerkin' 'em off. They gotta keep their clothes on. Yours are optional. You can touch 'em, they can't touch you. They do, dance ends immediately. Got someone right outside the door for each private dance. You yell, they're bustin' in there an' bustin' heads. Got me?

She nodded, pulling her bottom lip into her mouth.

"Damn, baby girl, keep doin' that an' you won't have to do much dancin'. Now do it or get out."

She grabbed her phone, which was on the cushion next to him, found another song and hit play.

O nce again, Dawg knew he was going to regret this decision. He shouldn't have let her into his place. He shouldn't have let her take her fucking clothes off. And now she stood before him only wearing panties, her tits all up in his face, her blonde hair falling past her shoulders, color in her damn cheeks and biting on that fucking goddamn lip.

His nostrils flared, picking up her flowery scent.

He was a stupid fuck. That's what he was. Why was he putting himself through this torture? Even with the few hours of practice she said she did, she still sucked at it and normally he would never hire someone like her. He wasn't fucking around when he said she was out of her element.

And though his brain kept telling him to kick her the hell out and stop wasting his time, his dick kept telling him otherwise. And, *fuck*, those tits of hers... and that mouth!

He wanted those pretty little lips wrapped around his rock-hard dick.

"I can touch you?" she asked again.

Fuck yes. "Yeah. Just can't grab my dick with your hands."

"But I can touch it with other things?"

Oh fuck yes. He swallowed the lump in his throat, so he could answer. "Yeah. But don't gotta do it, baby girl. Can put on your clothes an' leave."

She shook her head. "No, I want this."

His dick kicked in his pants and his balls got tight. *Fuck!* He wanted this, too.

"Don't got all day, baby girl. Gotta get downstairs to work."

She nodded, then moved. He slammed back into the couch in surprise when she climbed onto his lap and began to grind her ass against his dick.

Holy mother fuck.

"Baby girl..." he tried to say, but it came out more like a moan.

"Yeah?" she whispered into his ear, brushing her hard nipples against his chest.

"Fuck, baby girl..."

"Yeah?" She circled her hips above his. "You like that?"

Who the fuck was this woman? Was this some sort of trick?

"Yeah, I like." And against his better judgment, *again*, he urged her, "Get me off." He didn't think she could do it. She didn't seem skilled enough. Because of that and because he was a stupid fuck he continued, "Get me off without usin' your hands an' I'll hire you."

He heard her sharp intake of breath close to his ear. "Deal," she breathed as she continued to grind her hot, panty-covered pussy against his lap.

Her hands roamed over his chest, the pads of her thumbs brushing over his nipples as her hot, little mouth pressed against his ear. "You like that. I feel how hard I make you. I like it, too. I bet you want to taste how wet I am, don't you?"

FUCK!

She did *not* learn that from a how-to-strip video. No fucking way!

His dick kicked in his jeans, and the precum leaked out even faster.

He lost his breath when she whispered, "You want to stick that cock into my hot, tight pussy, don't you?"

Jesus fuckin' Christ.

He swallowed so he could tell her to get off him, that this was over. He was done because even though he was attracted to her, he didn't expect her to take him to his knees as much as she was at the moment.

"Tell me what you want to do to me..." she whispered in her honeyed husky voice. And that just pulled his balls up higher and tighter.

She might do it.

She just might make him come in his jeans! He was usually immune to this shit because he saw it day in and day out. But this woman...

"Tell me," she urged. "You want to bend me over and smack my ass while you're fucking me doggy-style?"

Fuck yes, he did.

"You want to..." she pressed her lips to his neck and licked down his throat.

He shuddered before he could stop it. "Fuck, baby girl," he groaned.

"Is that what you want to do, big boy? Fuck?"

She kept rocking on his lap, drawing her hot pussy back and forth over his throbbing dick.

He was about to blow his load in his jeans.

His blood deprived brain made him confess, "Yeah, wanna fuck."

"Me, too," she whispered, her breathing shallow, her nipples pebbled hard as they pressed into his bare skin.

Was she really turned on or just playing? There was no way she wanted him to fuck her.

His brain started to spin, once again thinking that this was some sort of trap. Blackmail. The Shadow Warriors MC setting him up for a hurting. Something.

He grabbed two handfuls of her hair and yanked her head back, so he could see her face. Her eyes were shuttered, her mouth parted, and a flush ran from her chest, up her neck and into her cheeks.

"You turned on, baby girl?"

"Y-yes."

Damn. "You wet?"

She stopped rocking her pussy against him long enough to lean back and show him the dark line that ran up the center of her panties. The line she traced with her own finger. "Yes."

The musky smell of her arousal made his nostrils flare. *Fuck!* "You don't fuck customers," he reminded her. And himself.

No, his girls did not fuck his customers. And Dawg didn't fuck his girls.

He had to get her off his lap. Get her dressed. Get her out of his apartment. And he had to do it soon because this was not how an audition was supposed to go.

Her voice was husky and thick when she declared, "You're not a customer."

"What're you sayin'?" She needed to spell it out loud and clear what she wanted. He was not ending up in a concrete box for doing something without her A-Okay.

No pussy was worth that.

He jerked her hair again, making her concentrate on him as he stared into her unfocused eyes. "Emma, gotta tell me this ain't a fuckin' game, an' you want me to fuck you. Need to say it out loud an' need to be sure one hundred fuckin' percent. Got me?"

"Yes."

"Yes, what?" he barked louder than he should have. But his blood was rushing in his ears, his dick was ready to blow, and his balls were in pain, needing a release.

"I need you to fuck me," she whispered, reaching between them and stroking his dick over his jeans.

What happened to the woman that came to the club this morning? The woman currently on his lap was not her. Not even close.

"Ain't on drugs, right?"

She shook her head, even though he still had a tight grip on her hair. "No."

"Ain't drunk, right?"

"No."

"You wanna fuck me?"

"Yes. Please."

Releasing her hair, he wrapped one arm around her waist, tucked one under her ass and pushed to his feet. He strode down the hallway, kicked open his bedroom door and dropped her onto his bed.

"Last chance, Emma. Gonna fuck a biker. Don't want you to regret it afterward. Got me? Don't wanna be one of your mistakes."

"I want this."

He squeezed his eyes shut for a moment, knowing this was a bad idea. But even with his eyes closed he couldn't get rid of the image of her in the middle of his bed, naked except for those soaked panties, blonde hair wild, eyelids heavy with need.

"Hurry," she encouraged.

Ah, fuck. This was going to go sideways. He just knew it.

He shoved his jeans down and stepped out of them, then climbed onto the mattress, staring down at the blonde vision sprawled on his bed.

His fucking bed. A *girl-next-door*, innocent-looking kindergarten teacher who did not belong there. She was no sweet butt or patch whore.

He shook his head to try to clear it. "You do this, you ain't gettin' this job. It's either dick or dancin'. Pick one. 'Cause I don't fuck my girls."

"I need the job."

"Think you need dick, too."

"Yes," she hissed. "But I need the job more."

"Then we ain't doin' this."

"No!" she cried and reached out a hand to him. "I need this, too. I swear."

"Emma, look at me. Really fuckin' look." He rose up onto his knees between her calves, and he flung his arms out wide. "I'm a biker who runs a strip joint. Got tats over the majority of my body. Fuckin' curse an' drink an' sometimes smoke a joint. Don't make a decision you're gonna regret later. Like I said, don't wanna be some bitch's mistake."

She pushed up to her elbows and let her gaze run over his body from the top of his head all the way to his knees. "Dawson, I see who you are. I want this. I'm not asking for anything but this moment."

Dawg's nostrils flared, and he gave her a sharp nod. His eyes dropped to her parted thighs and that telling sign of just how wet she was.

He wasn't afraid of much but there was something about this woman that scared the shit out of him. She might not regret what they were about to do, but he might.

"You touch yourself?" he asked her.

"Yes."

"You get off when you do it?"

"Yes."

He wanted to rip her panties off, but the doubt wouldn't leave the back of his mind. She needed to do it. Not him. "Panties off. Wanna see your pussy."

Lifting her hips, she pushed her panties down, then shoved them the rest of the way off with one of her feet. She cocked her knees and spread them.

He had been fucking wrong. This woman had no bush. Not even close. Smooth pink lips taunted him. And he wanted to tongue that little patch of blonde hair above them.

"Do you want me to touch myself now?"

Fuck yeah! "No." Dawg swore that was the hardest thing he'd ever said in his life.

But he had something else planned instead, and he was already teetering on the edge. Watching her finger her own pussy would just make him pop a nut before they even got started.

Instead he asked, "Like beards?"

"No."

"Gonna like 'em after this." With that, he dove forward, shoving his face between her thighs. After a quick inhale of her sweet fucking scent, he latched his mouth onto her clit and sucked hard.

She cried out as her hips shot off the bed. Separating her pussy with two fingers in a V, he ate her like a melting soft-serve ice cream cone.

She tasted just as good as one, too.

She was pink, hot, and slick. He barely paid attention to her loud moans and encouragement. Her fingers dug painfully into his hair and she shoved his face deeper into her pussy, grinding her hips against his face until her juices coated his lips and beard.

Yeah, that was exactly how he fucking liked it.

Holding her folds open with one hand, he shoved two fingers of the other deep inside her. *Fuck.* She was tight with just his fingers. When she clamped down around him, he just about lost his load on the bedspread.

He needed to be inside her, and he needed to be there right now. He plunged his fingers in and out of her a couple more times and with a last lick to her clit, he rose above her.

"Like beards?" he asked again.

"Yes," she breathed.

A smile pulled at his lips. "This is all gonna be on you, baby girl. Wanna know you want it every step of the way. The minute you don't want it, we're stoppin', got me?"

"Yes."

"Get a wrap outta my drawer."

Her head tilted in the direction of the nightstand. "A wrap?" she repeated confused.

"Yeah. For my dick."

She rolled onto her side far enough to be able to reach the nightstand and pull the drawer open.

"Careful of the gun. It's loaded, one in the fuckin' chamber."

She yanked her hand back as if something burned her and turned wide sky-blue eyes to him.

"Just be careful. Grab a wrap."

She rose up enough to peek into the drawer, then tentatively put her hand in and pulled out a condom. She rolled back into place, holding the wrapper up. "Now what?"

"Ain't a virgin, right?"

"No."

"Then roll that on my dick."

"You want me to do it?"

"Fuck yes." He was going to make her drive this whole fucking thing, so she knew how real this was going to be. The second that reality hit her, and she wanted him to stop, he was doing just that and kicking her right out the fucking door.

She rolled up to a seated position, ripped open the wrapper, and when she fisted her hot little hand around the root of his dick, he almost fell apart.

Damn.

She rolled the wrap down his length and tossed the wrapper off the bed onto the floor. He smirked. *Hell fuckin' yeah.*

As she was rolling back, he stopped her. "No." He shifted to his ass. "Fuckin' teased me with that lap dance. Now you're gonna do it again with nothin' but the wrap between us. Got me?"

She smiled and moved close enough where he could grab her and pull her onto his thighs.

"All you, baby girl. Show me how much you want this."

She circled one arm around his neck, shoving her hand into his hair at the back of his head. Holding his dick in her other hand, she rose up, positioned herself until the tip of his dick was tucked between her hot pussy lips and, in one move, sank down.

"Fuck. Me," he groaned, fighting the urge to shoot his load immediately into her tight, hot snatch.

"I am."

"Not what I meant, but we'll go with it."

As she rose and fell on him, the hard tips of her nipples dragged along his skin and he wanted them in his mouth, but she was too short for him to reach comfortably. Instead, with one hand on her ass guiding her up and down his pole, he snagged one of her nipples between his fingers and twisted. Her back arched, then she fell forward with a groan, crushing her lips to his.

Shoving her tongue into his mouth, she kissed him so hard, so deeply, that he swore she tickled his tonsils. But he wasn't complaining. He certainly fucking wasn't. He shoved back, pushing his tongue into her mouth instead, tasting every inch of her and letting her taste herself on his tongue. He trailed his fingers down the smooth skin of her back until he got to the cleft in her ass, then he dipped them lower, brushing across a place he wanted to explore at a later time. However, now wasn't it.

No way was he lasting much longer.

As she rode him hard, her pussy clenched and squeezed him until his brain turned to mush.

And the intense urge to make her his hit him in the gut.

With a grunt, he used his weight to roll her onto her back and he took over, slamming her hard, snagging a nipple in his mouth, sucking, flicking, scraping his teeth over one tip then the other.

She wiggled, screamed and called out his real name, spurring him on to take her harder and faster. When her legs wrapped around his hips, he slipped his hands under her ass and lifted her up enough so he could drive deep and hit her just right.

Then she exploded around him, clawing his back as she cried out, her body convulsing around him, trying to draw him deeper. He gritted his teeth, so he'd at least last until her orgasm was over, but it took every inch of willpower he had.

When she cried out, "Again!" he shook his head.

"Can't, baby girl... Can't..."

With one last thrust, he captured her mouth once more and his load shot out of him with such force that he swore he saw stars.

He broke their kiss so he could suck in some much needed oxygen and stared down into the face that would change his fucking life.

He just knew it.

And he wasn't sure he was happy about it, either.

CHAPTER FOUR

When Emma finally caught her breath, she dropped her gaze from the ceiling to the man who was now lying beside her, trying to slow his own ragged breathing.

Like he said, she should be regretting her actions since she did something so out of character for her. She simply didn't sleep with random strangers.

And she certainly didn't sleep with big tattooed bikers.

What the hell was she thinking?

"Damn, where did that come from?" he grumbled next to her, one arm thrown over his head, the other laying across his heavily decorated belly. His forehead still showed signs of perspiration.

Where did that come from? She honestly didn't have an answer. She had never been sexually promiscuous in her life. But she wasn't a prude, either. She enjoyed sex, yes. Though she couldn't remember enjoying it as much as she just had. With complete abandonment. And this man hadn't treated her like a breakable doll, he had given her everything he had.

Or at least that's what she thought. Did he have more? Did she want to find out?

"I don't know. I lost my head. I... I haven't been intimate with

anyone in a long time. I've been focused on... other things." She
rolled to her side and studied his large body sprawled on his back.
"Apparently, I needed this." Maybe it was all the stress she'd been
under for the past few months. Maybe she just needed to let loose
and forget all her problems, even if only for a little while.

"You ain't the only one."

She reached out and placed her palm on his damp chest,
watching it rise and fall for a moment. Her skin looked so pale
next to the colors of his tattoos. "Please don't think I used sex to
get this job."

He moved his hand up to cover hers. "Believe me, woman, us
doin' that has nothin' to do with you gettin' the job."

"I got it?" She held her breath, hoping for an affirmative
answer.

He reached up and brushed away a lock of her hair that was
plastered to her cheek as he studied her face. "Want the truth?"

"Yes. Please."

"Wanna tell you fuck no." He lifted his hand to stop her when
she opened her mouth to argue. "Gonna give you a shot. A trial
period. Got me?"

She smiled. "Yes!"

"Gonna get some of the girls to work with you an' teach you
some money-makin' moves. Start you off on daylight where the
clientele ain't so picky. See how you do."

As the excitement and relief rushed through her over that
news, she squealed and climbed on top of him, planting a big, fat
kiss on his lips.

He chuckled. "Hang on." He reached underneath her, pulled
off the condom, tied a knot in it and chucked it onto the floor.

Her first reaction was disgust at that move, but then it wasn't
her floor and she just got a job.

And had some awesome, stress-relieving sex.

With a big, burly, bearded biker who was probably an actual
pussycat deep down inside.

She tugged gently on his thick beard. "I have to admit, I kind of like the beard now."

He grinned. "Just kinda?"

"More than *kinda*."

He reached up and wrapped a lock of her hair around his finger. One of a few that had a bulky silver ring on it. "Lemme know when you wanna feel it again."

"Mmm." If there was a next time, she wanted him to spend a lot longer down there than what he did earlier. A *lot* longer.

He brushed a knuckle over her cheek. "When's the last time you had a man?"

"*Had* a man or had sex with a man?"

"There a difference?'

"Yes. It's been over a year and a half since I *had* a man. Longer since I've had sex with one."

"Makes no sense."

"Yes, it does when…" she hesitated. She was feeling good, she didn't want to bring that blissful satisfaction crashing down around her. Not now.

He frowned when she didn't continue. "Ain't gonna tell me."

"No, it's not your problem. It's mine."

"You end up as one of my girls, your problems become my problems. Got me?" When she didn't answer, he continued more firmly. "I hire you, you gotta spill it all. Got me? Gotta know what I'm dealin' with. Ain't bringin' unexpected shit down on me or the club."

"Okay."

"So, you wanna dance at my club, be prepared for me to be all up in your business, got me?"

Lord, it would be a relief to finally get all this off her chest, to have even the smallest of help. An ally. Something. She'd been going at this alone for so long…

But what could this biker do for her? For her problems?

"Lemme tell you how it all works… This ain't no nine to five. Got house fees. Gotta choice. Either you're payin' a stage fee an' keepin your tips or on rare occasion I'll accept a percentage of your tips instead. I'll discount your stage fee since you'll start out on daylight. Prime time's a lot higher. The house gets a percentage of each private dance. You're gonna hafta buy outfits, shoes, an' you're gonna hafta tip the DJ if they're playin' while you dance. That's only some of the costs, baby girl. You prepared to do that? Ain't a job where it's rainin' money. Your feet are gonna hurt. You're gonna be sick of perverts, men who wanna fuck you, take you to dinner, make you their girl. Ain't a walk in the park. Some women walk away because they're payin' more than their makin'. Got me?"

She rolled her lips under at his millionth "Got me?" "Got you," she answered.

"Start daylight. Stage fee will be twenty bucks a dance. You negotiate your private dances. More you make, more I make. Got me?"

"Got you," she repeated.

"Need sexy shit. No jeans. Platform heels. Gonna check to see if you can borrow some from the other girls 'til you got enough scratch to get your own. You're on the older side, but still got the innocent look so you got that goin' for ya. Bite that lip, give 'em a sultry look, shake your tits an' ass. Learn some moves an' you're gonna have 'em eatin' outta your hand."

She waited for his signature "got me." And when it didn't come she said, "Got you," anyway and giggled.

He lifted his head, his eyes narrowed. "Somethin' funny?"

"No."

"'Cause this shit's serious. Got me?"

She pressed her face into his chest and couldn't stop the laughter that bubbled up. Then something he said hit her. She lifted her head. "Hey! I'm on the older side?"

"How old are you?"

"I'm only twenty-nine!"

"Yeah. Old for this biz."

"Twenty-nine is not old," she exclaimed. "I'm younger than you!" He had to be at least thirty-five.

"Most of the dancers start out young. Eighteen, twenty. Start before they're poppin' out the kids, stretchin' shit out."

"So, I'm washed up before I even start?"

"Ain't washed up. My oldest girl's forty. She still got it goin' on. Popular with my regulars but she got skills." He traced his fingers down her arm. "Got kids?"

Emma closed her eyes for a moment and took a deep breath. He wanted her to be straight with him. It was part of the deal. But she wasn't sure if she was ready to tell him everything. "Yes."

"How many?"

"One. I'm doing this for her."

He nodded. "Times are tough. Got you."

"Yes, times are very tough. How about you? Do you have kids?"

"Suspect so."

Emma lifted her head and stared down into his green eyes. "You suspect so? You don't know?"

"One I'm pretty sure's mine. Wasn't told about her. Name ain't on the birth certificate so was adopted by the woman's new husband when she was an infant. Didn't know anything 'bout her 'til I heard a rumor."

"How old is she now?"

"Fourteen."

"And you've never met her?"

"No. When I heard 'bout her, went an' waited for her outside her school. Saw 'er from a distance. Soon as I saw her, knew she was mine."

"Then demand a DNA test."

He shook his head. "Her dad makes good money. Family's livin' large, big house, fancy cars, private school. She's got siblin's. Nothin' like my life. She got it good. Better than what I could give 'er. Probably go to college, make somethin' out of herself. She don't need a daddy who's got a stable of girls strippin' for a livin'."

"Her mother never told you she was pregnant?"

"No."

"Why?"

"'Cause fuckin' me was a mistake for her. Wanted to walk on the wild side for a hot minute. Didn't expect she'd walk away with a piece of me. We were both young an' stupid."

"Do you want to know your daughter?"

He didn't say anything for the longest time, only stared up at the ceiling. Finally, he murmured, "Best to let it go."

There was something in his voice that made an ache grow in her chest.

He didn't want to let it go.

And there was no way Emma was doing that, either. She couldn't let her daughter go, just like that. She was going to fight with every ounce of her being to get hers back.

He turned his head toward the nightstand and then sat up suddenly, making her tumble off his chest. "Fuckin' gotta get downstairs 'fore things go to shit." He rolled off the bed, yanked on his jeans, still leaving them undone. He dragged a hand through his hair and down over his beard. "You gotta go an' I gotta shower."

Emma blinked. She was being dismissed. Just like that.

A wham, bam, and not even a "thank you, ma'am."

"When can I start?"

He stared at her for a long, uncomfortable moment. He was going to change his mind!

She sat up quickly and took the matter into her own hands. "I'll be here tomorrow morning. Bright and early."

"Ain't no bright an' early 'round here. Ten-thirty. I'll get Dawn to come in then an' help get you ready."

She got to her feet. "Thank you, Dawson."

"Fuckin' Dawg."

"Sorry. *Dawg.* Dawson's a nice name." She gathered her own clothes, pulling them on as she found them.

"Been Dawg longer than been Dawson."

As she moved around the living room, she realized how much

she needed a shower, too. "Well, I like it."

"Fuckin' relieved."

She glanced up from buttoning her blouse. "What?"

"Fuckin' relieved that you like my name. Don't mean you should use it."

"Why not?"

"Ain't me."

She studied him for a moment. He was right. Dawson didn't fit the way he looked on the outside, Dawg did. But she liked it anyhow. It was a good name for a good man.

Biker. Strip club manager. Selfless father.

She just knew deep down inside he was a Dawson. And there was more than met the eye with the big, gruff man before her.

She finished closing her blouse, raced over to him, grabbed a chunk of his beard, pulling his head down with a yank, and planted a big, fat kiss on his lips.

"Thank you, Dawson!"

Before the surprise could be hidden from his expression, she grabbed her heels off the floor and dashed out the door. She ran down the steps barefoot and back to her car, trying not to scream out her joy at things going her way for once.

Things might be looking up!

Finally.

———

D awg leaned back against the bar, arms crossed over his chest, his jaw tight, his mouth curved downward.

This was a complete mistake.

His brain knew it. His instincts screamed it. But he, the stupid fuck that he was, ignored all the signs.

Why? Because the woman on stage right now screwing the pooch gave him a hard-on that wouldn't quit.

That wasn't the only reason why. Fuck no, it wasn't.

He saw something in her that he hadn't seen in a long time.

Problem was, it was the same thing he had seen in his daughter's mother.

Something he had wanted to hang on to but ended up being a pipe dream.

Stupid fuck that he was, he thought she'd settle for him. For a tattooed biker from the wrong side of the tracks.

Nope.

He'd been dead fucking wrong. Those couple of nights all those years ago, she only considered his dick a ride at the state fair while she held a fist full of tickets.

He'd been used.

Normally, he wouldn't have cared. Pussy was pussy. Something to bust a nut into. But he had hoped... *Fuck*, he'd thought there was something different about her.

But, fuck him, there wasn't.

And now he stood there staring up at Emma on stage, doing the worst pole dancing he'd ever seen, wearing shit that made him want to blow a fucking blood vessel. He didn't think it would bother him quite that much when she got naked on stage in front of other men.

But it did.

Even if it was for only two of his regular daytime customers and another few stragglers that had wandered in off the street. And none of them were really paying attention to the awful moves that *Ember* was attempting to do.

Good fucking thing for that.

Instead, their attention was drawn to the daylight girls he had scheduled today. Dawn and Kitty were currently working the room with their tits all pushed up out of their tops, trying to convince the customers to buy them a drink and then crack open their tight wallets for private dances.

Sometimes they would. Sometimes they wouldn't. Both of the regulars were pretty damn cheap. That's why they came in during happy hour to drink.

"Thank fuck," Dawg muttered when the song finally came to

an end and Emma practically stumbled off the stage only wearing borrowed platform shoes and a baby blue G-string that hopefully wasn't borrowed.

She was going to break her damn neck.

Dawg whacked his long-time bartender, Cubby, on the back and gave him a chin lift. "Got the girls' music list?"

"Yeah," Cubby grunted.

"Cocoa's up next," Dawg told him then rounded the bar and headed in the direction Emma disappeared. "Text me if you need somethin'. Gonna be busy for a bit."

"Gotcha, boss."

Out of the corner of his eye, he saw Dawn scoring a private dance on the other side of the stage. She held one finger up at him as he passed by.

One dance.

Cheap fucker.

Dawg lifted his chin in acknowledgment and, when he hit the back hallway, he saw Moose headed his way. "Dawn's got one on the line for a song. Green room. Got me?"

"Gotcha, boss."

The heavyset prospect continued past him to escort Dawn and her customer back to one of the private rooms. And then stand watch outside the door.

He needed more prospects working at Heaven's Angels. Especially ones like Moose. Though not super tall, the man held some bulk that could be intimidating. He also was a hard worker. He'd have to talk to Z about trying to find more DAMC recruits. They were cheap labor versus hiring people off the street.

He continued down the hallway and pushed through a door that had a sign on it that read "private." That lead to another short hallway and the first door on the right was the girls' dressing room.

He shoved open the door and walked in, not giving two shits who was in there.

He'd seen them all naked countless times on stage, so they

didn't care if he came into the dressing room. They couldn't be a prude and be a stripper...

Cocoa was putting the finishing touches on her makeup.

"Gotta be on stage, woman. Can't have no one on stage. Get out there," he barked.

Cocoa took her time as she finished applying her lipstick, rubbed her lips together, put the cap on the tube, threw it on the counter and then gave Dawg the middle-finger salute. "I'm going. It's not like there's a crowd out there. Probably be dancing for next to nothing."

"If you wanna dance later when you're gonna be rakin' it in, you better get your ass out there right now."

"Whatever, Dawg."

"Don't fuckin' *whatever* me."

Cocoa stepped away from the mirror and put her hands on her hips.

"Hold up. Let me see." Dawg inspected her from top to toe. The woman had the skin tone of her stage name. She was a rich chocolate brown with the biggest natural tits in his stable. Her ass was hard to ignore, too. She'd been working for Dawg for years and the woman knew what she was doing and made good money at it. "Lookin' good, baby."

Cocoa smiled. "I know it. You don't have to tell me." She approached him and lowered her voice. "She's in the bathroom crying. I tried to give her some pointers." She shook her head. "Don't think she's cut out for this, darlin'."

"No shit. Told her that. Figured she needed to find out for herself."

Cocoa reached out, grabbed his dick through his jeans and squeezed. "Mmm mmm. Say it every time... hung like a brotha, darlin'."

Dawg grinned. "*Am* a brother."

"Not that type of brotha. Shame you don't do your girls."

Dawg grunted. "Get the fuck out on stage."

Cocoa laughed. "One of these days, I'm gonna get me some

of that."

"An' your ol' man would kick my ass."

She winked and headed toward the door. "He doesn't mind sharing," she tossed over her shoulder.

"Right." Her husband was about five-six and maybe one hundred fifty pounds soaking wet. He was not kicking Dawg's ass anytime soon, but he still had to give her shit since she was happily married and would never cheat on her man no matter what she said.

He shook his head as he watched the door close behind her, then sighed. He glanced around the room and saw the women's clothes, shoes, makeup and all kinds of shit tossed around. It looked like a hurricane hit the dressing area.

"Fuckin' goddamn." He shook his head again and carefully headed through the disaster area toward the restroom that was dedicated to the dancers.

Not bothering to knock, he shoved the door open and stopped dead.

"It's occupied," came the tearful yell. Emma was perched on the closed toilet seat, her head hanging down, her face in her hands as her body shook.

"Don't give a shit," Dawg grumbled back and closed the door behind him.

She glanced up, her mouth hanging open. It was not a good look for her. The thick mascara she had applied earlier had caused black smears down her cheeks. Her lipstick had been chewed off her bottom lip. Her eyes were bloodshot and still rimmed with tears.

"Fuck," he muttered.

She had thrown on a silky red robe that was way too big for her and she looked like a little girl sitting on the commode as she cried.

His nostrils flared in his attempt to keep from yelling at her for being stupid and not listening to him in the first place. "What the fuck's wrong with you now? You got what you wanted."

"I know," she blubbered, fresh tears leaking out of her damn eyes.

Ah, fuck. He couldn't handle crying women.

"I was horrible up there, wasn't I?"

No point in lying and letting her think she had a shot at this. "Yeah, you fuckin' suck, baby girl."

Her eyes widened, and her mouth dropped open. "You couldn't be nice and lie about it?"

"Fuck no. Gotta hear the truth."

She reached into the robe pocket and pulled out a few balled-up dollar bills. "Two dances!"

"Yeah?"

"Two dances!" she yelled again.

Where the fuck was she going with this?

"Two dances and that's all I made!" She whipped the balled-up money at him. It bounced off his chest and onto the bathroom floor. "At that rate, I'll never get the money I need!"

Her body hiccuped and she let out a low wail that almost made the hair on the back of his neck stand up.

Holy fuck.

Emotional women sucked! That was the worst part of working with a whole shitload of them. Especially when they were all PMSing, which they all seemed to do at the same fucking time. Those where the days he needed to wear a Kevlar vest, a cup, and a riot helmet, while arming himself with pepper spray, chocolate and ear plugs.

He bent down and scooped the money off the floor. He unraveled the singles and smoothed them out.

He groaned. Eleven bucks. "This what you got outta both dances?"

"Yes!"

She was not going to like what he had to say next. "Owe me twenty-nine bucks."

"What?"

Once again her mouth was hanging open like a fish out of

water. "Yeah, discounted your stage fee to only twenty bucks a dance. You're in the red, baby girl."

"What?"

Maybe she needed her ears cleaned out. "Runnin' a business here. Can't afford to—"

Suddenly he was knocked backward. He grunted as his back slammed into the bathroom door and a spitfire was on him, pounding on his chest with her fists as she screamed nonsense, spit raining everywhere.

"What the fuck!" he shouted, trying to snag her swinging arms before she knocked him a good one or kneed him in the nuts. Finally, he captured her wrists and pulled her arms behind her back, holding her still. "Quit it!"

Then her body sagged against him and she began to cry uncontrollably, pressing her wet, snotty face between the opening of his cut and into his shirt.

"Fuck, baby girl," he murmured as he released her arms and held her tightly against him, otherwise she'd probably collapse to the floor. Her body heaved with each sob and her tears seemed endless.

But he stood there and held her until she was all cried out and became quiet, except for an occasional hiccup. Her arms slipped under his cut, wrapped around his waist and she squeezed him tight. "I'm sorry," came muffled from his now damp chest.

He combed his fingers through her hair and remained silent as she sniffled a few more times. He had a feeling she was using his Sturgis tee as a tissue.

Finally, she lifted her face. She looked like a complete fucking wreck, but she still made his chest pull tight and thoughts run through his head that had no business being there.

"Did I hurt you?" she asked shakily.

"No," he grunted, continuing to soothe her by stroking her long hair. He wanted to feel that silkiness all over his bare chest again.

"I don't know what came over me." Her shaking voice was thin, and it killed him. Twisted his fucking guts.

"Frustration. Desperation. Maybe even a feelin' of failure, baby girl. Don't know what's goin' on, but you're gonna fuckin' tell me."

She nuzzled deeper into his chest and didn't say anything for a long while.

"It's not your fault, and I took it out on you."

"I'm a big guy. Can handle it."

"Still..."

He leaned back and peered down into her face. "Go gather your shit. We're goin' up to my place where there's privacy an' you're gonna spill it. Got me?"

"Dawson..."

Dawg closed his eyes and blew out an impatient breath. "Haven't been Dawson for a long time... Go get your shit." He gently pushed her away and reached behind him to open the door. Then, with a hand to her back, he nudged her out into the dressing room and waited as she gathered her clothes.

"I need to get dressed and wash my face."

"Upstairs."

She fingered the robe she wore. "But this isn't my robe."

"I'll bring it back down."

"But—"

"Seriously, woman, you're tryin' my patience. Get your shit an' let's go."

She grabbed her belongings and held her street clothes in a ball against her chest. "I can just go home. You were right. I'm not cut out for this. I'll send you the twenty-nine dollars when I get it. I'm sorry for wasting your time."

"Emma," he growled. "Ain't gonna tell you again."

"I thank you for the opportunity, but—"

Before another word could escape her lips, he grabbed her and threw her over his shoulder. She squealed in surprise, but he didn't give a shit.

The fucking woman didn't listen. He was tired of talking, so now he was taking matters into his own hands. With her struggling against him, he strode out of the dressing room, toward the back of the club, out the door and up the steps to his apartment. He paused only long enough to avoid taking a foot to the dick, to dig his keys out of his pocket, unlock the deadbolt and shove the door open. He slammed it shut, latched the lock, took two long strides into the living room and then tossed her over the back of the couch where she landed with a bounce on the cushions, her hair flying all over the place.

"What—"

"Shut up," he barked and moved around to the front of the couch just as she was pushing herself up to a seat.

"That's so rude!"

He planted his hands on his hips. "Damn right it is. An' so's not listenin' to what I'm tellin' you."

"You're not the boss of me!"

He stopped himself before he shouted that he was. Because in reality, he wasn't. He needed to remind himself of that.

Just because he stuck his dick in her once, didn't make her his.

Fuck no, it didn't.

When she went to stand up, he pointed at her and bellowed, "Sit the fuck down. Ain't movin' from that spot 'til you tell me everything. Got me?"

"Dawson..."

"It's fuckin' Dawg!"

She lifted a hand and then dropped it back into her lap. Her head bowed, and she whispered, "Sorry."

Fuck. Now he felt like a complete shit.

"Look at me. Don't give a shit what you call me, as long as you tell me what the fuck's goin' on."

She lifted her red-rimmed blue eyes to his. "Why do you care?"

Good question. Why the fuck did he care?

Because he was a stupid shit, and he knew the moment he'd stuck his dick in her his life was going to change.

That's why he cared.

CHAPTER FIVE

Emma stared up at the man who loomed over her with a frown on his face, his brow furrowed, and hands on his hips, just waiting for her to spill her secrets.

"Can I get dressed first?"

"No."

She raised a hand to her cheek. "Can I wash my face?"

"No."

"Are you always this bossy?"

His lips twitched slightly, then he grunted, "Fuck yeah."

Great. She sighed. "Where should I start?"

"The beginnin'."

"Maybe you should take a seat then," she suggested, waving a hand at a worn leather recliner nearby.

"Fine where I'm at."

"I'd prefer you sit down." She didn't need a big tattooed biker standing over her as she tried to tell him a story that was painful. "Please," she added softly.

A look she didn't recognize crossed his face, then he finally gave her a sharp nod and settled into the recliner that faced the couch. At least now there was some distance between them and she might be able to think a bit straighter.

She cleared her throat. "I have a daughter."

"Know it."

She frowned. "Are you going to let me tell you?"

His lips twitched again, and he sat back. "Go."

She took a deep inhale and began to speak. "I was eighteen when I met him." Because of her grades and her SAT scores, she had received a scholarship and some grants to attend a college she wouldn't have normally been able to afford. Especially since her grandmother who raised her couldn't help her financially, either. But it was a college where her future husband's family had no problem footing his bill. "I was a freshman and met him at a frat party—"

He leaned forward with a jerk. "Him?"

She shot him a look.

His eyes widened as if he hadn't realized he'd spoken out loud, and he said again, "Go."

"Handsome, smart, from a good family..."

His fingers curled into fists on his thighs. "He beat you?"

"Dawson," she chided him for interrupting again. "Do you want to hear it or not?"

"Sorry. Go."

"I was too young to realize that I was too young to make life-altering decisions. Like marriage and family and..."

"And?"

She blew out a breath. "I thought I was in love. Anyway, long story short, by the time I graduated college, we were engaged, living together, and I was expecting." She sat back and chewed on her bottom lip as she remembered how she felt when she found out she was pregnant.

Excited. Elated. Hopeful. That's how she felt. She couldn't wait to be a mother. Even though her career would be put on hold for a little while, she thought it would be worth it.

"And then Lily was born." She would never forget the moment

the nurse placed her newborn in her arms. "You can't know how precious... what a gift..." She glanced up and saw Dawg's face was as tight as a drum.

No, he couldn't know how precious bringing a life into the world could be. He never had the chance to see his daughter being born, to hold her during that first breath. To watch her take her first steps. Hear her first words. To create that bond with a life that was a piece of yourself. Her chest ached for his loss. For never knowing the love that you felt as a parent.

Because he was never allowed to be one. He'd been denied that opportunity. Most likely because of who he was and where he came from, how he chose to live his life.

He had been treated as a mistake that needed to be erased.

And that was downright cruel.

She swallowed the lump in her throat. "After Lily was born, our marriage suffered, but I didn't know why. I mean we *were* young and being new parents *was* stressful. But something else was going on and because I was so caught up with taking care of my daughter, I missed it. Maybe it was my fault, for being blind, for not paying attention. I don't know..."

"Emma."

Her name on his lips and the way he said it drew her attention. His green eyes looked dark, troubled, his jaw tight.

"He cheat on you?"

"It was worse than that." Because it was *oh-so* worse. Never in her wildest dreams could she imagine what the man—who she loved, who she married, who she had a child with—was plotting.

In fact, even now, she had a hard time wrapping her head around it. She couldn't imagine what kind of human being did what he did. A selfish bastard, that was who.

"He have a kid with someone else?"

She made a noise before she could stop it. She pressed her fingers to her lips to prevent anything else from escaping. Closing her eyes, she pictured her baby girl. Her daughter in her crib. Wobbling across the floor taking her first steps. Smashing the cake from her first birthday into her mouth but missing and getting it all over her chubby chin and cheeks as she laughed with glee. Then the cake from her second birthday and the third. Even the fourth.

And Emma had no idea what was going on all that time. None.

In the end, all she knew was that she failed her daughter. She had been too blissfully unaware.

"Emma," Dawg urged, his voice low and tight, no more than a rough whisper, spurring her to continue.

"No, that's the funny part." Which really wasn't funny at all. "He didn't have any other children. They couldn't."

"What do you mean?"

Emma lifted her gaze to meet Dawg's head-on. "The woman he was... *seeing* for years behind my back couldn't have children. Though they tried. And tried. So they..."

Emma squeezed her eyes shut, stinging tears threatening to spill once more, her throat closing up. She didn't know if she could continue. It was like ripping the wound open all over again to expose something that was painful, raw, unbearable.

"Betrayed me," she finally finished, her voice catching.

"How?"

Saying the words made it feel like a knife being shoved into her heart all over again. "They... stole my daughter."

"What the fuck!" Dawg bellowed, jumping up from his seat, his face a mask of pure unadulterated rage, his hands clenched tightly into fists. "What the fuck you talkin' about?"

Emma dropped her face into her hands and shook her head. She couldn't talk about it anymore. She couldn't put it into words. Those words cut her like a million shards of shattered glass.

Dawg rushed over to her, dropped to his knees, grabbed her face in his big hands and forced her to look at him.

His furious expression, the hardness in his eyes, his flaring nostrils made a shiver of fear skitter down her spine.

He gave her a slight shake. "Emma! What the fuck you talkin' about?"

She breathed, "They took her."

"Who?"

"My husband and his... his *girlfriend*."

"When?"

"A year and a half ago."

"Why didn't you stop 'em?"

If it had only been that easy. "I couldn't."

"What do you mean?"

"He snuck out in the middle of the night and disappeared."

Though, her husband was kind enough to leave a note explaining why and that she shouldn't be worried, that her daughter would be safe with him. And, by the way, not to bother looking for them since she'd never find them. *Bastard*.

"Where?"

"I don't know!"

"What do you mean you don't know!" he shouted.

"Exactly what I said," she shouted back in frustration. "I have no idea where they are."

"What the fuck! That's impossible. Hire someone to find 'em."

"I did! I fucking did, Dawson! I spent all of my money on investigators. On attorneys. I did..." She ground the heels of her palms into her eyes and took a shaky breath.

"Have to be somewhere..."

"No. They left the country. They disappeared somewhere other than the States. The trail went cold in South America and I ran out of money. I lost my house. I lost my car. I lost everything because I spent every cent trying to find them. Trying to bring my daughter home."

Dawg sat back on his heels, dragged a hand through his hair and blew out a breath. Then he pushed to his feet and began to pace restlessly.

"That is why I need this job, Dawson. I *need* this job. I need cash." She rose to her feet and stepped into his path, gripping his leather vest within her fingers and shaking it. "I *need* to find my daughter!"

Dawg stood staring down at her, his breathing fast, his eyes narrowed. "You're fired."

"What?" That was the last thing she expected to come out of his mouth.

"Gonna find your daughter."

And that was the second to last thing. "How?"

"Know people. Cops. A lawyer. Men who are good at findin' people who don't wanna be found."

Emma shook her head. "I can't let this become your problem."

"Too late."

"Why's that?"

He cupped her cheeks in his hands and stared down into her face. "Knew the minute you walked into my club, baby girl. The second I looked into those eyes when you were in my bed, when my dick was inside you... you were mine. I take care of my girls..."

But she wasn't one of his girls, he... "You just fired me."

"An' I take care of *my* girl."

His girl? What was he saying? "I'm not your girl, Dawson."

"The fuck you ain't."

"I need you to be my boss not my... boyfriend." Even the word tasted weird on her tongue. "I just need a chance to earn enough cash to rehire the investigator. So he can continue—"

"No."

Her head jerked back. No? Just no? "No what?"

"No, got it covered. Got you covered. Gonna get your daughter back."

Emma tried desperately to tamp down the hope that bubbled up from his words. He sounded so confident. Like he could do it. Like he could actually find Lily and bring her home. But he was a biker. A strip club manager. What kind of connections could he possibly have?

What could this man do that the police, the FBI and even INTERPOL couldn't? He was delusional to think he could do something they haven't been able to.

"I don't want to be in debt to you, Dawson. I can't be."

"No debt. Doin' it for you. For your girl."

"But you don't even know me."

"Fucked you. Know you."

They had sex once and now he *knew* her? Really? "That simple?"

"Yeah. That simple, baby girl."

"I can't afford—"

"Already said you ain't payin' shit, baby girl. Got you covered."

"I can't just allow you to help me and not do anything in return."

"Ain't gonna strip. You'll chase away my customers."

She blinked at his honesty. "You don't sugar coat anything, do you?"

"Fuck no. You need to pay me back, you'll do it in a different way, got me?"

"What do you mean? How?" He better not had meant sex. She was not going to sell her body, even to get her daughter back. Not to this biker or anyone else.

Though, she had to admit, during her most desperate times she'd considered it. Even though she had been appalled at the thought, she'd considered anything that would mean getting her daughter back. *Anything.*

So far, the police hadn't been much help, FBI could only do so much, and INTERPOL didn't have her missing daughter at the top of their priority list. What was more, the investigator she had hired didn't work for free.

"Gonna rehire you," he finally said with a frown.

"You just fired me," she stated, surprised.

"Yeah, as a dancer. Gonna hire you as a hostess. Wear a sexy dress, show some cleavage, get the girls to show you how to wear some makeup to highlight your *girl-next-door* look, nothing slapped on too thick. Work the room, make sure the girls are doin' what they're supposed to be doin', make sure the customers are happy. Comp 'em a drink if they're tippin' heavily. Flirt, smile, but no dancin'. Make 'em feel welcome."

She could do that! And she didn't have to get naked!

"Gotta learn to walk in heels. Gonna set you up with one of the girls to go shoppin'." He lifted his hand before she could interrupt him. "Gonna cover your expenses like your clothes an' heels. Any makeup you need. Got me?"

"Yes, so how much is this going to pay?"

"Nothin'."

"Nothing?" He expected her to work for free? That wasn't going to happen. Not as long as she was in her right mind.

"Gonna get your daughter back. No matter what it costs. This is how you'll make it up to me. Got me?"

"But... I have rent... expenses."

"Nope."

What? "Uh, yes."

"No. Gotta spare room. You're movin' in. Livin' expenses will be covered 'til we get your daughter back. Once we do, can find your own place again."

"Wait." She lifted a palm and glanced around the living room. "You want me to live *here*?"

"Yeah. Gotta spare room."

He already said that. That didn't mean she was just moving in! Into a stranger's apartment. Someone she'd only known for not even a couple of days. "Yes, but—"

"No shit, woman. Wanna find your daughter?"

"Yes!"

"Willin' to do whatever you gotta do to get it done?"

"Yes!"

"Then gotta do what I say. No lip. No backtalk. No nothin'. Got me?"

"Uh..."

"Gonna get some prospects to move your shit into storage if you got too much. Basics come here for now."

"Um..."

He lifted his hand again to stop her. "No lip. Got me?"

No matter what he wanted, she was asking this question: "You don't expect me to sleep with you?"

"Bedroom door will be open. You wanna climb into my bed an' fuck me, ain't gonna complain. You don't, ain't gonna complain. Ain't takin' payment out in sex. Never needed to pay for pussy an' ain't gonna start now. You wanna climb on my dick, it's on you. Do it 'cause you wanna, not 'cause you gotta. Yeah?"

"Yeah," she echoed him on a breath, her heart racing at everything he just said.

She just got a job, sort of, a free place to live, sort of, and this man, this *biker*, stated he was going to get her daughter back. She hoped that wasn't "sort of."

This couldn't be real.

None of this could be real. She had to be caught in some sort of alternate reality. She was just having some weird dream.

She reached into the black leather vest with the dirty patches he was wearing and pinched him.

He jerked. "What the fuck?"

"I'm just making sure this is all real."

"By pinchin' me?"

"Yes. I can't very well pinch myself, right? If I'm dreaming, I'd only imagine myself doing it."

He snorted. "You're crazy, woman. But got a better way for you to tell this is all fuckin' real." With that, he dropped his head, jerked her closer and crushed his lips to hers.

He took advantage of it when she gasped, slipping his tongue in between her lips and exploring her mouth thoroughly. She clung to him as her knees went weak. His rough beard scraped against her skin, his tongue took control of her mouth, his erection pressed into her belly. He grabbed one of her hands and shoved it between them, curving it over his hard-on. He lifted his head slightly, his lips just above hers.

"Real enough for you?"

"Yes," she whispered, his heat, his hardness making her squeeze her thighs together.

He let her go and stepped back. "Good. Door will be open at night. Your choice what room you end up in. Got me?"

"Got you," she answered, her voice a bit breathless at the thought.

"Not obligated to do anythin' but be the club's hostess, baby girl."

"Okay."

"Can help keep shit clean 'round here, though. Ain't gonna bitch if you do."

"Okay," she repeated as if in a trance.

"Got the rest of the night off. Go home an' pack. Need your address. Prospects will be there first thing in the mornin' to grab your shit. Party at church tomorrow night. Will get Moose to run the club. Gonna take you an' introduce you 'round. Gonna talk to Diesel an' Kiki. Maybe even Bella's ol' man, who's a pig."

She had no idea who he was talking about. And before she could ask, he continued.

"Cover yourself up for the party at church. This club you can let it all hang out. That club, no. Got me?"

She shook her head. "I'm confused." This club, that club. A church. A pig. She had no clue what the hell he was talking about. Her head was spinning.

"Won't be for long, baby girl. Promise. If you got a lease, break it tomorrow an' let me know how much I need to pay."

"But—"

"No lip."

Right. No lip. She wasn't allowed to argue with anything he said or did. But he was going to get her daughter back. That's what he said. So for now, she'd follow his rules.

Then once she had Lily back in her custody, she could go on with her life as scheduled. Find another teaching job, find her own place. Tip her life back right-side up.

She could deal temporarily with his overbearing bossiness.

Who knew her savior would be wearing a leather vest, big black biker boots, worn jeans, a bunch of clunky silver jewelry and sporting a heavy beard, as well as a plethora of tattoos?

Not her.

CHAPTER SIX

awg eyeballed the blonde with the killer curves, stunning blue eyes, and a mouth that could make a grown brother cry, as she worked the floor. She'd borrowed a slinky midnight blue, *cling-to-every-curve*, low-cut dress from Savannah and had bought herself a pair of strappy, sexy heels with the cash he'd given her before she'd left this morning.

And he'd been sporting a raging hard-on almost all afternoon. Hell, almost from the minute she walked out onto the floor.

Jester and Rooster had brought over some of her shit earlier. In fact, he'd still been in bed and half-asleep when they arrived. They carried her stuff into the spare bedroom and quickly split after telling him they had left her in the rental office of her complex breaking her lease like he told her to.

He was sure that was going to cost him a pretty penny but watching Emma talking to his customers, making them feel *very* welcome... he knew it would be worth every fucking cent.

His patrons could have *Ember* in the afternoon and evening, but come late night and early morning, Emma was going to be all his. And only his.

He had told her it would be her choice to climb into his bed and that would remain true. But if it was up to him, she'd be underneath him, and sometimes on top, too.

He checked the clock hidden behind the bar and then said to Cubby, "Got a party at church. Moose's in charge. Any problems, text me."

"Got it, boss."

"Just make sure there ain't any problems."

Cubby gave him an answering chin lift and a grunt as Dawg walked from behind the bar and over to where *Ember* was talking to one of his regulars.

The man's eyes were glued to the pale globes of flesh that were practically spilling out of the cups of her dress. He stepped up to Jack and slapped him on the back. "She treatin' you well, Jack-o?"

The man reluctantly raised his eyes to Dawg. "Sure is. Though when I asked her for a private dance, she refused."

"Yeah, she's just here to make sure you're happy. But not *that* happy."

Jack laughed, and his eyes landed back on Emma's tits. When the man licked his lips, Dawg fought the urge to smash his fist into his face.

"Now I gotta steal her away, my man. Got business to take care of."

Jack smirked. "Sure. *Business.* No wonder she isn't agreeing to a private dance."

"Right. To get over your disappointment, givin' you a drink on the house."

"Not sure if that's a fair trade, Dawg."

"Agreed. Ain't a fair trade, but will have to do." Dawg lifted his hand and caught Cubby's attention. He lifted a finger, tipped his chin toward Jack, and the bartender nodded in acknowledgment.

Dawg slipped an arm around Emma's waist and planted a possessive hand on the curve of her hip. "Now, we gotta go. She'll be here tomorrow night, Jack. See you then."

"Yeah, Dawg, you lucky bastard."

Dawg shot him a grin, then steered Emma away from the stage

and toward the back of the club. Before he opened the door to the private hallway, he tipped his head down and said in a low voice, "Gotta go upstairs an' change outta that dress, baby girl. Jeans. Regular shoes. Cover up your tits. Got me? Goin' to church."

Her eyebrows furrowed. "What kind of church do you attend?"

He grinned again, this time in amusement, and shook his head. "One for hellions."

He escorted her through the back area, out the back door and up to his apartment.

"Prospects moved your shit into the spare room. Gotta share a bathroom since this ain't no high-dollar penthouse. So keep your woman's shit to a minimum in there, got me?"

"I'll try to stay out of your way."

That wasn't quite what he wanted, but he didn't correct her. Instead he went into the kitchen, grabbed a beer from the fridge and knocked the cap off on the edge of the counter. "Wear closed shoes. Boots, if you got 'em. Gonna take my sled."

"What's a sled?"

He paused, the bottle halfway to his lips. "My bike."

"Should you be drinking before we get on your motorcycle?"

He snorted, then took a sip of his beer. The cool brew went down smoothly. "Yeah. Makes me steadier."

"I doubt that."

"Never doubt me, baby girl."

With her lips pursed as if she was about to backtalk him, she pinned him with a stare for a moment, then headed down the hallway to her room.

Not even an hour later, Emma was handing him her helmet after dismounting from his Harley. She pulled the elastic band out of her hair to let it fall around her shoulders.

That did not help his throbbing dick. The ride over wasn't long from Heaven's Angels to church, but having her pressed against his back during the ride had him almost purring as loudly as his sled's engine. She had done well for never being on a bike before.

Not that there was a lot to do. Just hang on tight.

That she did.

He placed the helmet on the seat, yanked his skull bandana down his face and tucked his glasses into the collar of his T-shirt.

"This doesn't look like any church I've ever seen before," she said staring at the steel door that led into the clubhouse. "What does the sign say over the door?"

Her hand felt so tiny in his when he grabbed it and pulled her over to the entrance. "Read it now."

"Dirty Angels MC... Down and dirty 'til dead." She dropped her gaze to him. "What does that mean?"

"Family. Brotherhood. That's what it fuckin' means."

"Is that your club motto?"

"Yeah, baby girl, it is."

"You have that tattooed over your heart."

His head jerked back. "Yeah." He hadn't realized she'd inspected his tattoos that closely.

"How long have you been a member?"

"Long time. Now, enough with the fuckin' questions." He reached for the door handle. "Stick close, got me? Want you in my sight at all times."

She pulled back on his hand. "Is it dangerous?"

"No. But you're fresh meat an' some of the hang-arounds an' prospects might come sniffin'."

She frowned. "Sniffing?"

"Any of 'em get pushy, you yell for me. Might think you're one of my girls."

"You bring the dancers here?"

"Normally, yeah."

"To do what? Entertain?"

Dawg yanked open the door and the music being piped into church from the outside courtyard hit them hard since the volume was louder than normal. But then Dirty Deed's, Nash's band, was playing *I Drink Alone* by George Thorogood. So that made sense. That was always a *turn-it-up-to-full-blast* song.

"Yeah, baby girl, they *entertain*," he finally answered her *what-felt-like-millionth* question as he dragged her inside.

The pool tables were occupied, a dart game was in full swing, and there was a crowd around the club's private bar.

A voice yelled out from the left. "Dawg, where's your girls? You only brought one tonight?"

Dawg's eyes narrowed as he swung his gaze in that direction. It landed on Badger, one of the newer prospects.

"Stand right there," Dawg said in a low voice to Emma. "Don't move, got me?"

He released her hand and moved toward the pool table before she could answer.

He snapped his fingers high in the air to get the attention of all the prospects playing pool. "Listen up an' listen good. See her?"

All eyes left him and landed on Emma, who surprisingly still stood exactly where he left her.

That was at least the second time today that she actually listened to him. Imagine that. A woman that followed directions. They were hard to come by.

"Asked you assholes a question. Didn't hear an answer yet."

"Yeahs" came from the *wet-behind-the-ears* bikers around the table.

"Ain't touchin' her." Dawg heard a few complaints muttered.

"She ain't off limits if she's a stripper," Badger claimed. "Can't touch the sweet butts, but was told your girls are fair game."

Dawg pinned him with his gaze. "She's off limits," he clarified slowly to make sure they did not mistake his meaning.

"Brother, why d'you bring 'er if we can't touch the fresh m—"

Before Badger finished his question, Dawg had fingers wrapped tightly around the newest recruit's throat. Eyes wide, his hands came up instinctively and clawed at Dawg's wrists.

"Prospect, you questionin' me? Need a reminder you're lower than a piece of shit stuck to the bottom of my fuckin' boot?" Dawg pushed the prospect away by his neck and Badger stumbled back. "Makin' this super fuckin' easy. She talks to you first, you can answer. She don't, don't say a fuckin' word to her. Got me?" He waited for their answers. "Got me?" he bellowed.

"Got yous" and "yeahs" answered him.

He nodded, then strode back to Emma, who watched him with her eyebrows so high they were clinging to her hairline.

"You need anything. *Anything.* Your toenails painted. Air in your tires. Mud cleaned off your shoes by one of their tongues. Get any one of 'em that's wearin' a vest that says 'prospect' to do it. They say no, you tell me. Got me?"

"Got you," she whispered, her gaze bouncing off each of the prospects as they went back to their pool game. She grabbed his arm and leaned in closer. "So what's a prospect?"

"A nobody."

"Doesn't Moose wear one of those vests?"

"Yeah. Moose's a good one. He's gonna make it. Some of those over there won't."

"Are they like a frat pledge?"

"A what?"

"Never mind." She shook her head then turned it toward the front of the room. "Why is everyone looking at us?"

He grinned. "'Cause you're fuckin' beautiful. An' they're jealous you ain't with them."

"Dawson..."

"Fuck!" he barked. He lowered his voice. "Don't call me that here."

"Why?"

"Just don't."

She grinned up at him. "Are you going to say please?"

"Fuck no." He grabbed her elbow and steered her toward the private bar. "Let's go. People you gotta meet."

———

eople she "gotta meet." There sure were a lot of them. Her head was spinning with all the names and faces, both men and women alike. All staring at her with curiosity and also glancing at Dawg with sly, knowing looks.

Which she had no idea what that could be about.

The best part was when she got to hold the cutest baby named Zeke. She had no problem remembering his name. Emma had shoved her nose into his downy hair and inhaled deeply. She missed that sweet baby smell.

From what she gathered, this was the MC's clubhouse and some of the members lived upstairs, some lived other places, like Dawg. Dawg had also shown her the public bar at the front of the property, The Iron Horse Roadhouse. When she was being introduced to some of the bikers, she was told who ran what. Like a body shop and a towing company. And Zeke's mother, Sophie, ran a bakery with another woman who had dark long hair.

The women seemed openly friendly and welcoming. The men didn't hide their interest.

Emma sipped at the rum and Coke that the dark-haired woman behind the bar had made her. A shiver ran through her when she tasted how strong it was. Dawg slipped a hand beneath her hair and wrapped his warm, long fingers around the back of her neck.

"Okay, baby girl?" he asked against her ear.

"Yes, it's just strong. She must be trying to get me intoxicated."

"Yeah," he murmured. "Loosen you up a bit."

His deep voice and warm breath so close to her ear made her shiver like the strong drink. It also didn't help that he kept brushing his thumb across her skin. She shook herself mentally. This biker shouldn't have an effect on her like he did. "What was her name?"

"Bella."

"Bella," Emma repeated in a whisper. "Beautiful name for a beautiful woman."

"Yeah, she is. Gonna talk to her ol' man."

"Who's her *ol' man?*"

"A pig."

Emma blinked. "Does *ol' man* mean husband?"

"Same shit."

"And her husband's a cop?"

"Her ol' man is, yeah."

"What's she doing here, then?" It seemed that it would be a conflict of interest for a cop to have a significant other as part of a motorcycle club.

"She's DAMC born an' bred, baby girl. She's family."

"And her... *ol' man* doesn't mind her being here?"

"He minds."

"But she does it, anyway?"

"Ain't got a say."

Emma pursed her lips, thinking about what Dawg just said. "Is he going to be able to help me?"

"Dunno, baby girl. Gonna ask 'im. In the meantime, gotta find Diesel."

"I didn't meet him yet?"

Dawg chuckled. "No. You'd know if you'd met him."

"He sounds... interesting." Especially with a name like Diesel. "Is that his real name?"

"Yeah."

"Is he here tonight?"

"Probably outside. Don't let his ol' lady out of his sight."

"Why? Is she untrustworthy?"

Dawg snorted and grinned down at her. "No. She's pregnant."

Emma blinked in surprise. That was a weird reason. "So?"

"So... since he found out, he don't let her out of his sight," he repeated, like that answered her question.

"I don't understand. Why?"

"Jesus, the fuckin' questions! Because he's just like that. Keepin' her safe."

"From what?"

"From..." His eyes slid to the side as his words drifted off.

"From?" she prodded.

"Nothin' for you to worry 'bout. Got enough problems on your plate."

That she did. But she was still curious about why a man would have to follow his pregnant wife... ol' lady... *whatever* around like a guard dog.

And what did she need protection from? Just what was this club involved in?

Maybe she should rethink letting Dawg help her. Maybe they were doing some illegal activity which would only make things worse for her.

Oh boy, she just gave up her apartment, too. Maybe she could convince the complex office to—

"Baby girl."

"Huh?" She looked up into Dawg's deep green eyes which were crinkled at the corners as if he was amused.

"Gotta stop bitin' that lip of yours before I do somethin' that'll make you blush."

She released her lip and glanced around quickly. "Here?"

"Here." He pinned his lips together, tucked a lock of her hair behind her ear, then jerked his head toward a side door. "C'mon. Gonna go talk to D."

———

Emma sat on the top of a wood picnic table under an open pavilion that was not far from a stage where a band played. An actual live band. They were good, too. Dawg had said the band's name was Dirty Deeds and that one of his "brothers" played and sang in it. She was starting to pick up on some of the language Dawg used in regards to his club. Like brother. Ol' man. Ol' lady.

And speaking of ol' lady, even in just the glow of the roaring bonfire, she could see Diesel's headed in her direction. Emma's eyes slid to where Dawg was talking to this 'D' in the shadows next to the pavilion. Even though Dawg was a big guy, Diesel was even bigger. Big as in huge and scary.

Not the type of man you'd want to meet in a dark alley.

When Dawg introduced her to Diesel, he just grunted as he took a good look at her. It was almost as if he was scrutinizing her. Though, she wasn't sure if she passed inspection or not since she got no reaction from him at all.

Dawg was right about Diesel keeping an eye on his woman. The man's eyes tracked the petite woman as she crossed the court-yard and approached Emma.

"Hey," Jewel said and hauled herself up next to her on the table. The woman wore a snug black camisole that had large white letters proclaiming she was a "bad ass biker bitch" across her chest.

"Hey," she greeted the woman back. "I'm still learning these biker terms. You're Diesel's ol' lady, right?"

The dark-haired woman smiled. "Yeah. Sure am." With a groan, Jewel leaned back, unfastened the top button of her shorts and then sighed with what sounded like relief. "Sorry. Shorts are getting tight."

"Please excuse my curiosity, but are you officially his wife?"

"No. Not legally."

"So, you're his girlfriend?"

"An ol' lady is more than just a regular piece. It's almost the same thing as being a wife."

"A regular piece?"

"A regular piece of ass is like a girlfriend; however, they're not officially claimed. But, either way, your man ends up in your bed every night. They're not out sticking their dicks in every hole that's available."

"Claimed?" Emma squeaked. Another term she needed to be "schooled" on, but she wasn't sure if she liked the sound of that one.

"Yeah, your man can take it to the table and claim you, which means you become an official ol' lady."

None of that sounded appealing. At all.

Jewel lifted her hand with a laugh. "And before you ask, taking it to the table means they go in front of the Executive Committee and request a vote."

That was the most bizarre thing she ever heard. Well, maybe not the most bizarre but pretty damn close. It sounded like the women were treated like property.

And that couldn't be right. It was the twenty-first century; no man owned a woman. Right?

"Are the guys loyal to their ol' ladies? Once they're officially claimed, I mean."

Jewel hesitated. "For the most part." She shrugged. "Like a marriage, there's no guarantee."

Emma glanced over at the two men standing at the corner of the pavilion, talking. "How long have you known Diesel?"

"My whole life. We were both born into this club."

"Oh wow!"

"Yeah."

"I guess you like being a part of the club, then."

"Wouldn't want anything else." She placed a hand on her slightly rounded belly. "Especially now."

"Congratulations, by the way. Dawson... *Oh damn!* Sorry. Don't tell him I called him that!"

Jewel's eyes widened, and she barked out a laugh. "Dawson?"

"Well, that's his name."

"It is?"

Emma looked at Jewel in surprise. "You didn't know that?"

"Hell no!"

Oh double damn. Emma's heart began to race in panic. "Oh Lord. Please don't tell anyone."

"How did you find out what it was?"

"It's listed like that on Heaven's Angel's business license. I did a search online for a contact name..."

"Holy shit."

"Please, *please*... don't say anything. He didn't want me to call him that here."

The corners of Jewel's blue eyes crinkled. "Just here?"

"Well, everywhere. He gets annoyed when I do."

Jewel nodded then made a twisting motion at her lips like she was locking them, then she tossed the invisible key away. "I won't say a word. Promise." Jewel leaned back and crossed her ankles, glancing over to where Dawg and her ol' man were talking.

"Daw—*Dawg* told me that you're pregnant. How far along are you?"

Jewel tilted her head and studied her for a moment. Finally, she said, "Four months."

"How exciting! I was walking on air when I found out I was pregnant!"

"You have a kid?"

"Yes, a daughter. Lily. She's seven."

"You don't look old enough to have a seven-year-old."

"Oh, I am."

Jewel's eyes narrowed. "But didn't the prospects just move you into Dawg's place this morning?"

Emma wondered how she knew that, but then from what she could tell so far, it seemed to be a close-knit club. She imagined news traveled fast. "Yes, they did."

"You want your daughter living over a strip club?"

"No... No, it's just temporary..."

"Until what?"

Emma shook her head. The fact that she allowed her daughter to be stolen from her was embarrassing. It shouldn't be, but it was. It made her feel like such a failure as a mother. How could she not protect her own daughter better? So, she wasn't sure she wanted to talk about it with people she didn't know. People who might judge her.

"You don't mind your daughter living over a strip club even temporarily?" Jewel asked again.

Damn, that made her sound like an even worse mother! "She's... not with me."

"Where is she?" Jewel asked then raised her palm. "Look, I

don't mean to pry. If you don't want to tell me, that's your business. But I have a feeling that whatever it is, it's what your man's talking about with mine."

"He's not my man."

Jewel pursed her lips as she studied Emma for a moment. "No?"

"No. We just have a..."

"A?" the woman prodded.

"An arrangement." Emma guessed it could be called that. Honestly, she didn't know what it should be called.

Jewel's brows pinned together. "Are you his new house mouse? Because if so, I didn't know he was looking."

Another term she didn't know. It was like these people had their own language! "What's a house mouse?"

"Usually someone who needs a place to live, but normally is a bit younger than you and is related to the club in some way. Instead of paying for rent, food and shit like that, she keeps the brother's place clean, does chores like grocery shopping, beer runs, and does the cooking. It works out well since none of the females in the DAMC can live at church."

"Huh. He did ask me to clean up around his place," Emma murmured.

"Has he asked you to cook yet?"

"Not yet."

"Doesn't mean it isn't coming," Jewel said.

"Has Dawg ever had a house mouse before?"

"Not that I know of."

"Do you think I'm his house mouse?" Emma asked in a panic.

Jewel laughed. "It's not a bad thing. It's certainly not like being a sweet butt or even one of his strippers."

Emma rolled her lips under. She figured she better not tell Jewel that was how she met Dawg, by begging to become one of his strippers. "What's a sweet butt? That's a weird term."

"A sweet butt puts out to any of the brothers. Sometimes we call them patch whores. They do that in exchange for being allowed to hang around the club and party, shit like that."

The woman was just a wealth of information. "Why would a woman want to be used like that?"

Jewel shrugged. "I don't know. In hopes to become an ol' lady, maybe? To drink for free? To get access to dick?"

"Wait. The men share these women?"

"Yeah. Gross, right? And Dawg's girls, too. The prospects can't touch the sweet butts, but Dawg's girls are free rein."

Emma's eyes slid back to where Dawg was standing. She did a double-take when she realized that both men were staring in their direction with serious looks on their faces. "Do most of the bikers take advantage of using these sweet butts and the strippers?"

Jewel followed her gaze. "If you're asking me if Dawg does sweet butts and strippers, you'd have to ask him."

"He told me he doesn't do his girls."

"Yeah, that's one of his rules now after..."

"After what?"

"Shit got sticky with one of them. Hard to scrape off a woman when you employ her."

"Sounds messy," Emma said, now wanting to ask a million more questions. Questions Jewel probably wouldn't answer for her.

"Yeah, so why's Dawg talking to D? And why'd you move into his place this morning? And why'd he bring you here tonight?"

"Woman," came a loud bark nearby before Emma could answer.

She twisted her neck to see the massive man named Diesel standing at the end of the table, Dawg by his side. Both wore very deep frowns.

"What?" Jewel answered.

"Quit the yappin'. Got work to do. Let's go."

"Now?" Jewel asked.

Diesel grunted, "Yeah."

"I can catch a ride home."

The big man cocked an eyebrow in his woman's direction. "Know better than that."

"I'm fine. It's safe here."

"Long as my kid's in your belly, ain't riskin' it. No lip. Let's go."

Jewel sighed and rolled her eyes. "I can't wait until the Warriors are all..." She shot a quick glance at Emma. "*Gone* and I can live a normal fucking life." She pushed to her feet. "Welcome to the sisterhood, Emma." Then she gave Emma a wink and patted Dawg on the arm. "She's sweet."

"Right," Dawg grumbled.

Emma waited until Diesel and Jewel left, then she turned to Dawg. "Who are the Warriors?"

"'Nother MC."

"Why can't she live a normal life with them around?"

"None of us can. 'Nough questions."

She agreed. She had asked enough questions for the evening. Though, there was at least one burning question she needed an answer to.

"Gonna grab a beer. Want somethin'?"

"Yes, please." She needed a drink and to process everything she'd learned so far tonight. Which was a lot, and the night wasn't even over yet.

CHAPTER SEVEN

D awg propped his head on his pillow and shoved a hand under the sheet to grab his nuts. He listened to Emma rustling around in her room, digging through her shit. For what, he didn't know or care. He just knew his sac needed to be drained, and she was a viable candidate. First off, she was just feet away in the next room. Second, she was smoking hot. And lastly, he didn't want to stick his dick in anyone else right now but her.

And if he did, he knew he'd have a tough time not thinking about Emma while he did so.

Before he had wandered into his room to shuck off his clothes and climb into his large, empty bed, he'd reminded her once more that his door would be open.

But she had seemed distracted and maybe even a little overwhelmed after being at the party at church. That was to be expected since she didn't know shit about the MC world and tonight had been somewhat of a rude awakening.

She had handled it well. Just like being on the back of his bike. Just like becoming the Heaven's Angel's hostess.

She seemed to adapt easily to new situations. Was flexible.

Fuck yeah. He liked that about her.

But that was clearly not the only thing he liked. Fuck no. He closed his eyes, his fingers finding the root of his dick, which had been at a half chub since he slipped under the sheets in anticipation of her possibly joining him.

He heard the hallway bathroom door click closed. Then the water run. Hopefully, she was washing the rest of the makeup she had worn downstairs earlier off her face. It hadn't been put on heavily, but he liked her better without any makeup at all and she hadn't removed it before they went to church.

He spread his legs wider and found a steady rhythm with his palm. He imagined Emma wearing that clingy dress from earlier while he pushed her against a wall, shoving that silky fabric up over her ass and fucking her from behind.

Yeah. Just like that.

Little noises coming from between those bitable lips of hers.

He swept away the bead of precum on the head and squeezed his dick tighter. Fuck, she had a tight snatch and he couldn't wait to feel how hot and wet it got once more. He tilted his head back on the pillow as he envisioned her tits swinging and her nipples puckered every time she had tried to "audition" for him. And again, when she was on stage yesterday. Nipples that were made for his mouth.

He told her he wasn't going to help her out in exchange for sex. And he wasn't. But, *damn*, it was hard to hold himself to that. He wanted to help her because she had gotten the shaft from her husband. Or ex-husband. Whatever the bastard was. And no parent should be stripped from their child's life without a valid reason.

A curse slipped through his lips. He didn't need to think of that guy and all that shit while he was jerking on his johnson. Fuck no...

He needed to concentrate on Emma instead. Who may very well be naked in his shower right at that moment. Her skin wet and slick as she sudsed herself up, running her hands over her own tits, down to her little pink pussy, around the back...

He stroked faster, his hips lifting off the mattress with each down stroke of his palm.

Fuck. If she didn't climb into his bed and onto his dick tonight, he'd need to invest in a vat of lube, because it was going to be difficult to live in the same apartment as her and not get any. And it wasn't like he could invite any other women up while Emma was staying with him.

Fuck no, he couldn't. His damn sex life was now on pause. The only person who could press "play" would be Emma herself.

"Um..."

Dawg's eyes popped open and he released his dick. "Jesus," he muttered. Caught red-handed.

"I... uh..."

He sat up, adjusting the sheet over his lap. Not that it hid the evidence of his raging hard-on. Not that he really wanted to hide it from her, anyhow. Especially since she was apparently taking advantage of his "open door" offer.

Fuck yeah!

"I was wondering if you had a spare toothbrush? I can't find mine."

Fuck noooo!

She wasn't standing in his doorway wearing some old oversized T-shirt because she was going to climb onto his dick.

Life couldn't be so fucking cruel.

"Really want me to get up an' get you one right now?"

Her eyes dropped to his lap. "I... Just tell me where it is."

"Where spare toothbrushes are kept, baby girl. Check the medicine cabinet."

"Ah... okay. I'll..."

"Baby girl..." he said softly.

Her eyes lifted to his. "Yeah?"

"That all you wanted?" Because the flush running up her neck into her cheeks and her nipples beading under the thin, worn cotton were screaming something different at him.

"Yes."

"Sure?"

"Yes. Just a toothbrush," she mumbled, her hand clutching her throat. "I... I'm going to go brush my teeth."

"Door's gonna be open." *And my fuckin' dick's gonna remain hard, damn it.*

He barely heard her "okay" as she hurried back to the bathroom. He waited for the door to slam shut but it didn't. But it did sound like she was fumbling around in there, cursing. Then the water was running again, and he could hear her brushing her teeth.

He lifted his hand and told it, "Fuck. Guess it's just you an' me."

His hand didn't answer.

He settled back against the pillow and began all over again, rewinding the visions in his head to give him fodder to jerk himself off. He pictured the sexy little mole she had on the outer curve of her left breast that he wanted to lick and suck. He imagined running his tongue down to her belly button and sucking on that, too. Then lower to suck on her...

He groaned.

"Dawson..."

What the fuck! Again?

What the hell did she need now? A razor?

He opened his eyes and glanced in the direction of the doorway, where once again she was standing there in that ugly-ass T-shirt that should be thrown in the trash. It didn't do her hot little body any justice.

"Fuck, baby girl. Better be in here for one reason an' one reason only."

"I..." Her words caught as she walked farther into his room, ripping her T-shirt over her head. Revealing the fact that she only wore lacy pink panties underneath.

Damn.

When she reached the foot of his bed, she stood staring at him, not saying a word. Her lips were parted, her blue eyes hooded, her nipples as hard as fucking pebbles, her chest rising and falling quickly.

"Thank fuck," he muttered and pulled back the sheet. "C'mere, baby girl. Looks like you got a problem that you need me to fix."

"I do," she whispered, the color high in her cheeks.

He patted the bed next to him. "C'mon. Tell Dawg what it is."

"I couldn't get what you were doing out of my head."

"Like that?"

"Yes," she breathed.

He kicked the sheet from him completely, showing her just how much she affected him. He had never released his dick when she interrupted him the second time. So, as she watched, he began to stroke again. From root to tip. Fisting, squeezing.

He couldn't believe how fucking hot it was that she watched him.

His voice caught as he demanded, "Tell me how much you like it."

"A lot."

"Make you wet?"

"Yes." She climbed onto the bed and between his spread legs.

Before he could finish an upstroke, she knocked his hand away and began to take over. Her hand was a hell of a lot smaller than his, but felt so much fucking better.

Then she dropped to her belly and her hot little mouth took him deeply.

He lost his breath as she wrapped her lips around him, sucking hard. His hands automatically dug into her hair as her head bobbed up and down on his dick.

"Baby..." he groaned. "Ah, *fuuuuck*..."

It had been a while since he'd gotten head. And even longer since he got a blowjob that was as good as she was doing. Damn, the woman had some skills. Skills he hoped came naturally and not because she sucked a lot of fucking dicks.

He pushed that thought out of his head and peered down his body. He couldn't see Emma's face, and he wanted to. Gathering her hair firmly into a ponytail with one hand, he pulled it away. And when he did, her eyes hit his. The way her mouth was stretched around him... *Fuck!*

The fingers she had encircled around him at the base squeezed so hard his hips popped off the bed. But she didn't release him. Oh no, she fucking didn't. She sucked him harder and faster, her tongue flicking over the head of his dick every time she hit the top.

He couldn't take anymore. He didn't want to blow his load down her throat. He'd leave that for another time since he didn't want to miss out on the opportunity to sink deep inside her. He wasn't sure how many more chances he'd get to do just that.

After fucking her the other day, he hadn't been able to stop thinking about doing it again.

Now he was getting that chance. He tugged on her hair. "Baby girl..." Him pulling on her hair didn't stop her from continuing with her mission for him to lose his fucking mind. "*Fuck*... baby girl... Emma..."

She smiled around his dick.

"Ain't funny, Em. Gotta stop." She seriously had to stop. He groaned when she pressed a finger in the sensitive area between his balls and his asshole as her cheeks hollowed out from sucking him so hard.

What the fuck?

What was she doing? *Oh... Oh fuck.*

"Emma!" he barked, rolling up to a seat and yanking on her hair even harder. Relief flooded him when she finally released him with a wet popping sound.

"You didn't like that?" she asked with a smile.

"Ain't about likin' it..." He released her hair and rolled to his side enough to reach the drawer in his nightstand. Feeling around, he found a wrap and pulled it out.

Within seconds, he had it open and rolled down his dick, which was throbbing, his balls tight. At least wearing a condom would help keep him from blowing his load in three seconds flat. Yeah, maybe extend it to a whole ten seconds.

As he watched her rip off her panties, he said, "Promise I'll return the favor next time, yeah? Right now—"

He fell back onto the mattress as she shoved him hard.

Then just climbed the fuck on him. Held him in place and sank her hot, wet pussy onto his dick.

He grunted and grabbed her hips as she began to move, her head thrown back, all kinds of sounds coming out of her mouth. Whimpers and sighs and... *Fuck!* And those tits! Bouncing up and down, teasing the shit out of him.

"Baby girl, gotta slow down."

"No," she moaned.

No? She just said no? Just like that?

"Yeah, Em, gotta—"

"I'm coming," she cried out, grinding down on him hard.

No shit. That was quick. And she wasn't lying, either. Because suddenly she was pulsating around him and soaking his dick, too.

But, *oh damn*, that was going to make him come. He clenched his jaws in an attempt to hold it off, digging his fingers deeper into the flesh around her hips.

Then she collapsed on his chest, like the orgasm had stolen all the bones from her body.

He stilled. She stilled. Okay, he was good. He just needed a minute. Just a few seconds... She rolled her eyes up toward his.

"Ah, fuck," he muttered, then came. "*Goddamnit.*"

She hid her giggle against his chest. After a moment, she glanced back up at him. "You didn't want to come?"

"Not that fast. Fuck no."

She patted his chest. "But I came, so you're good."

No, he wasn't "good." He just blew his load in less than a minute. There was nothing good about that. Not only because it was embarrassing but because he wanted to enjoy being inside her longer.

"Next time you'll last longer."

Next time? "Yeah," he said, keeping his voice steady. Though he really wanted to fist bump her instead since she just announced there was going to be a "next time."

She slipped off him and to his side, her head still on his chest, her hand planted on his gut.

Damn, her cuddling against him felt good. He ripped the condom off, knotted it and dropped it to the floor.

"That's gross."

"What?"

"Dropping that on the floor!" she exclaimed in disgust.

"Where you want me to put it?"

"In the trash."

"It'll get there... eventually. Ain't movin' right now."

"Why?"

"'Cause you're in my bed. Don't wanna miss a second of it."

She jerked against him. "I... I don't know what to say to that," she breathed.

"Don't say nothin'. Just enjoy it." He curled his fingers around the back of her head and pressed her closer to him.

His heart thumped heavily in his chest at the thought of her sleeping next to him every night.

He closed his eyes. What was he thinking? He hardly knew the woman. And she didn't come from his world.

He'd been there, done that. And didn't even have a fucking T-shirt to show for it.

Once he helped get her daughter back, he was sure she'd be on her way. Marching right back out of his life. Living above a strip club was no place for a kindergarten teacher and her young daughter.

"I know I asked a lot of questions earlier... but I need to ask a couple more."

A lot of questions? The woman could rattle them off like a machine gun.

He combed his fingers through her hair, smoothing the silky strands across his chest. "Shoot."

"One of the ladies—"

Dawg snorted loudly.

She whacked him lightly and started again. "Jewel asked if I'm your house mouse."

Dawg tilted his head down to study Emma. "Did she now?"

"Yes. Am I?"

"She tell you what a house mouse was?"

"Yes."

"Brothers don't normally sleep with their house mouse. Though, sometimes shit happens... but, no, ain't my house mouse. Hired you to be the hostess for my club. Wanna cook me a meal, ain't gonna say no. Wanna scrub the toilet, ain't gonna stop you. But, baby girl, that ain't required. Just like bein' in my bed ain't, either. Want you here 'cause you wanna be, not because you hafta be."

"Well, I have to admit the sex has been nice."

"Nice?"

"Yes, nice," she answered on a soft sigh.

"Just nice?"

"Well, it *was* a little quick." She smirked up at him.

Dawg frowned. "But you're gonna let me make it up to you." He wasn't asking her; he was telling her. He wasn't giving her the chance to change her mind. He might be a stupid fuck when it came to this woman, but he wasn't *that* stupid.

"Yes, I'd like that," she said softly.

Dawg grinned up at the ceiling. "While you're here, want you in my bed every night, baby girl. You okay with that?"

"Yes. I'd like that, too."

His grin widened to a smile. "Don't ever feel obligated. The minute you want out, you tell me. Ain't forcin' myself on nobody."

She pressed a light kiss on his chest. "Okay. I'll let you know the second I'm done with you."

He jerked his head up to stare at her and her body began to shake. "Think you're funny."

A cute little snort escaped her. "No."

"Yeah, you do."

She sobered. "I have another question. What happened with the discussion with Diesel? Can he help?"

With a sigh, he relaxed back against the pillow again. "Got D workin' on it. He'll pull through. His crew's good."

"He has a crew? What does he do?"

"Runs a security company."

"Security. Like alarm systems?"

"Not quite. Though he's good at installin' 'em. Did the system downstairs for the club. But he's moved on from shit like that. Has built a crew that's got a lotta skills. They get shit done. Like I said before, they can find people who don't wanna be found."

"Sounds expensive."

"Again, you ain't payin' for it."

"But you are."

Dawg didn't say anything for a moment. He and D hadn't talked payment since the man usually did shit for the brothers for nothing. However, Emma was an outsider and he wasn't sure if D would cover it or expect Dawg to. But he would. He'd cover D's expenses without a doubt, because he was sure that was going to cost a shit ton. Diesel was planning on sending at least two of his guys to talk to the PI that Emma used. Then from there pick up the trail where the PI quit once Emma had run out of funds.

He wasn't sure just how cold that trail was, but they'd find out. And Dawg had no doubt if anybody could find Emma's ex, it would be them. D said he'd put Hunter and Walker on the job.

Then follow up with Mercy if need be.

Emma's ex was going to regret ever taking her little girl.

"Got it covered. Just gotta be a good hostess for Heaven's Angels an' not worry 'bout a thing. Got me?"

"Hard not to worry..." She chewed on her lower lip.

"Know it, baby girl. Your ex wouldn't hurt 'er, right? Outta spite or anything?"

"No, I doubt it. I don't know about his girlfriend though."

"At least she wasn't your best friend, stealin' your husband an' your kid."

"She can have my husband. I just want Lily back."

"Ex."

She tipped her eyes up to him. "What?"

"Ex. Said husband."

When her eyes slid to the side, a knot grew in his gut. "Ain't officially an ex, is he?"

The warm breath she exhaled in a rush swept across his bare chest. "No, when I ran out of money, I couldn't afford my attorney, either. Everything I had, everything I made, went into finding Lily. I figured I could get the divorce papers filed later, when I recovered financially."

"Fuck," he muttered.

"Sorry."

"Ain't gotta apologize to me, baby girl. Gonna get that taken care of, too."

"How?"

"The DAMC's attorney. She'll take care of the legal shit."

"The club has an attorney?"

"Yeah."

"Why?"

He shrugged. "Legal shit."

"Like representing people in court?"

"That an' business shit. The DAMC's got a lot of businesses. A lot of irons in the fire."

"You must keep her busy. But, Dawson, I can't afford her, either."

He sighed. "Not gonna tell you again. Got it covered."

"But—"

"She's part of the club. She'll help you out."

"Oh. The club doesn't pay her?"

He had no idea how much she charged an hour, or if she would even bill him. "She's Hawk's ol' lady."

"Hawk... I met him tonight."

"Yeah," he grunted.

"Diesel's brother with the mohawk."

"Yeah."

"And the woman who was stuck to his side was—"

"Yeah, Kiki. Smart. Capable. She'll get shit done. Also, gonna stop at the pig pen tomorrow an' talk to Bella's ol' man."

"The cop."

"Yeah," he grunted.

"The cops haven't helped much," she said softly.

"Yeah, just wanna run a few things by 'im."

"Dawson..." she whispered, reaching up to cup his cheek.

"Yeah?"

"I want to thank you for everything."

His nostrils flared as his chest got tight. He grabbed her hand and brought it to his lips, pressing them against her knuckles. "Nothin' to thank me for yet. Can do it after we get Lily back." He dropped their clasped hands to his chest and squeezed hers gently.

"You don't know how much that means to me."

She was wrong. He did.

Dawg closed his eyes and saw his own daughter walking out of the school's entrance the day he tracked her down. She had been wearing a plaid skirt and a maroon polo shirt. What looked like a school uniform that all the girls wore. Her dark blonde hair was pulled back into a ponytail and he wanted to see if her eyes were the same green as his.

As she had bounded down the steps at the end of the school day toward the curb, he fought to keep himself from getting out of his truck and calling out to her. His hand had been on the door handle when he saw the vehicle she approached. A top of the line Mercedes sedan, a male in a suit behind the steering wheel. Caitlin's smile was wide when she opened the passenger side door and climbed in after throwing her book bag in the back seat. Then the man leaned over and gave her a kiss on the cheek. Dawg watched them as they drove off.

A few minutes later he followed, eventually parking down the street from their huge home in an upscale neighborhood.

That's when it hit him hard that he had nothing to offer his daughter.

Nothing at all.

He drove away not allowing himself to look back. He never returned to the school, and he made sure to stay out of that particular neighborhood.

He didn't belong there.

Not only that, but seeing her and not being able to talk to her or have anything to do with someone who was a piece of him, ripped him apart and twisted his gut painfully.

He hadn't spent one fucking moment with his daughter and it pained him to be kept in the dark, to be kept *from her* for all those years. So, yeah, he could understand the hurt Emma was going through.

And that shit just pissed him the fuck off.

CHAPTER EIGHT

s Emma sat facing a metal desk, Dawg slouched in the chair
next to her, his thighs spread so far apart his knee almost
touched hers. The uniformed man on the other side of the surprisingly neat and organized desk had asked her questions. Lots of
questions. Mostly the same ones the police at her local station had
asked her right after Lily's abduction.

But Dawg knew this cop. This Axel. An interesting name for a
police officer who lived with one of the DAMC women. *Bella.* Yes,
the dark-haired beauty who worked at the bakery in town. The one
who was behind the bar last night at what Dawg called "church."

Axel kept his face skillfully masked as he'd questioned her, but
every once in a while, he'd shoot a curious glance over at Dawg,
then return his attention quickly back to her. Maybe he couldn't
understand why or how Dawg was involved in all this.

Though, honestly, Emma wasn't sure why, either. Why he cared
so much whether she ever found her daughter. But he did, and his
determination to get Lily back made all the questions Axel asked
her easier to swallow.

After a while, Axel was quiet, typing information into the
computer on his desk.

Emma held her breath, hoping he would find something that the other officers had missed.

When he sat back and scrubbed a hand over his short dark hair, her stomach sank. His blue eyes swung to Dawg. "Just *how* do you know each other?"

Dawg slowly leaned forward in his chair, thick, tattooed arms crossed over his broad chest. "Does it matter?"

"Well, she's a kindergarten teacher, Dawg. She kind of doesn't..." He drifted off and eyeballed Emma, who, unlike Dawg, was on the edge of her seat so she sat straighter in her chair.

"Don't what?" Dawg growled.

Axel lifted a hand in a placating fashion. "Truth is, she doesn't seem to fit... your lifestyle."

Dawg grunted. "Your brother's DAMC, Axel. Your woman is, too."

His brother was part of the MC? That was odd.

She opened her mouth to ask questions in regard to that, but Axel continued with a nod. "I know that. That wasn't what I meant."

Dawg's eyes narrowed. "Meant what? 'Cause I run Heaven's Angels?"

"Well, that, too. I didn't expect you to—"

"To what?"

"End up with someone like Emma."

Her head jerked up as her spine stiffened. She repeated, "Someone like me?"

"Not a stripper, I guess," Axel clarified with a frown.

"Don't do my girls," Dawg grumbled.

"We're not together," Emma quickly added. Then she ignored the heated stare coming from the big man in what seemed like an extremely small seat next to her. "He's being very kind by helping me."

"*Kind*... So, you're not *together*?" Axel asked her the question but stared at Dawg.

"We're together," Dawg answered.

Axel sat back and laughed. "*Shiiit*. Another one bites the dust."

She didn't like the sound of that, even though she wasn't quite sure what the officer meant. "No..." Emma quickly said. Her head twisted toward Dawg. "No. That's not what this is... I'm..." How the hell did she explain their situation?

Axel smiled. "Got it." Then he sobered quickly. "Well, anyway, the bad news is I don't have any info. Looks like it's now considered a cold case for your local PD. It's been over a year now?"

Emma nodded, gnawing on her bottom lip.

"A cold case?" Dawg asked.

"Yeah. It was passed on to the FBI, who passed it on to INTERPOL. But, unfortunately, nothing new has been added to the file in over eight months." He turned to Emma. "Your daughter's in NCIC. Her case is listed as a parental abduction."

"What's NCIC?" Emma asked.

"It's the FBI's database for crime information. She's considered a missing person, but..."

"But?" Dawg barked.

Axel's brows pinned together as he considered the man across the desk from him. "But..." He turned back to Emma again. "You weren't divorced, right? You were living in the same household when he took her?"

"Yes, but I didn't give permission for him to take her. Or take her out of the country, for Christ's sake. I had no idea! He *stole* her."

Axel lifted a hand again, this time trying to pacify her. "I know. I'm sorry. It must be extremely difficult. And I assume that once she's found you'll be able to get full custody of her and a restraining order against your husband."

"He needs to be arrested," she mumbled.

"Agreed," Axel answered. He stared at Dawg for a long moment. "Guess you got Diesel on this, right?"

"Y—"

Dawg's hand shot out and latched onto her arm to stop her from answering.

What was that about?

Dawg growled, "Gonna do what needs done to find the bastard."

Axel sighed. "Which means you got D's crew on this."

"Just means we're gonna do what needs done to find the bastard," Dawg repeated.

"Then I'm surprised you even bothered coming in here today."

"Figured I'd give you pigs a chance to do the right thing."

Axel's eyes narrowed, and his nostrils flared. "Do you think a local PD is equipped to find a missing child in some foreign country?" He leaned forward and lowered his voice. "That's why the fucking FBI was notified. Her PD took the right steps, did all they could do. Someone who abducts a child and flees the States usually has some sort of financial backing."

Dawg pushed to his feet, snagged Emma under the elbow, and pulled her up as well. "Guess we're done here."

Axel rose, too, his hands landing on his hips above his gun belt. "Look, I'll contact the FBI, try to light a fire under their asses. I'll do what I can. Get the captain involved. Maybe he can make some calls, too. Not sure if it'll do any good, though. They get thousands of cases."

"Thank you," Emma said, even though any hope she had before coming to the police station was now dashed.

"Dawg, take her to Kiki. She's going to need an attorney to file paperwork for full custody. And for that restraining order I mentioned. Have her file for divorce while she's at it. Do what you have to do to make sure once Lily is back on American soil, she's protected."

Dawg grunted. "She'll be protected."

"Protected by the legal system," Axel clarified.

Emma didn't miss the tightening of Dawg's jaw as he steered her away from the desk with his hand firmly on her upper arm.

"Right," he grunted again.

"You're welcome," Axel called out.

Dawg flipped a hand in the air over his shoulder. Emma tried to turn and thank Axel again, but Dawg was dragging her quickly toward the entrance.

"He was trying to be helpful and you're being rude."

"He ain't helpin'."

"Yes he was, and he actually seemed to care."

"Right. Don't trust the pigs."

"Well, I don't have a choice."

"Gotta choice." He pulled her outside and over to his bike. He grabbed the helmet and handed it to her, then mounted, heeling the stand up.

"Diesel isn't going to do anything illegal, right? I can't risk getting Lily back only to lose her for some crazy reason."

"Get on."

She gripped the helmet tighter. "Dawson, I can't risk losing her again once I get her back."

He jerked a thumb behind him. "Get on my sled."

She took a deep breath of the humid mid-July air. "It's hot."

"Yeah."

She stared down at the black helmet in her hands. "Do I have to wear this?"

"Put it on an' get on the fuckin' bike."

"Why are you so grumpy?"

"'Cause it's fuckin' hot an' you're just standin' there. Sweatin' my balls off while I'm waitin'."

She reluctantly yanked the helmet over her head and opened the face shield. "I'm getting on. Hold on to your impatient sweaty balls. Sheesh."

His head tipped down as he stared at the bike's gas tank and, after a moment, he shook it. With a sigh, Emma planted her hands on his shoulders and climbed on behind him. Once she was settled tightly against his back, she wrapped her arms around his waist.

"Probably doesn't help by wearing a leather vest in the summer. It's probably giving you swamp ass, too."

His body jerked and after a moment, he said, "It's a cut."

"A what?"

Dawg hit the starter, and the bike roared to life, the vibrations of the engine making her whole body tingle. She slapped the plastic shield down over her face.

"Don't fall off," he yelled.

He twisted the throttle, and she yelped as the bike shot forward, making her hold on tighter as he pulled away from the station. As they rode through the streets of Shadow Valley, she realized he wasn't heading in the direction of Heaven's Angels.

Even though it was early yet, she needed to get ready to be on the club's floor as the hostess soon. She wanted to make sure she was holding up her end of the deal.

She lifted the shield part way. "Where are we going?" she yelled over the noise of the wind and the exhaust.

"Just hang on."

Oh, she was hanging on, no doubt about that. Having her arms wrapped around the big man in front of her felt good. It felt right, even though the vest she was plastered against had patches that clearly stated in no uncertain terms that he was a biker and what club he belonged to. In fact, they were the exact same patches he had tattooed onto his back.

Her life had been turned upside down for the past year and a half. But it was weird that it seemed to right itself whenever she was with Dawg. She'd never been with a man like him before. And never would have guessed that she would ever be.

But here she was, on the back of a Harley, clinging to a burly biker. And sleeping with him, too.

Last night, and again this morning, he had made up for his initial minute man routine and then some. In fact, her inner thighs were still smarting from the brush burn from his rough beard.

She smiled, heat rushing through her, as she remembered him with his head between her legs, making her orgasm several times. *Several.* Good ones, too. Yes, she really, really liked his beard now. Even if it did make her a bit sore in her most sensitive spots.

Not realizing she had closed her eyes during that replay in her

DOWN & DIRTY: DAWG

mind, she popped them open and saw they were headed out of town.

She had no idea where they were going. But before long, her stress seemed to melt away as he took her on a ride through the countryside, over hills and hugging the curves of the road. The longer they rode, the less she wanted to head back to reality.

Being on the back of what he called his "sled" felt like freedom. She wished she wasn't wearing the helmet because she needed to feel the wind in her hair and on her face. She opened the shield and tipped her face toward the sun, closing her eyes once more to enjoy its warm summer rays.

Every once in a while, Dawg would lay a hand on her knee and squeeze. And sometimes he'd even let it linger which sent butter-flies fluttering in her belly. Not only did he have mad skills with his tongue, but his fingers were a close second.

She let the vibrations of the bike soothe away her worries. For some reason, the man in front of her made her think everything was going to end up all right. Maybe she was foolish in believing that. But she had to hold on to at least that thread of hope.

All those months of begging people to help her and they would, but only if she could write them a fat check or hand over a wad of cash. She understood it, though. Her problems weren't theirs. They, whether it was her attorney or her investigator, had a business to run, expenses to pay.

But the man in front of her, the biker, the strip club manager, the person she least expected to help her, was giving her every-thing she needed. He was being generous with his time and his connections. And for what?

He'd known her for only a split moment. That was all. And he had taken everything she'd told him about Lily's abduction as truth, never once questioning her. Not once.

But she'd never be able to repay him for his generosity. And that wasn't fair to him.

Suddenly the motorcycle slowed, and Dawg pulled off into a wooded area into what looked like a state park. The parking lot was half full since, even though it was hot and humid, it was still a beautiful day and it was early yet. The real heat would hit later in the afternoon. But by then, both of them would be inside the air-conditioned club.

After looping the bike around the paved lot, he walked it back-ward into an empty spot, kicked the stand down and shut the engine off.

He yanked the bandana that covered his mouth down his face. "Get off."

She did what she was told and couldn't wait to remove the helmet. When her head was finally free, she shook her hair out and sighed with relief. "I don't want to wear that."

"Gotta wear it," he said, climbing off his bike.

"You don't."

"Yeah," was all he grunted, took the helmet from her and hung it over one of the handlebars.

She glanced around looking for any indication of their location. "Where are we?"

"A park."

Emma shot him an exasperated look, and he smirked.

"Stop here sometimes on club runs."

"What's a club run?"

"When we all go out ridin' our sleds together," he answered.

"That sounds nice."

He chuckled. "Yeah, it's nice."

"You guys do that often?"

"When the weather's good, yeah."

She looked up at the tall trees that lined the lot. At least there was shade where he parked. "So, what's special about this park?"

"Gonna show you."

"Don't we need to get back? I need to get to work."

"Don't worry, I know the manager."

"Well, sometimes he can be a bit of a grump," she answered Dawg as he grabbed her hand and pulled her along behind him.

"Was he grumpy when his face was buried in your cunt this mornin'?"

Her mouth dropped open.

"Was he grumpy when his dick was makin' you squeal?"

"I didn't *squeal*."

"The fuck you didn't. So loud my ears were ringin'. Musta been doin' somethin' right."

Emma giggled. "Must have."

As he led her along, she watched her footing as they traveled along a narrow dirt trail through the woods. She was glad she had thrown on a pair of sneakers this morning. Every time they'd pass hikers coming the opposite direction, they'd stare at Dawg wide-eyed. She guessed he wasn't the sort of man you met along a trail in the woods. At least voluntarily. Then their eyes would land on him gripping her hand tightly as he pulled her along behind him and they would give her a look that almost seemed to be out of concern.

She'd just smile and trudge along after him, trying not to trip. Because if she did, he'd most likely continue to drag her over the tree roots and exposed rocks. He probably wouldn't even realize he was hauling dead weight behind him.

She giggled at the image of a Neanderthal dragging his woman by her hair into his cave after clubbing her.

Mine.

Woman. Mine.

When she was least expecting it, he came to a dead stop and before she could slow her forward motion, she slammed right into his back.

"Hey!" she yelled at him. "A little warning would be nice."

He said nothing, and she moved around him to see what he was staring at.

"Oh," she breathed.

He had taken her to a waterfall deep within the woods. It was absolutely stunning. Breathtaking even.

"C'mon," he grunted, then releasing her hand, climbed out onto a nearby boulder that overlooked the falls.

"Are you supposed to do that?" she called out as she watched him choose his footing carefully as he picked his way over the large rock.

He dropped to a seat, twisted his head toward her and held out his hand. "C'mon!"

She carefully climbed up onto the rock and when she reached him, he snagged her hand, tugged her in front of him and demanded, "Sit."

She settled between his spread legs and he wrapped one arm under her breasts, pulling her back into his chest. The other snaked around her lower belly. With a sigh, she relaxed, leaned back, and let him take her weight.

"This is beautiful," she whispered, peeking over her shoulder at him.

He was staring out over the falls, his green eyes dark in the low light caused by the shade of the trees. "Yeah."

"I never knew this was here."

"Then gonna have to bring your girl here when she gets home."

When she gets home.

Emma's breathing stuttered, her heart did a flip and suddenly the tears welled up in her eyes. What did she finally do right in her life to deserve this man? One who did not fit into any of the molds of acceptable society, but seemed to be more caring than the ones that did.

The waterfall became a blur as she leaned her head back against his shoulder and his arms tightened around her even more.

"Emma," he murmured next to her ear.

She sniffled and wiped at her cheeks. "Yeah?"

"You got dealt a shitty hand. Gonna make it right. Got me?"

"Yeah, Dawson, I got you." She twisted in his arms. "But I'm not sure why you feel you need to do that."

"'Cause..." He stopped, his face got hard, and he didn't say anything for the longest time. "Just because."

Just because.

Just because he was Dawson. A good man. A caring man. A man nicknamed Dawg who, on the outside, could probably scare most people with a pointed glare, but inside had an enormous heart.

Oh Lord, she'd only known him for three days and...

She reached up and stroked her hand along his beard, the texture of it coarse and wiry against her fingers.

"I won't ever be able to repay you."

"You'll find a way," he said softly.

Emma had a feeling what he meant had nothing to do with money.

CHAPTER NINE

A sharp pain shot through Dawg's chest as he watched Emma work the floor. It wasn't the first night she worked where the club was packed solid. Two of his girls were currently on stage and were raking in the tips. Especially when they "played" with each other. Though neither were lesbians, they knew what the men liked and didn't mind playing them, since it paid off. The evidence being the numerous dollar bills being thrown their way.

Cubby was busy behind the bar serving beer and drinks as fast as he could. The VIP rooms had a steady flow of customers and dancers going in and out of their doors. Moose was busy playing bodyguard outside of them, making sure that none of the girls got manhandled. Dawg had even called in a couple more prospects to help be bouncers for the night.

The floor was crowded, the cash was flowing, and Dawg should be very pleased, but he fucking wasn't.

Ember was wearing a long sleek royal blue dress that she had borrowed from one of the girls, which worked perfectly with her blonde hair. The clingy dress had strategic slits in it, so when she moved a bare thigh would show, the flesh of her hip, or the curve of a breast. The back was open all the way to the top curves of her ass. The front plunged practically down to her fucking belly button. He had no idea how her tits weren't falling out of it. One of the girls must have shown her the magic of double-sided tape.

But even so, he knew she wore *nothing* under that fucking dress. It would be impossible to do so. The only thing under that scrap of fabric was Emma herself.

And he did not like that at all.

He downed a shot of whiskey, then gritted his teeth as she moved from one customer to the next with a huge smile on her face, her eyes sparkling. They were all beckoning her over to them, vying for her attention.

He did not like that at all, either.

In fact, he fucking hated it.

But she was doing what he "hired" her to do, and that was work the crowd. Make her customers happy without getting naked. Encourage them to drink more, tip heavier.

When they begged her for a private dance, she'd call over one of the other girls and set them up. The dancers were making better money than they had in a while. That put her in good favor with them. And she had wormed her way into their hearts as she had his.

Again, the club was packed.

It couldn't be Emma bringing in all the business, could it?

Were all these fucking men coming in to see her? To try to steal her away from him?

"Cubby," he barked.

The bartender paused in mixing a drink. "Yeah, boss?"

"Why d'you think the place's packed tonight?"

With a smile, Cubby finished topping off the glass with a squirt of pop from the dispenser gun. Then he jerked his chin toward Emma. "Think you found your golden goose, boss."

"She ain't even gettin' naked," he muttered.

"Don't think she needs to be. It's the chase they like. She ain't giving anything up, so they want her even more. Temptation at its finest. They're enjoying the pursuit."

"Think so?"

"Yeah, boss. She's like the untouchable and they all want to be the first one to score."

Fucking nobody was "scoring" with her. Nobody.

His gaze pinned on the man who had an arm around Emma's waist and his hand spread over her ribcage, having a deep conversation with her tits.

Fuck.

If she was on stage, the place would probably be a ghost town. Her dancing would chase them away. But working the crowd? Cubby was right. She was just out of reach for them. It was like dangling a carrot in front of the horse. Or donkey. What-fucking-ever.

From across the stage, Emma's eyes met his, and she arched an eyebrow at his scowl. Then she returned her attention to the man who was now pawing at her hip and threw her head back. He could almost hear her throaty laugh over the music from where he stood.

Fucking bullshit. That's what it was. Bullshit.

Dawg watched with narrowed eyes as Emma playfully dragged her fingers through the customer's hair while bending over to whisper something in his ear in that ball-tightening voice of hers. The man finally lifted his gaze from her cleavage as Emma waved a hand at Savannah, who rushed over and escorted the man back toward the VIP rooms.

She landed another fucking sale. Just like that. A touch. A laugh. A whisper. And they were putty in her hands.

Suddenly, Emma was on the other side of the bar from him, frowning. "Why are you grumpy now? You're having a great night. It's busy. The girls are happy. Cubby's even raking in the tips."

"You bend over like that, he can see your tits."

She glanced down at her dress then back up at him. "Okay?"

"You bend over like that, he can see *your tits.*"

"Okay? If I was on stage, he'd see my..." She shrugged, making the objects of this discussion jiggle beneath the thin, glittery fabric. "*Breasts,* anyway."

"Ain't on stage."

"No, but—"

"Woman," he growled.

Then she laughed. *Laughed.*

"Not funny."

"Daw—*Dawg,* I'm doing what you hired me to do."

"Know it."

"I'm doing it well."

"Know that, too." She was doing it a little too well.

"So, stop being a grump."

"Ain't a grump."

"Well, you sure look like one. You'd have a handsome face if you'd stop scrunching it up like you've been sucking on a lemon."

"Don't like 'em touchin' you."

"It's harmless. They're just being friendly."

Right. Friendly.

"Should fire your ass an' just make you my house mouse 'til all your shit's settled."

Her eyes widened. "What?"

Yeah, that's what he should do. Lock her up in his place and only let her out when he was with her.

Fuck! He couldn't do that, but he was sorely tempted.

"Who did your makeup?"

Her delicate brows rose in surprise. "Cocoa. Why?"

It was perfect for her. Just enough to emphasize her *girl-next-door* looks. Hell, if he didn't know better, he might wonder if she was a virgin himself.

His gaze swept the floor and the crowd of men filling the room. *Fuck.* Maybe they all thought she was a virgin and wanted to be the first one to pop her cherry!

No. Nobody at her age was a virgin anymore. Were they?

"Are you okay?" she asked, a look of concern on her face.

No, he was not okay. All these men wanted to stick their dicks in Emma.

A blood vessel throbbed at his temple.

Nobody was sticking their dick in his woman, except him.

His head jerked back. *His woman?*

Fuck him. She was here only temporarily. Just until she got her daughter back. He needed that reminder tattooed onto his forehead.

Fuck! He needed that tattooed onto his dick instead. So every time he looked at it, touched it, took a fucking piss, he'd be reminded of the truth.

She was not his woman. She'd never be his woman. She was only in his life for a short while. He was a means to an end for her.

He wanted to smash his fist into a wall. He wanted to beat someone to a bloody pulp. He grabbed a bottle of Jack and a shot glass and rushed around to the open end of the bar and toward the back of the club, ignoring everyone who called out a greeting. Including Emma calling out his name.

He moved past Moose standing guard outside the Red room.

"Boss," he called.

Dawg ignored him, too. Whatever the prospect needed he could handle it himself.

Right now, he needed to down some whiskey and numb his brain. He needed to get his thoughts back on business and off Emma.

And that fucking dress she was wearing.

And her tits practically hanging out.

And those slits in that dress that played a sexy peek-a-boo with his customers.

And that man's hands on her as she flirted with him, got him worked up, probably sporting a fucking hard-on while thinking he'd score with her.

He shoved the door to the back area of the club open and slammed it behind him. He took long strides into his office and slammed that door shut, too. None of it made him feel any better.

With a growl, he whipped the shot glass across the room and it shattered into a thousand pieces as it crashed against the wall. He untwisted the cap off the bottle and brought it to his lips, letting the smooth amber liquor slide down his throat, warm his belly, coat his jealousy.

She'd been in his life a little over a week now. Barely over a fucking week. And he'd totally lost his shit over her. Lost his damn mind.

He didn't want any other man touching her, looking at her, *thinking* about her in the same way he did. Not even his customers.

When he lowered the bottle, he realized he'd guzzled a third of the whiskey in seconds flat. He barely stopped himself from chucking the bottle across the room, too.

He knew it wouldn't take long for D's crew to locate her daughter. Maybe a couple of weeks, a month at the most. They were good. They weren't going to waste time. And then she'd be gone.

Gone.

Fucking gone.

Out of his life. Out of his bed.

What the fuck was about her that got under his damn skin?

"Dawson."

Her low, honeyed voice washed over his addled brain and he squeezed his eyes closed. He couldn't look at her. Not yet.

"Did I do something wrong?"

Yeah, you got under my skin, you crawled into my chest an' burrowed yourself in deep.

That's what you fuckin' did.

You climb into my bed every night an' make me wish that you'd do that every night for the rest of my life.

That's what you fuckin' did.

Every time you fuckin' laugh or give me a smile that's meant just for me, it rips me apart because I know you're only here for a little while.

That's what you fuckin' did.

You made me want you desperately with every fiber of my being. Like a fuckin' drug.

That's what you fuckin' did.

You call me Dawson instead of Dawg, no matter how many times I tell you not to.

That's what you fuckin' did.

That's what you'll continue to do.

'Cause you're you, Emma.

You're you, baby girl. An' I want you for the rest of my fuckin' life.

"I... I don't know what to say."

He opened his eyes and spun on her. "What?" Did he say all that shit out loud?

Holy fuck.

"I never know what to say when you're in a mood like this. If I did something wrong, I'm sorry. But I'm honestly not aware of doing anything, but what I was hired to do."

Oh, thank fuck. That had been all in his head. And that's where it needed to stay.

He blew out a breath. "Baby girl, you didn't do nothin' wrong. Everything you're doin' is right. You're packin' the house. You're bein' the perfect hostess. You're makin' the customers happy. It ain't you."

No, it ain't you. It's me.

A muscle in his jaw ticked. It was him. Him. He allowed this to happen. He opened the fucking door and let her in. Hell, dragged her in. He got involved with her life, her problems.

For some crazy reason, he wanted her to discover that there was more to him than what other people saw.

He wanted to be her fucking hero. He wanted to be the one that could do what no one else could do for her.

What he couldn't even do for himself.

How could he accept his own daughter being ripped from his life, but he couldn't accept Lily being ripped from hers?

He was fucked up.

He didn't even realize she'd moved closer to him. He'd been too caught up in his own fucked up thoughts.

Her hero.

What a stupid fuck he was. Someone who peddled pussy to horny men would never be anyone's hero.

She stepped toe to toe with him and looked up with her heart-stopping blue eyes. "I don't want to make you unhappy. I know I forced myself into your life, begging for you to help me... Desperation makes people do things they normally wouldn't do."

"Like sleepin' with me?"

She dropped her gaze. "No."

He reached out, grabbed a handful of her hair, pulling it back enough to tip her face to his, forcing her to meet his eyes. "Sure 'bout that?"

"Yes, I'm not sleeping with you for any reason other than I want to. I swear. You..."

"I what?"

His eyes were drawn to her throat as it undulated when she swallowed hard. "You make me feel things I haven't felt in a long time. I had shut that part of me down a while ago. I never expected to find it again with you."

His heart began to beat so hard that he thought she could hear it over the thumping of the music that seeped through the walls.

"Emma," he murmured.

"Yes?"

"Ain't lyin' to me, right?"

"I have no reason to lie to you, Dawson. You told me it was my choice to sleep with you. My only obligation was to be your hostess."

"So if I wanted to fuck you right now, you wouldn't say no."

Her lips curved just slightly at the ends. "Do you?"

"Fuck yes." He dropped his head until his lips were just above hers. "Want to push you against a wall while you're wearin' one of those sexy fuckin' dresses an' take you from behind."

"What's stopping you?"

With a growl, he grabbed her shoulders, spun her around and shoved her backwards. She stumbled in her heels, losing her balance with a gasp. Her arms reached out, and she caught herself against the nearest wall. He rushed forward, pinned her to it, his mouth against her ear. His now hard dick pressing against the exposed skin above her ass.

"Gonna do it. Want it?"

"Yes," she hissed.

"Pull your dress up. Show me your ass."

Grabbing the fabric of her dress, she shimmied it up her legs over her hips and gathered it around her waist.

Her ass was perfect globes, ripe for his handprint.

"Should spank that ass of yours so when you go back out on that floor, I know an' you know what I've left behind. My hand markin' your ass as mine."

She shuddered beneath him, pressing her bare ass against his crotch. "I've never..."

The blood rushed into his ears. "Never what?"

"Never had that done to me."

Dawg's dick kicked in his jeans. "Never been spanked?"

"No."

"Bad girls like to be spanked. You a bad girl, Emma?"

He cupped her ass and spread her cheeks apart, thrusting against her. He needed to get his dick out and take her right where she stood.

"Yes, I did something to piss you off out on the floor, so I must be bad. Maybe you need to show me how bad I was."

Her husky, breathless voice, her words made his head spin. She wanted him to spank her.

What happened to his sweet, *girl-next-door* Emma?

Was working in his club corrupting her, changing her?

He released her abruptly and moved behind his desk. He pulled his chair out and sank down into it. He glanced over at Emma, still frozen where she stood against the wall, her dress pulled up, her face flushed, her eyes unfocused.

"Get over here." He patted his thighs. "Across my lap. Gonna give you what you deserve."

Without hesitation, she came to him willingly, draping herself over his legs, her ass bare and beautiful, her dress gathered at her waist, her blonde hair falling almost to the floor.

Her body trembling.

He slipped a finger over her crease and into her cunt. She was soaked. Her trembling wasn't from fear. Fuck no, it wasn't. She wanted everything he was about to do to her.

He pulled his fingers from her, now slick with her arousal, and dragged them back over her tight little hole. That was going to be his, too. But not now, not here.

That would take some time, preparation and patience. Right now, he had none of that.

Instead, he raised his hand and dropped it down hard. His palm cracking against her flesh made her yelp and squirm in his lap, which did not help with how hard his dick was.

As her skin turned a slight shade of pink, he turned his attention to the other pale cheek. When he smacked that one, he could feel the sting in his own hand, so it had to be worse for her.

But this time she didn't yelp. Instead she groaned and ground herself against his hard-on.

Her fingernails dug into the denim covering his thighs, but she kept her head down, and using her toes, she tilted her ass higher.

"Again," she groaned.

He bit back a grin. "Fuckin' naughty girl, yeah?"

"Yes. So bad. I need you to teach me a lesson."

He ripped open the top drawer in his desk and found what he was looking for. A ruler that had been shoved deep in the back. He had almost thrown it out after finding it in the used desk when he bought it. But he hadn't. And he was so glad he never did. He finally had a use for it.

"Rulers were made for bad little teachers. Weren't they?"

She turned her head, brushing the hair out of her eyes. She stiffened when he saw what he was holding.

"Dawson…"

He brought the ruler down on her ass. "Name's Dawg."

"Dawson…" she breathed again.

"Dawg," he repeated as he struck her other ass cheek. She jerked on his lap.

"Dawson… please."

"Please what? Stop?"

"No," she moaned. "Don't stop."

He struck her twice more with the ruler, once on each cheek. Just enough to leave a mark, then he tossed it onto his desk, letting his fingers brush over the slightly raised welts.

Her ass looked fucking beautiful like that.

"Get up," he ordered.

She scrambled from his lap, her hair wild, her bottom lip caught between her teeth, her face a mask of ecstasy.

Who knew his baby girl would like it like that?

His balls were so tight, in such pain, his dick so hard. He couldn't wait much longer.

Raising his hips out of the chair, he unfastened his jeans and shoved them down his thighs, just enough so she'd be able to ride his dick.

Grabbing her wrist, he spun her around and pulled her backwards.

Then reality hit him and, before he could stop her, she sank down, her wet heat surrounding him. All the oxygen fled his lungs as her tight sheath squeezed him, clenched around him.

"Nobody gets that but me," he growled in her ear. "Got me?"

"Dawson..."

"Got me?" He needed to hear it.

"Yes. Got you."

He sank his teeth into the smooth flesh at her neck as she rose up and down, crying out every time she sank deep. He reached around her, finding her clit, teasing it, making her grind hard down onto his lap, soaking him.

Fuck. There was nothing between them. Nothing. It felt so fucking good.

But it was so wrong.

He tried to stop his spinning mind. Tried to think responsibly. This wasn't right.

It wasn't right.

Emma continued to ride him hard and while his thumb played

with her slick nub, his fingers found where they were joined. He dug his other hand into her dress, cupping her tit, thumbing the hard bead of her nipple. She arched her back, dropping her head back onto his shoulder, her breath coming out in hot puffs of air.

Nothing felt as good as when he was inside her. When he became a part of her.

But he had to pull out before he came. He needed to think straight.

Which went to shit when she rode him harder, faster, drawing all the blood from his brain down into his dick. She called out his name over and over, her nails digging into the skin of his arms.

He had to tell her... "Em..."

He had to stop her... "Em..."

Then she arched her back even more, reached down and grabbed his balls, calling out, "I'm coming!"

Ah fuck.

He shoved his face into her neck and, with a curse, blew his load deep inside her.

So much for pulling out.

Why did she have this effect on him? Made his brain turn into fucking mush? Made him lose control?

"Em..."

She turned her head, smiled, squeezed his cheeks together and planted a big fat kiss on his lips. Then she pushed to her feet and tugged her dress down, wiggling it back into place. "I'm going to go clean up and get back to work."

Then she was gone, and he was left sitting in his office chair with his dick in his hand.

"Fuck, baby girl," he muttered to the empty room.

Fuck!

————

D awg shoved open his bedroom door and was surprised to see what greeted him. Emma laid on her belly on his bed, reading a book. Totally naked.

His eyes immediately were drawn to her ass. He was pleased to see some marks remained from earlier, but worried he'd been too rough.

"You okay?"

"Yes. Why?" she asked distractedly, not pulling her attention from her book.

"Thought maybe you were layin' on your stomach 'cause your ass hurts."

She twisted her head and checked out her own ass. "No. I'm fine."

"So you didn't mind that?"

A smile crept across her face. "No. I was actually surprised by how much I liked it."

Thank fuck.

He shucked his cut and laid it over the nearby chair in the corner of his room. He sat down, unbuckled his boots and yanked them off. Then he approached the bed, tossing the package he'd carried with him into the room onto the bed next to her.

Emma picked up the box, her brows furrowed. "What's this?"

After Emma had gone back onto the floor earlier, he'd cleaned up and headed out to the nearest drug store to buy emergency contraceptive. "Don't want to be one of your mistakes."

"Is that..." Her words drifted off as she read the box.

"Gotta take it soon."

She frowned and tossed it back toward him. It bounced off the mattress and fell to the floor. "I don't want it."

Dawg leaned over, picked it up and chucked it back on the bed. "Emma, we fucked up."

"No. We didn't."

What the fuck? If he needed to take the brunt of the responsibility so she didn't feel guilty, then he'd do that. "Then I fucked up."

She shook her head. "No. You didn't."

"Emma, we didn't use a wrap."

"I'm well aware of that."

Did she just roll her eyes at him? "Can't risk it. Can't have—"

She pushed herself up and tucked her legs underneath her to the side. He lost his breath as he studied her sitting there, completely naked, in the middle of his bed. He wondered if he'd ever get used to seeing her like that.

He hoped not. Because it got his blood boiling every time.

"Dawson, be rest assured I would never keep you from your child. But you don't have to worry about that. I'm on the Depo shot."

His head jerked back. "The what?"

"A birth control shot. I get it every three months."

"It works?"

She gave him a small smile. "I sure hope so."

A weird mix of emotions clashed in his head. On one hand, he was glad they were covered and there'd be no chance of any accidents. On the other...

Dawg stared at the woman who looked so right in his bed. He imagined her belly round with his child. One he'd get to know from the second he or she was born. One he'd get to help raise, have a say in everything the kid did. One he'd even get to help name.

He remembered how everyone had been there when Z's kid was born. Everyone had celebrated. The whole club wanted a hand in raising the fourth generation of the DAMC.

Dawg didn't come from either founding member's bloodline. But he'd been a part of this club since the minute he could be a prospect at eighteen. He'd become a fully patched member little over a year later. He'd been a member longer than most of the brothers who currently sat on the Executive Committee. Everyone except for Ace.

So he still was a big part of the DAMC family. Blood or not.

He might not have been born into the club like Diesel or Hawk, or Dex, Jag or even Zak. But the DAMC still ran deep through his veins.

It was important to him that this club survived, continued long after the generation before them was gone. He, as well as the rest of the brothers, were determined to not let rival MC's like the Shadow Warriors snuff out their fire.

The DAMC had deep roots in Shadow Valley and once he landed here as a wayward teen, he never left. Never planned on leaving. There was nowhere else he'd rather be.

He'd be *Down & Dirty 'til Dead*.

The club would continue with Zak's kids, Hawk's, Jag's and soon Diesel's. It helped that women like Ivy and Jewel, even Diamond, were women who were born into the club and were willing to bear the next generation. None of them had reason or a desire to leave.

Zak and Hawk were lucky to find women who eventually, after a little convincing, blended easily into the club lifestyle.

But the club life might hinder Emma's career, might put a kink in her fight for custody of her daughter. And he didn't want to be the reason for her failure in either of those things.

"Dawson."

He focused on the welcoming hand she had outstretched in his direction.

"Are you going to just stand there or come to bed?"

He glanced at the clock. It was almost three AM. "It's late."

"I know; I was waiting up for you."

"Didn't have to."

"I wanted to."

What had he done right in his life to deserve this woman?

He finished undressing, throwing his clothes in a pile on the floor then settled on the bed next to her, laying on his belly the same as her. Both of their heads turned toward each other.

She began to lightly trace his club colors that were tattooed onto his back. "Do all of you have these tattoos?"

"Yeah, baby girl."

"Why?"

"Easy for someone to steal your colors. Your cut. Harder to take 'em from you when they're inked into your skin."

"Do you have to do it?"

"No."

"So why do you?"

"Shows loyalty. To the club, to the brotherhood. To the lifestyle. Prospects ain't permitted to do it. Not until they're fully patched. But once you're fully patched an' wanna buy out your membership or are forced to leave, you can't wear your colors."

"Your vest?"

"An' the tats on your back. Anything to do with the MC."

"How do you get rid of that large tattoo if you leave?"

"Two ways..."

"Which are?" she prodded.

"Removin' 'em or coverin' 'em up."

She winced. "Ouch."

"Yeah. Ain't pleasant either way. Coverin' 'em up is the better way, *if* you get to choose."

"Would you ever leave?"

"Why you askin'?"

She lifted a shoulder in a half-assed shrug. "Just curious."

"No. This is my family. Never leavin'."

"What about your real family?"

"The DAMC is my real family, baby girl."

"I meant your blood relatives. Father? Mother?"

Blood wasn't always family. Family wasn't always blood. That was something he discovered from very young.

"Father was a drunk, took off with some bitch when I was five. Mother found a new man, also a fuckin' drunk, who thought I was his competition. Been on my own for a long time."

"How long?"

Why did she need to know this shit? This wasn't a conversation he liked to have. "Long time, baby girl."

"How long?" she asked again. She wasn't going to let it go until he answered. She had a little stubborn streak. And a head full of endless questions.

Dawg blew out a breath. "Since I was thirteen."

She pushed up to her elbows and started down at him. "Thirteen?"

"Bounced 'round for a while. A couple aunts. An uncle. A distant cousin. They all got the shits of me an' put me out. Ran across a biker one day from an outlaw club, he bought me a beer even though I was sixteen. Talked up his club, the lifestyle. When I heard all that, I knew what I wanted. Ended up at his place."

"So he was nice enough to take you in?"

Dawg closed his eyes and sucked in a deep breath. That biker had an ol' lady that he hadn't touched in ages since he was too busy sticking his dick in any snatch that had a pulse. So his ol' lady had turned her eyes on Dawg. At first, losing his virginity to an older, more experienced woman seemed like a bonus. Until it wasn't.

To remain living with them, he had to service her just about every night like a fucking stud dog. Her ol' man encouraged it, since it got her nagging ass off his back. But after a while, Dawg couldn't get it up because there was nothing about her that he found attractive and he ended up back on the street after being beaten to within an inch of his life by the biker himself. He still had a small scar from a cut on his temple made from a large ring while being backhanded.

He drifted from there. During his seventeenth year, he landed in one bed after another just to keep a roof over his head and food in his gut. But he kept moving.

Until the day he stumbled into Shadow Valley and ran into a club hang-around the same age as him named Crow, who didn't look like he would fit into a typical MC, who also introduced him to Ace, Pierce, and Grizz. Then the second he turned eighteen, they handed him his prospect patches, assigned him a room above church, and put him to work. And his life got better from there.

The only other hiccup was finding out last year that he had a daughter named Caitlin.

Other than that, life was good. He studied the woman who could make his life even better if she gave him a shot.

"Gotta confess somethin', baby girl."

"What?"

"You're a teacher, so it might make you look at me differently."

Her blue eyes studied him. "Tell me. It can't be that bad."

"Don't got my high school diploma."

She shrugged and continued to mindlessly trace the tattoos on his back. "A GED is just as good."

The motion was soothing, and he could lay there all night, enjoying her soft touch. "Don't got that either."

Her fingers stilled. "You didn't finish school at all?"

He didn't know why he felt the need to confess all his secrets to her. Things that no one else knew and might never know. Not even his club brothers. "Nope."

"How far did you get?"

"Em... got kicked out of the house at thirteen," he reminded her.

"Thirteen," she repeated in a whisper, then her eyes widened. "Oh my God."

"Right. Ain't even a high school dropout."

She lifted her head and stared at him. "But you run a successful business."

"Which consists of naked women dancin' on a pole."

"But you have the smarts to run it well, keep it profitable."

"Didn't say I was dumb, just a dropout."

"Baby," she whispered, running her fingers through his beard.

His eyes narrowed. "You just call me baby?"

Her lips curved upward. "Yes, I did."

"That a "poor baby" baby? Or "baby, I wanna fuck your brains out" baby?"

She tilted her head and her smile grew. "Which do you want it to be?"

"The fuckin' second one."

She bit her bottom lip and, with a growl, he tackled her.

One minute she was giggling, the next she was moaning.

He couldn't figure out which one he liked best.

He'd just have to keep making her do both.

CHAPTER TEN

Steel, with his hands and bare feet wrapped with athletic tape, was beating the fucking snot out of a heavy bag that hung in the corner of D's large warehouse, which was home to In the Shadows Security.

"Can't wait 'til Slade gets that fuckin' gym open," Mercy grumbled next to Dawg.

Diesel grunted in agreement. "Needs to quit bendin' Diamond over an' givin' her dick every five minutes. That's why shit ain't gettin' done faster."

Dawg's eyes slid to Diesel, then back to Steel, as D's man punched and kicked the bag with a power that was impressive. And a little scary if Dawg had to admit it.

"You're always in your office porkin' your ol' lady an' you get shit done," Mercy muttered. Mercy's cold eyes landed on Dawg. "Heard you're gettin' some from that sweet little thing whose daughter went missin'."

"Heard you ain't gettin' nothin' but your own fuckin' palm since no woman in their right mind wants to look up into that ugly-assed face of yours when you're huffin' an' puffin' on top of her."

A smile that didn't quite reach his gray eyes crept over Mercy's face as he grabbed his dick through his jeans and shook it. "The dick makes up for the face."

"True that. Easy for 'em to close their eyes, right?"

"They don't like my face, I can give it to 'em from the rear."

Diesel snorted and smacked Dawg on the back. "C'mon, brother, got fuckin' business to talk about."

"Want me in there, boss?" Mercy asked.

D gave the large, scarred man a chin lift. "Yeah."

Mercy followed them down a corridor off the large open area of the warehouse as they headed back to D's office.

When Diesel shoved the door open, Jewel lifted her head from the desk and blinked at them.

"You in here sleepin'?" Diesel barked.

She gave her ol' man a frown. "If you haven't noticed, I'm pregnant. Your kid's suckin' the life out of me."

Dawg bit back his laugh and shot Jewel a smile. "Hey, Jewelee."

"Hey, Dawg." She got up from the chair and moved around it to stand between Dawg and D's former special ops guy. "How's Emma?"

"Good. You?"

"Getting fat and cranky." She glanced over at Mercy. "Hey, handsome. How's it hanging?"

"A little to the left," Mercy answered with a poker face. He glanced at Dawg. "See? She'd do me from the front."

Diesel sank his bulk into his office chair with a grunt.

"The scar gives him character," Jewel agreed with a wink. "I'm sure it's only scary when he's making his 'I'm coming' face.'" Then she squeezed her eyes shut and let out a big orgasmic cry while twisting her face up.

"Somethin' you ain't ever gonna see. *Out*," Diesel barked at Jewel.

"*Jesus*. Good thing I love you, asshole."

D swatted a hand in her direction as she walked out of the office.

"Woman," he bellowed. Jewel paused and looked over her

shoulder at him. He softened his voice. "Don't leave the warehouse, got me?"

Her lips twitched and her eyes crinkled as she gave him a nod. Then shut the door behind her.

D stared at the closed door for a moment then grumbled, "Fuckin' women."

Dawg snorted. Diesel was crazy about Jewel. No matter how much he bitched about her or pretended she was a pain in his ass, he loved her to death. No fucking doubt about it. That man would do anything for the woman and though he wasn't thrilled about her becoming pregnant, he wouldn't hesitate to kill for her and his unborn kid.

And Dawg knew D worried constantly about her getting snatched again by the fucking Warriors. Especially now that she was pregnant and even more vulnerable.

No matter what, Dawg never wanted to see that happen. The huge man would lose his shit and go on a fucking rampage worse than Godzilla in a Japanese town.

However, the Warriors had been quiet ever since Dawg, D, Jag and Hawk, along with D's crew went into their midst to extract Slade from the outlaw MC. But then, that day there had been a lot of carnage left behind. A clear message to the rest of those assholes that the Angels were done with their bullshit.

Even so, the nomad club was probably not done fucking with the DAMC. Dawg couldn't imagine they ever would be. But he also had a feeling that the man with the scarred face leaning against the wall was on a mission. And that mission included exterminating every Warrior he and the rest of D's "Shadows" came across in retribution for everything the fuckwads did to Kiki, Jazz and Jewel.

Payback was a black-hearted, son-of-a-bitch named Mercy.

"Trail went cold..." D started, and Dawg's stomach sank.

"In Brunei," Mercy finished.

Dawg's gaze swung to the former Delta Force operator. "Where the fuck is Brunei?"

"Small nation on the island of Borneo," Mercy explained.

"Run by some fuckin' sultan," D added.

He didn't even know where the island of Borneo was. He'd never had a geography class in his life, but he was keeping that to himself and he nodded like he knew. "A sultan?"

"Yeah, won't give a shit about any American girl. Especially one with her father. If they're still there, we can get in an' out with no one the wiser. If they moved on..."

"When will you know?" Dawg asked Mercy.

"Hunter an' Walker are headed there now," Mercy answered. "Problem is, there are plenty of other countries Americans can hide an' not worry about extradition. Cuba bein' one. Russia. The Western Sahara. Hell, Mongolia. Even fuckin' Iran an' Afghanistan. Though, don't think the boys want to take a trip back down memory lane into those hell holes."

Dawg lifted a hand. "Hold up. Were they plannin' on contactin' the governments in these places first?"

"Fuck no," D grunted.

"Nope," Mercy confirmed. "This mission's goin' to be of the shock an' awe variety. Get in, get the girl, get the fuck out."

"Maybe not so neat," D muttered, raising a brow toward Mercy.

That made a smile curve at Mercy's mouth. Though his smile looked not only crooked, but sinister from the scar that ran diagonally across his face and pulled up one side of this lip. "It'll be neat. Painless."

"Don't want Lily witnessin' any shit, D. Don't want her scarred for life."

"Like me?" Mercy asked.

"No, mentally scarred, not just stuck with an ugly puss like yours."

"She ain't gonna see shit," D confirmed, giving Mercy a look, whose expression reminded Dawg of stone.

"Emma's gonna get Kiki to file for full custody, so when Lily comes back, there ain't goin' to be any issues," Dawg told them.

"Not goin' to need that. But let her do it, anyway. The man will never return to American soil. Guaranteed. But she doesn't need to know that."

Diesel nodded at Mercy's word. "Guaranteed. An' agreed, your woman don't need to know. Better she not know any fuckin' details."

"An' when the FBI asks how Emma got 'er back?"

"We'll come up with a story. Might even be true," Mercy said. "Girlfriend got knocked up, didn't want to be saddled with the man's kid anymore, put her on a plane back to her mother. Simple."

Dawg didn't think it was that simple, but he wasn't going to argue. Whatever it took to get Lily back was okay with him.

"Ain't divorced yet, right?" D asked.

"Right."

D's eyes met Mercy's as he gave his man his orders. "Death certificate. Got me? Man died in a tragic accident, girlfriend don't wanna raise another woman's kid, ships her home. No problem with custody. No problem with the fuckin' divorce. The widow gets the man's shit. Life insurance, any assets, whatever."

"If he didn't change the beneficiary," Mercy murmured.

D shrugged. "Either way. She's free of 'im. Kid'll be safe. No fuckin' worries."

Mercy nodded. "An' the girlfriend will never show her face in the good o' US of A, either. She's a fugitive."

"Yeah," D grunted. "Lemme know when you hear from Hunter or Walker."

"Got it. I'll be on standby. Will head out as soon as I get a twenty." Mercy pushed away from the wall. He whacked Dawg on the back as he passed, saying, "Got your six, brother." He headed toward the door. "Get your woman's girl back an' you'll get grateful pussy for the rest of your fuckin' life. *Guaranteed.*"

Dawg doubted that. As soon as Emma got her daughter back, she'd be getting her life back in order. He was sure Emma wanted to be a good role model for her girl, not raising her kid over a strip club where she only had to walk down the steps to be the Heaven's Angels' hostess and have men pawing at her.

"Spill it. What's she to you?" Diesel asked him once the door closed behind Mercy.

"Nothin'."

"Ain't nothin'. Makin' too much of an effort for *nothin'*."

Dawg stayed quiet, hoping the club's Sergeant at Arms would drop it.

But that wasn't good enough for D. "Known her less than a couple weeks, right?"

"Right."

"My guys' asses are on the fuckin' line headin' into some of these countries, got me?"

"Yeah."

"So ain't fuckin' *nothin'*. Not gonna continue this mission if she's nothin'. If she's nothin' send 'er on her way. Ain't attractin' trouble for the club or my business for *nothin'*, got me?"

"I gotta cover it, I'll cover it."

"More than you got."

Dawg stared at Diesel with dread. The man knew what Heaven's Angels was pulling in revenue wise every month since he sat on the DAMC's Executive Committee. So he knew that Dawg wasn't hurting for scratch in any way, shape or form. But what Dawg had banked wouldn't be enough?

Fuck. He had almost five hundred grand tucked away in his personal account. And Diesel knew that, too, because the club got ten percent of the net income every month from all the DAMC businesses. And Diesel was no dumb fuck. The strip club was one of the DAMC's top earning businesses.

The big man shrugged. "Three men in several foreign countries. Payin' people off, payin' for info, special equipment, travel, expenses. Also had to pay off the fuckin' P.I. since Emma owed 'im money. Wouldn't spill any shit 'til he was made whole. So, made 'im whole. By the way, she was wastin' 'er scratch on that fucker. Didn't do much besides trace some airline tickets an' ping the husband's

DOWN & DIRTY: DAWG

phone. Phone ended up ditched at an airport. Asshole never woulda found your woman's girl, but woulda kept suckin' her dry."

Dawg's jaw got tight. Emma said she lost her house and her car trying to pay for the guy's help. The cage she currently drove, and the one now parked in his back lot, had to be no more than a five-hundred-dollar clunker. It wasn't safe for her or her daughter. She'd need a better ride when Lily was back in her custody.

"Paid 'im for nothin'?" Dawg asked, fighting the urge to smash shit on D's messy desk.

"Yep. Didn't do nothin' more than any computer geek could do. With her knowledge, Ivy woulda done a fuckin' better job."

"Guess I gotta go visit the fucker."

Diesel shook his head. "Guy got his fuckin' money an' a lesson 'bout takin' advantage of a desperate mother. Got me?"

Dawg dragged his fingers through his beard. "Yeah, got you."

"So, tell me again how she's fuckin' *nothin'* to you." He pinned his dark gaze on Dawg. "In your bed?"

"Yeah."

"Plannin' on keepin' 'er there?"

Dawg took a deep inhale. "Dunno, D. Like you said, only been a little over a week."

"Might have to talk to Z 'bout switchin' up the club. An' when I say club, ain't talkin' the DAMC. I'm talkin' your club. Ain't gonna raise a seven-year-old above a club like that. Got me?"

"Since when're you worried 'bout how a kid's gonna be raised?"

Diesel sat back and scrubbed a hand over his short dark hair. "Since I put one in Jewel's belly." He tapped his temple with a beefy finger. "Makes you think."

"Yeah, that it does," Dawg said softly. Because if his own daughter was a part of his life, he wouldn't be raising her over a strip club, either.

"If this is gettin' serious, start thinkin' about who's gonna take your place. Got big shoes to fill, though. Which sucks. Heaven's Angels brings the club a fuckload of scratch. Needs to keep runnin' like a fuckin' machine."

"Yeah." If he did what D was suggesting, which was handing over the management of Heaven's Angels to one of the other brothers, what the fuck would he do? He had to do something to bring money into the coffers. He wasn't a damn mechanic, so he couldn't work at Shadow Valley Body shop. He wasn't an ink slinger, so he couldn't work with Crow. And he was no bartender, so The Iron Horse was out. Ace didn't need anyone at the Shadow Valley Pawn, either.

There was always Shadow Valley Gun Shop and Range. Pierce was lying low, keeping away from church, so it might be a good idea to get in over there and work on taking over that business. Then if they needed to push the former prez out of the club, it could be done a lot easier. The gun shop was one of the reasons the Committee decided not to strip the asshole of his colors. But if someone else could step in without a hitch...

He'd need to talk to Z. See what his opinion was on the subject.

But right now, he didn't need to figure that out. Once he knew Lily was on her way back home, then he'd have to see where he and Emma stood.

Though, if it was up to him, he knew exactly where Emma would end up every night.

The same place Dawg laid down his own head.

Guaranteed.

E mma stood in the reception area of a small law firm that sat in the center of town watching Dawg give an attractive woman a welcoming hug. With long dark hair and blue eyes, she kind of looked familiar.

"When are you going to shave off that shit?" the younger woman asked, tugging on his beard.

"Ain't gonna," he grumbled when he released her and smoothed his beard back in place.

"You wouldn't be so ugly if you did."

"I like it," Emma said softly, attracting her attention.

Dawg stepped back to Emma's side. "Em, this is Jayde. Zak an' Axel's baby sister."

"I'm not a baby," Jayde chided him. "I have my Bachelor's and now an actual job!" She stuck out her hand and Emma shook it. "Welcome to the sisterhood."

The sisterhood. "That's not the first time I've heard that," Emma murmured.

Jayde's eyes slid to Dawg, arched a brow at him, then her gaze landed back on Emma. "Right. Well..."

"So, your brother's the cop?"

"Both my brother and my dad are part of Shadow Valley PD."

"And Zak..." Emma gave Dawg a questioning look. "That's your MC's president, right? The one with the baby?"

Before now, Emma hadn't put two and two together. Even though they did all look alike. However, two cops and an MC president in the same family? Weird.

"Yes! Zeke! Oh my god! Baby Z is *sooooo* adorable! I want a baby!" Jayde squealed, bouncing on her toes.

"Gettin' knocked up's the easy part, Jayde. Raisin' 'em ain't."

"Like you would know," Jayde huffed.

"Wouldn't. But ask your fuckin' mom an' pop. Guessin' they'd tell you raisin' you three was a pain in their ass."

Jayde waved a dismissing hand. "Axel and I are the good ones. Z's the one that gives Dad a headache. Well... Now that Axel's with Bella, though... I don't think he's thrilled with that." She smiled. "So I guess that means I'm the only good one."

"Right, an' now you're workin' for Kiki, who's the club attorney. Mitch probably ain't likin' that, either."

"He's not, but he agrees it'll at least look good on my resume."

Kiki peeked out of her office door and beckoned them. "Okay, come on back you two."

Dawg put a hand to the small of Emma's back as they headed in the attorney's direction.

"Sorry," Kiki said as she returned to her desk. "Got stuck on a call. Close the door, Dawg, will you?"

When Emma saw Kiki at the party at church a week ago, she'd been wearing casual clothes. But now she wore professional attire even though her skirt was snug and a bit shorter than Emma would wear. Plus, the stiletto heels the woman wore... The woman would probably have no problem dancing in the platform shoes that the girls danced in on stage.

But as Kiki sat down behind her desk, Emma knew there was no way this woman would ever be in a jam enough to have to dance in a strip club for money. Being an attorney and owning her own firm probably made a lot more than a typical kindergarten teacher. A lot more.

Dawg closed the door behind Emma and then hurried to help her into her chair. She frowned, wondering why he was hovering like he was. He sank into the chair next to her after sliding it over within a few inches of hers.

Kiki's eyebrows rose as she noticed it, too. Her gaze bounced from Dawg to Emma and back to Dawg, and then a small smile curved her lips.

"Dawg, do me a favor and tell Linc, next time you see him, that Jayde has baby fever, and he needs to stock up on wraps. Mitch will skin him alive if he knocks her up." She pursed her lips. "On that note, Z and Axel might, too."

Dawg's head jerked. "Linc's doin' her?"

Kiki sighed. "I don't think so, but you know they've been eyeballing each other for a while now. And it wouldn't hurt for him to be prepared. But, honestly, I think Linc doesn't want a hassle from Mitch and Axel. And, of course, Z. Last thing you want to do is get on your president's bad side, right?"

"Yeah, makes sense. He's young. Don't need all that fuckin' headache for just some pussy."

"Well, I wouldn't call Jayde 'just some pussy' but I know what you mean." Kiki grabbed her glasses off her desk and slid them on her face. "Still, it's a good idea to make sure he's prepared... just in case."

Emma watched with curiosity as Dawg's eyes were drawn to the woman who went from looking like a sexy attorney to a naughty librarian with just one accessory, her glasses. His mouth opened, shut, then he twisted his head to stare at Emma for a long awkward moment before reaching down and adjusting himself.

Did Kiki turn Dawg on?

Kiki cleared her throat, drawing both of their attention. "*Okay* then... so I drew up the divorce complaint, the custody petition, a request for an accounting of all marital assets and, of course, a restraining order. We'll need to appear in front of the judge and I'm sure he'll have questions for you, Emma. Are you up for that?"

All of that sounded expensive. "How much is all of this going to cost me?"

"I... uh..." Kiki slid her glasses down her nose and peered over them at Dawg.

"Nothin'," he grumbled next to her.

"But—"

"Told you it's covered," he grumbled in his "no lip" voice.

"Right," Kiki said, waving a hand around. "Don't worry about that for right now. I think the club's covering any filing fees and I'm working pro bono."

"Pro bono? Your time is worth something!"

"Yes, but if you're a part of the club—"

"I'm not a part of the club!" Emma exclaimed, cutting her off.

Kiki turned surprised blue eyes to Dawg. "I thought..."

"Yeah, it's covered," Dawg said again in a tone that didn't invite an argument.

She protested anyway. "Dawson!"

"Dawson?" Kiki repeated.

"Fuck," Dawg muttered with his brows pinned together.

"I like it," Kiki said, chuckling.

"I do, too," Emma agreed with a smile.

"Fuck," Dawg muttered again.

"Anyway, Emma, I need you to sign some papers and I'll get the petition for divorce filed, and the rest of the paperwork. Then I'll let you know how soon we can talk to the judge for the PFA."

"PFA?"

"The restraining order. It'll be for you and for Lily, too. It shouldn't be a problem to at least get a temporary one. Permanent?" She shrugged. "The man abducted your daughter and left the country without your permission. Parent or not, that's unacceptable. The judge should see it the same way. Plus, once he's back in the States, he should be charged, so that will help the judge decide on the permanent one. Then once Lily turns eighteen, it'll be up to her whether to see her father or not. Just a warning, he could file for supervised visitation." Kiki lifted a hand before Emma could protest. "Doesn't mean he'll get it."

Dawg reached over and grabbed her hand from her lap, squeezing it. "Ain't gettin' it. Guaranteed."

"Well," Kiki continued, "Here's the thing you two have to consider... Dawg not only manages a strip club, but lives above it, and you're working there, too, right?"

Emma nodded, "But it's just temporary."

"Which part?" Kiki asked.

"All of it. Well, not the part where Daw... Dawg's the manager."

Dawg cut in. "Yeah, it's all temporary. Gonna talk to Z."

Kiki's eyebrows rose. "About what?"

"Movin' an' findin' something else to do other than the club."

"Like a new business?" Kiki asked, clearly surprised. She wasn't the only one. This was the first that Emma was hearing this.

Dawg shrugged. "Not sure yet. Gonna talk to Z."

None of this made sense. Why would Dawg give up a business he'd managed successfully for *years* for her? Was he thinking this was more than a temporary situation?

Her plan had always been to find a new apartment as soon as Lily was returned to her custody. And to find another job doing what she was meant to do, loved to do, what her degree was in, which was teaching.

He had no reason to cause a total upheaval in his life for her.

She appreciated everything he was doing for her and she certainly appreciated the time they spent together being intimate, but if he was thinking long-term...

Was he thinking long term?

Her gaze slid to the left to where he was sitting so close to her. Then it dropped to their clasped hands.

Oh Lord, he was thinking long-term!

He was a tattooed biker who managed a strip club.

She had a daughter to raise...

Her heart began to beat furiously.

He was certainly not the ideal father figure for Lily.

What kind of judge was going to give her full custody of her daughter if they were living with a man like Dawg? He could be the kindest, gentlest man in the world and he would still be judged by what was seen on the outside. The beard, the tattoos, the cut, the biker boots and worn jeans, the clunky silver rings on his fingers of a skull and more...

It was what he represented, not who he actually was inside.

Her husband's family had money and lots of it. His parents, Lily's grandparents, could fight her for custody claiming that she was an unfit mother, a bad influence. That Emma made bad choices... like even temporarily living with and working for Dawg.

The one person who has helped her the most, just might have hindered her. And not because he meant to. Clearly the man had nothing but the best intentions.

"Dawg," she whispered, scared that accepting his help had been a huge mistake. A colossal mistake.

He must not have heard her because he went on to say, "Got somethin' else to run past you, Keeks."

"What?" Kiki removed her glasses and placed them on the desk blotter.

"Ain't just thinkin' 'bout movin' for Lily. Thinkin' about my parental rights for my own daughter. Fightin' for visitation."

Kiki's mouth dropped open, and she sat back in her thick leather desk chair. "You have a daughter?"

Emma didn't blame the woman for her reaction. Hers probably looked similar since she had no idea that Dawg was going to bring that up today. Or ever. She had no idea that he was even thinking of getting to know his daughter. Not after the conversation they'd had.

"Yeah."

"Dawg," Kiki breathed, then groaned. "Why didn't you tell me? I could've started working on this a long time ago."

"Doin' criminal defense." The hesitation before his answer was a telling sign to Emma. He hadn't considered it until now. Or this last week. When he originally told her about his daughter, he thought it was better for her for him not to be involved in her life.

Crap. And her thoughts about raising Lily with him were the exact same as his were about raising his own daughter. He didn't think he was good enough.

Kiki's voice dragged her out of her thoughts. She realized that she was squeezing the crap out of Dawg's hand and relaxed her fingers slightly.

"Dawg, I'm the club's attorney. You know I handle everything for the MC now. Which would include something like this. So you better believe I'm going to help you out on this. There's no reason you shouldn't see your biological daughter. How old is she?"

"Fourteen."

The man missed out on fourteen years of his daughter's life. Emma couldn't imagine that.

Again, Kiki looked a little shell-shocked. "Fourteen and I haven't heard a word about her?"

"Just found out 'bout her myself last year. Didn't think I'd want to interrupt her life. Got it good where she's at."

"Are you listed as her father on the birth certificate?"

He shook his head, his fingers twitching within Emma's. It was her turn to give him a reassuring squeeze.

"So, you didn't know anything about her until recently?"

"No."

"Dawg... Are you sure she's yours?"

"Ain't had a test yet, but saw her. Positive she's mine. Gut tells me so."

"Wow." Kiki sat back and rubbed a hand over her forehead. "Do any of the guys know about her?"

"Nope. Just Emma, and now you."

"How did you find out?"

His eyes slid to Emma for a moment, then back to Kiki. "A friend of 'ers let it slip."

A friend of hers let it slip? Hers? As in the mother's? From the way Dawg talked, the mother's friends wouldn't be running in the same circles as Dawg. Emma wondered if there was more to it than that.

"Okay, well... First thing we need to do is get a DNA test ordered to establish paternity. She'll fight it, of course. Then once paternity is established, I'll petition the court for visitation. It might be a problem when it comes to you not only managing Heaven's Angels, but living above the club, too. That may give them ammo to keep you out of your daughter's life. They could say that you're unfit to be a parent. Even just for visitation. I don't know. I'll have to talk to some other attorneys I know that specialize in family law. But again, if you're thinking about moving and giving up the club..."

"Givin' up Heaven's Angels. Not the DAMC."

"Right, that's what I meant. Even so, Dawg... when it comes to custody or visitation rights... just you being a part of the DAMC, even though it's not an outlaw club, might hinder both you and Emma. I'm just warning you now. I hope I'm wrong, but..." She shook her head. "Life's unfair sometimes, as we all know."

"Right," he grunted. "Lemme know what I gotta do to get it done."

"I will, Dawg. As long as everyone stays out of jail, you and Emma will be my top priority. *Got me?*" Her pretty blue eyes twinkled as she said the last.

"Got you," Dawg chuckled. "Appreciate it, Keeks."

Kiki rose from her seat. "You know I'd do anything for you guys," she glanced over at Emma, "and the sisterhood. You're all family."

Emma's gaze dropped to the diamond on Kiki's left ring finger. "I've been meaning to tell you since I first spotted it, that's a very beautiful ring." And very huge, too. It had to have cost a fortune.

Kiki's eyes got soft, and a smile drifted over her lips. "Yes. My ol' man's very generous."

Dawg's hand settled on the back of Emma's neck under her hair and he squeezed gently as he said, "Hawk's world revolves around you."

Kiki shook her head. "No. I think it's the opposite."

"When you gonna give him babies?"

Kiki laughed. "It isn't my turn. Jewel's unexpected news screwed up the betting pool. Ivy was supposed to be next. So I've got time."

"Not so sure 'bout that. Though, doubt Hawk'll be passin' out like D did when he heard the news."

Kiki's laugh filled the office and it made Emma smile. "Diesel passed out when he found out Jewel was pregnant?"

"Oh yeah," Kiki said. "He dropped like a tree onto the pavement. Luckily he's hard-headed so he wasn't hurt."

"Wow."

"Yes, it was a wow moment, all right," Kiki agreed as she escorted them back out into the lobby where Jayde was texting furiously on her phone.

Kiki tilted her head toward the younger woman and raised her eyebrows at Dawg. "See? Make sure you talk to *you-know-who* if you see him before Hawk does," she whispered. She raised her voice, "Jayde, who are you texting?"

Jayde glanced up in surprise, then slapped the phone face down on her desk. "No one... A friend."

"Uh-huh," Kiki said. She turned to Emma and Dawg. "I'll let you guys know when I need you back in here."

"Thank you for everything," Emma said.

Kiki gave her a smile. "It's my pleasure. I might not be a family law expert, but I'll do my best to get your family back together. For both of you."

Dawg steered Emma out of the law office and out to the curb where his bike was parked.

She took the helmet from him but didn't put it on. Instead, she watched him mount his "sled." "Dawg..."

His head twisted back to her with a frown. "*Now* you use my name when nobody's 'round?"

Emma grimaced. That wasn't what they needed to discuss. And she didn't even know where to begin...

"Does she turn you on? I saw what you did when she put on her glasses."

Holy crap, did she sound jealous? Was she jealous?

Did she have any reason *to* be jealous?

She bit her bottom lip and Dawg's eyes were immediately drawn to the gesture. His eyes darkened and his arm snaked out, grabbing her at the waist and pulling her to him.

"Wasn't her, baby girl." He brushed his thumb over her bottom lip, pulling it from between her teeth. "She slipped on those glasses an' suddenly I saw you doin' the same fuckin' thing, but only wearin' a half-open button-down shirt and biting that lip when you did it. Hot as fuck."

"Oh," she breathed.

"Kiki's hot as fuck, too, but if I had those same thoughts 'bout her, Hawk would kill me with his bare hands. Wouldn't blame 'im one fuckin' bit, either. Now you know how I feel when my customers are eyeballin' you like a piece of hard candy they wanna suck on. Got me?"

Ooooob. "Dawg..."

He cocked an eyebrow at her. "Really? Em, stop fuckin' 'round an' get on the sled. Need to take you home."

"For what?"

"So I can be in the A/C when I answer the thousand questions you got in your fuckin' head right now. But first gonna fuck you."

"Oh," she breathed again. And suddenly, it wasn't just the sun's heat making her warm.

"Yeah, *oh*. Get the fuck on. If you haven't noticed, it's like a thousand degrees out here an' doubt you wanna suck sweaty dick."

Emma bit back a laugh and pulled the helmet over her head. Dawg helped secure it and she slipped on the bike behind him. She wrapped her arms tightly around him as he took off, heading back toward Heaven's Angels and his apartment.

She agreed, *sweaty dick* didn't sound the most appetizing. However, nothing was stopping them from taking a long shower together first.

CHAPTER ELEVEN

D awg grunted as he thrust against Emma's ass. The water was turning cold, but he didn't give a shit. Em's pussy, hot as hell, made up for it as he pumped in and out of her. She had her hands and cheek pressed to the shower wall, her ass tilted enough to give him the perfect access to her cunt so he could fuck her thoroughly.

Water dripped off his brow, into his eyes, off his beard and down his chest. He had both arms wrapped around her, one hand gripping her tit firmly, two fingers twisting her pointed nipple. His other hand was tucked between her legs, his fingers brushing against where they were connected while his thumb teased her clit.

The sounds coming from between her *so-fuckin'-sweet* lips drove him crazy. Drove him to fuck her harder, faster. But he was determined to take his time. Make this last.

He wanted every second he spent inside this woman to last a lifetime.

He shoved his face into the crook of her neck, using his chin to shove away her wet hair so he could get to her delicate skin. His tongue traced the line of her neck, then he pressed his lips against her and sucked hard enough to leave a mark. That action caused a reaction within her that made him groan. Every time he sucked or bit her, she'd clamp down around him, as if trying to draw him deeper. Though he wasn't sure that was possible.

He was already in deep.

So fucking deep, he doubted he'd ever be able to claw his way back out.

"Baby girl, you're squeezin' me so fuckin' tight," he murmured against her wet skin.

She reached up and wrapped a hand around the back of his head, in a husky voice encouraging, "Bite me again."

His dick twitched inside her. His baby girl liked rough play. Not all the time, but when she was really worked up.

And right now, her body was humming like a live electrical wire against him.

"Gonna come?"

"Yes, if you... bite me," she groaned.

Dawg slowly sank his teeth into the tender spot where her neck met her shoulder and Emma exploded, crying out, her fingernails digging painfully into his scalp as her body convulsed around him.

Fuck, when she did that, he had a hard time not losing it himself.

But he was getting used to how responsive she was, how much she loved sex, which he thought surprised her more than it did him. Knowing her body and anticipating her reactions better now, he could last longer, make sure she didn't only orgasm once before he lost his load. Fuck no, he made her come multiple times each time he fucked her.

And she ate that shit up.

So did he.

Every day that passed, every minute he spent with her, made him realize he never wanted any other man to experience what Emma gave him. Because every time they fucked, she didn't hold anything back. She gave him her all.

And that right there got him in the fucking gut.

She gave *him*, Dawg, everything she had.

That got him thinking once more: what he did to deserve her? Was fate fucking with him? Teasing him with a woman he couldn't get enough of? Giving him hope that she would stick, only to rip her away because of her circumstances?

Or his?

"Em," he growled.

She let out a little noise of complaint when he pulled out, but he only did it long enough to turn her around in the tight shower. Then he pressed her back against the wall, jerked her legs up around his waist and plunged into her once again.

His fingers dug into the soft flesh of her ass as she wrapped her arms around his neck, grabbing handfuls of his hair, arching her back to press her beautiful fucking tits into his chest.

His rhythm stuttered when she ripped his head back and bit the side of his throat.

He squeezed his eyes shut and stilled, trying not to come. But it was hard. *So hard.*

No way was he done with her. Not yet.

"Can't get any deeper than that, baby girl," he groaned, letting her weight drop a little farther, grinding hard against her.

"Baby, you feel so good inside me," her honey-smooth voice whispered near his ear.

She normally didn't say much during sex. Made a lot of noises, fuck yeah, but talking? No. So when she said shit like that, he appreciated every word that came out of her mouth.

He pressed his forehead against hers and sucked in a breath as he slowed this pace, savoring her tight heat, her soft skin, her baby blues. Everything about her.

"Think that feels fuckin' good? You should be me. Ain't no better feelin' then bein' inside you, Em. None."

"When you say things like that..." Her words drifted off, but he needed to hear her finish her thought.

"Tell me," he encouraged.

"You make it difficult..."

"To what?" His heart thumped heavily in his chest.

She shook her head. "Not now."

Fuck.

Whatever she was going to say wasn't what he thought. So, yeah, he didn't want to hear it now.

Because in this shower, it was just the two of them. No one else. Reality could wait its asshole-self outside the bathroom door. But right now, this was his time alone with her. No customers, no ex-husbands, no Shadow Warriors, no clubs of any kind, no worries about their daughters.

It was just them. Every time they fucked, it was their break from the craziness that surrounded them.

Even though, for the most part, Emma acted like she had her shit together and was dealing with Lily's abduction as best as she could, he knew on the inside she was ripped apart and worried constantly.

He'd catch her just staring at an object, lost in her head. Chewing on her bottom lip as she thought about her daughter. Or sometimes she'd try to hide her tears, thinking he didn't see her crying.

He did. It tore him apart, too. And each and every tear she shed over Lily made him want to kill the bastard that much more.

He wanted to go with Hunter and Walker to Brunei or wherever Lily was. But he had no passport. No training in being covert. He could fuck everything up.

Because like D would turn into a beast if Jewelee was ever snatched again, Dawg would be the same way... kicking in doors and busting fucking heads.

He'd blow the whole mission.

So he needed to let those men do what they did best. And he needed to take care of his woman, be her support, and remind her that people did care.

Especially him.

"Dawson," she murmured against his throat.

He realized he had slowed his thrusting to almost a complete stop.

"Yeah, baby girl."

"The water's freezing."

He hadn't even noticed until she said it. But it sure as fuck was.

He turned off the shower and without breaking their connection, stepped out, carried her over to the sink, propped her ass on the edge and took his time to get her worked up once more.

She clung tightly to him as she came once more, and he finally let go. And when he glanced up in the mirror at the two of them, he saw two people who looked like they belonged in totally different worlds.

But maybe they could make it work.

Hawk and Kiki couldn't have been more different. Sophie and Z were, too. And look at them now.

Perfect examples of how no two puzzle pieces were ever the same, but somehow when placed together they fit seamlessly.

He'd never put a puzzle together in his life, but he was willing to try.

———

Emma collapsed on Dawg, her breathing as ragged as his. After they had dried off from their shower, they had moved to the bed for round two.

Dawg rubbed a strand of her long hair between his fingers, marveling on how it felt like silk draped over his chest.

Funny how the chaos in his head quieted during moments like these. He hoped it was the same for her.

"We need to talk about some of the things you said in Kiki's office," she murmured, her breath sweeping over his still heated skin.

"My dick's still in you, wanna talk 'bout that shit now?"

She rolled her head until her chin was planted on his chest and she locked her gaze with his. "Yes, before I need to go downstairs. I don't want it distracting me when I work the floor."

Right. Because soon he'd need to share her with the rest of the world again.

Reality was creeping in with each passing second.

But what she brought up first made it close in around him like a hand squeezing his throat.

"You're not giving up your club or your place for me and Lily. First, I owe you, you don't owe me. Second, I've disrupted your life enough as it is. There's no reason for it. I'll find a place, a teaching job. You have a good thing here, Dawson. You're successful, the girls tell me how good you are to them and they rely on you. I'm not going to screw that up."

His chest tightened. "Ain't screwin' up anything." This kind of talk made his dick soften faster than normal and he slipped out of her with a disappointed sigh.

She traced her fingers over his collar bone and up his throat. "It doesn't make sense to flip your life upside down for me. I don't even know why you'd want to do it."

"Not just doin' it for you, Em." Though, she was a major part of it. "This whole thing with you an' Lily got me thinkin'."

"About what? Reevaluating your life?" She combed her fingers through his beard and he lifted his chin to give her better access. He loved when she did that. It made him want to purr like a mountain lion. "There's nothing wrong with the life you live. It may not be for everyone but it's your life, Dawson."

"Your daughter's important to you..." he began.

"Of course she is."

"Mine needs to be important to me, too," he admitted. It hit him then that he'd opened up to this woman more than he'd ever opened up to anyone else in his life.

Her fingers stilled. "Your daughter spent the first fourteen years of her life not knowing you exist. Are you sure you want to get involved now? Flip *her* life upside down? She might not want anything to do with you. She might feel betrayed by her mother for lying to her all these years. She probably thinks her stepfather is her real father."

"Don't make it right," he muttered.

"I agree. It doesn't make it right. Not at all. What her mother did was wrong. For you. For Caitlin. But she may have done what she thought was best at the time. Just like me coming to you and begging for a job. Do you think I wanted to be a stripper? No. But I need to do what's best for my daughter, which is bring her home. And to do that, I need money. So I was ready to do whatever I needed to do, even get naked on a stage in front of strangers." Before Dawg could answer she lifted her hand to stop him. "Now, maybe Todd thinks he's doing what's best for Lily. I don't know. I don't know what he's thinking, besides being a selfish prick. But he very well may have thought I was a horrible mother."

There was no way Emma was a horrible mother, not even close. "Doubt it, baby girl. Look what you're doin' to get her back. A horrible mother wouldn't go to all that trouble."

"Maybe. Maybe not." Her fingers continued on their journey brushing through his beard. "But to give up everything you've known for... how long?"

"Fifteen years."

"Right. Think long and hard about giving up everything you've known, what you've built for the past fifteen years, Dawson. I'm not sure if you should give that all up for Caitlin. And especially not for me and Lily. You've only known me for a little over a week. This place has been a part of you longer than your daughter has been on this earth. Make sure whatever decision you make, you don't regret later."

Fuck, he told her the same thing about her decision to sleep with him. He'd needed her to be sure, so she wouldn't regret it later. Now she was flipping that around on him.

"Regret being in my bed, baby girl?"

"No."

She answered him without even a hesitation and something

swelled deep inside him. Something he wasn't sure he'd ever felt before.

He grabbed her hand to stop its motion, then lifted her fingers to his lips, brushing his mouth along the tips.

"Emma," he murmured. "Never want you to regret bein' with me. Got me?"

"I just said I didn't."

She thought he meant only in bed. It was more than that. "Not now. Later. Don't wanna be the one to hurt your chances gettin' full custody of Lily. Don't wanna be the reason anyone would call you an unfit mother. Because you on your own are not. With me by your side..." He let that hang and laid her hand on his chest, covering it with his.

"My daughter comes first, Dawson. No matter what," she said softly.

Of course she did. He'd expect nothing less from Emma.

His mother never made him a priority. Having a man in her bed, taking care of the lot rent and being able to buy her cigarettes was the most important to her. Whether that man was a drunk or not. His mother couldn't care less whether that man was good to her son. Or even a good influence. To her, Dawg was simply an inconvenience.

What if one day Caitlin found out the truth and he'd never come forward? What if she found out that he knew about her but didn't do shit about it? Would she feel the same way about him as he did about his mother? Would she feel unwanted?

He didn't want that. All children should feel wanted, loved.

Right?

He opened his mouth to tell her how he knew that Lily would be first on her list but he'd like to be on her list, too. Second, third, whatever. As long as Emma could slip him somewhere into her life, he wanted to be a part of it.

Maybe, just maybe, he could build a life, a family with Emma, Lily and Caitlin, too.

He closed his mouth and stayed silent as the ache in his chest grew. He wanted to build something he'd never had. Something he never thought he would have until a honey-smooth, husky voiced kindergarten teacher showed up in his club begging for a stripper job.

"Did you ever think about approaching her mother, telling her that you know, and asking for visitation? It doesn't have to be court-ordered, you know. She might be agreeable."

"Doubt she'll be agreeable."

"You don't know that until you ask."

"Yeah, baby girl, she kept Caitlin a secret, so I can pretty much guess what her answer will be. A big 'fuck you.'"

"It can't hurt. Especially if you're going to proceed in court, anyway. Try to be civil first. Approach her, see if she's even willing to consider it. It also might give you an idea of what kind of fight you might have on your hands."

What Em said was true. He might want to get a read on Regan.

"You know if you establish paternity, you might have to pay back child support. I'm not sure on how all that works."

He wasn't, either. Especially since Regan kept him in the dark all those years and allowed her husband to adopt her. Or that's what he heard. He didn't know if the adoption was true or not. "Yeah."

"It might be a lot."

"Yeah," he grunted.

"Are you prepared for that?"

"Got the money."

"Another reason why you shouldn't be financially covering anything for me. You need to cover your own expenses. Not mine."

"Got the money, Em. Ain't a problem. Club's got fat coffers, worse comes to worse. A lotta that comes from my club. Z would have no problem agreein' to get shit settled for me. An' for you. 'Specially now he's got a family of his own. He gets it."

"I'm still having a hard time wrapping my head around why any of you would spend resources like that on me and Lily."

Dawg rolled quickly, taking Emma with him until she was flat on her back and he was perched above her, practically nose to nose. "How many times have the women welcomed you to the sisterhood?"

"Too many."

"Think there's a reason for that?"

She got quiet.

"Asked you a question," he prodded.

"I think you're expecting me to stick around after Lily comes home."

She thought right. "Yeah."

"I think we need to discuss that, too."

Fuck. "Em..."

She reached up and cupped his chin. "Dawson..."

"Don't wanna fuck up your chances with all the legal shit, but also don't want you to walk outta my life. Got me?"

There. He said it. He laid it out for her.

"You want a relationship." Not a question, but a confirmation.

"Want you in my life, baby girl. An' before you argue again 'bout how we've only known each other not very long... Fuckin' know that. Lemme tell you somethin' 'bout us Angels. We're fuckin' stubborn. Hard-headed. An' when we see what we want, we go for it. An', baby girl, I want you. Nobody but you, got me?"

"Why?" she asked softly, her eyes shiny and filling with what he knew would soon spill over and down her cheeks.

Fuck. He hated when women cried. Especially Emma.

Though he wasn't quite sure how to answer her question, he gave it a shot and hoped he didn't sound too much like a stupid fuck.

"You're good for me, Em. Never thought I'd say that to any woman. Never thought I'd want somethin' long term with one, either. But I'm gonna be thirty-six years old. Built a successful business from the ground up. Found my family, my brothers. But I need somethin' else. Didn't realize it 'til you walked in the door, lookin' all awkward as fuck. You got to me, Em, not just in the dick, but here."

He slapped his hand on his chest over his heart. "Never thought it could happen to me. Saw my brothers goin' down left an' right. Gotta admit, kinda laughed at 'em, 'til I saw how their women were right for 'em. Perfect. Made 'em whole. Made 'em better. Complete. Maybe I'm soundin' like a fuckin' pussy sayin' all this. An', honestly, don't give a flyin' fuck. But I tell you shit I've never told anyone else an' that's sayin' somethin'. Never spilled my guts to just any snatch in my bed before. An' you know why? 'Cause they were just pussy. Nothin' more, nothin' less. That ain't you, Emma. Ain't just pussy. You're so much more than that. An' now I'm done talkin' 'bout this shit before I grow a pair of tits an' my balls disappear into my cunt."

The whole time he was spilling his guts, her mouth hung open, her eyes were wide and her face had become pale.

He must have scared the shit out of her. Because his speech scared the shit out of him. But it was said, and he wasn't taking it back. Not that he could even if he wanted to.

"Dawson," she whispered.

He closed his eyes, waiting for the rejection. Waiting for her to tell him that this was all just temporary. That they'd never be a thing. That he was a means to an end. That there was only one reason why she was in his life.

And that reason wasn't him.

Because why the fuck would she want to spend the rest of her life with someone like him? An uneducated biker and strip club manager.

She wouldn't.

"Dawson, look at me."

Fuck. The ache in his chest was now unbearable. She just needed to put him out of his misery. Pull the trigger...

Tell him he's a stupid fuck for even thinking those thoughts.

"Look at me!" she demanded loudly.

His eyes popped open, and he saw something in her face that made his gut twist and his heart stop.

A lone tear rolled down from the corner of her eye, disap-

pearing into the blonde hair that was spread out around her like a
satin cape.

"I didn't realize it until you started talking..."

That I'm a stupid fuck?

"Just how I felt..."

An' you wanted to run out of the room screamin'?

"And I'm not sure I should tell you this..."

She was killing him. This hesitation, this uncertainty.

"But..."

HOLY FUCK!

"Dawson... I think..."

"Emma," he finally barked because he had no more patience
left. None. Zip. Zero. It was like she was digging a knife slowly
into his heart. The pain was deep and unbearable.

"I love you."

His head jerked back.

What?

Wait. What?

He glanced over his shoulder to make sure no one was behind
him. That she wasn't saying that to anyone else but him.

She reached up and cupped his cheek. "Does that freak you
out? Because I have to admit that it freaks me out a bit."

Fuck yeah, it freaked him the fuck out. It was the last thing he
expected to come out of her mouth.

"Fuck, baby girl," was the only thing he could say because, fuck
him, he had no idea how to respond to the bomb she just dropped.
He already had flayed himself open enough to her.

Instead, he lowered his head and took her mouth, licking her
bottom lip that now belonged to him, tangling their tongues,
exploring every part of it. She groaned as he took the kiss deeper.
He dug his fingers into her hair, fisting them tight, holding her
down, claiming her as his.

Because now there was no doubt she was his. And no matter
what happened in their life with the shitty hands they've been
dealt, he knew one thing for sure, he was not letting her go.

Not now. Not ever.

When he finally broke the kiss, she stared up at him in a daze. "I need to get to work."

"Yeah." They both did. But the woman just admitted something that almost blew his brains out. He needed to respond to that. "Gotta tell you somethin', baby girl."

"What's that?"

"Never had anyone tell me that before."

"But—"

He knew where she was going with that, so he cut her off. "No, Em. Not even her." His mother had never said those three words to him. Not once that he could remember. "So let me tell you how fuckin' special that is to me. An' I also gotta say that if what I'm feelin' is love, then," he sucked in a breath, steeled himself then admitted, "I love you, too. Just wanna let you know."

She smiled and she brushed her fingers over his brow. "That took a lot for you to say."

"Yeah."

"Then I'll cherish that." She planted a kiss on his cheek, then wiggled out from beneath him. "But now I have to go put on a slutty dress and flirt with other men."

For fuck's sake.

CHAPTER TWELVE

Dawg gritted his teeth as he watched the woman he fucked almost fifteen years ago climb out of her overpriced shiny new SUV in the driveway of her overpriced huge house.

She looked good. But nothing like when she was nineteen. Now she looked well-put together, dressed like she had money, her hair was perfectly in place, and she looked pampered.

Nothing he would've been able to give her. Not back then, maybe not even now.

Fuck no. He could only offer her dick, and the future of living over a damn strip club.

That wasn't what she wanted from him. And he didn't blame her, she had it good now. She probably wanted for nothing and ran in circles that would never give him the time of day. Though, he was sure some of the men in her "circles" were some of his loyal clientele.

But, hey, as long as they tipped his girls good, he didn't care what side of the tracks his customers were from.

The women in her circle wouldn't give him a second glance unless they were looking for a night with a bad boy just for shits and giggles. Or looking for revenge on a cheating husband. And thank fuck he'd taken one up on her offer one night last year during a dry spell. The rich bitch he did that night just happened to know Regan and slipped about Caitlin's real father possibly being an Angel when she saw his cut.

A few casual questions later and Dawg had put two and two together...

He'd climbed off his sled and now stood there waiting, arms crossed over his chest.

She had seen him. He was hard to miss. And he was sure it wasn't very often that a biker wearing a DAMC cut sat on his Harley at the curb of a million-dollar mansion. Or however much that house cost.

In fact, "wasn't very often" probably meant never.

He was surprised none of the neighbors had called the cops yet for a suspicious person. But he kept an ear peeled for sirens just in case. Though he wasn't doing anything illegal, he didn't know any of the cops in this wealthy area outside of Pittsburgh. So he might end up tased, batoned or even thrown in jail for just looking at a pig sideways.

Then his day would suck even more than it already did.

Regan slipped her sunglasses down her nose as she stared at him from next to her vehicle. Even from where he stood, on public property to make sure he wasn't trespassing, he could tell she was muttering under her breath.

Probably calling him every name in the book.

Well, he was calling her the same shit in his head. So they were even.

With a large visible sigh, she yanked her purse over her shoulder and stomped in his direction. "What the hell are you doing here, Dawg?" she asked in an angry whisper when she got close enough.

"Surprised you remember me," he said, even though he had no doubt she would never forget him. Especially when she popped out his kid. "Need to talk."

"Now? There's absolutely no reason to reminisce about *good times*."

The sarcasm in her voice made him grimace. "*Was* it good for you?"

Color flooded her cheeks, and she pushed her sunglasses higher up her nose. She twisted her head left and right, probably making sure none of her neighbors saw her slumming with a man of questionable character.

"You look good, Regan."

Her head jerked back. "I'm married."

"Know it. Don't wanna fuck you, just tryin' to be civil."

Emma had reminded him before he'd left to remain calm and be civil since you drew more flies with honey. That's what she said, and he would try to stick with that plan.

"Why are you here, Dawg?"

"Like I said, need to talk."

"We have nothing to talk about."

He pinned her with a stare. "Doubt that." Then he shut up and waited.

After a few seconds, her face became pale and her lips thinned. Even through her big, fashionable sunglasses he could see her eyes widen when it hit her why he was there. "I'm going inside. You need to leave."

As she turned, he snaked out a hand and snagged her wrist, keeping her right where she stood. "No."

"No?" She tugged on her arm and he let her go. He didn't need to add on assault charges.

"No. Came here for a reason. Stayin' until I say my piece."

She tugged her purse higher up her shoulder. Maybe she was afraid he'd try to snatch it. "What could we possibly have to talk about after fifteen years? We slept together once."

"Three times," he muttered.

She grimaced as if that number made it even worse. "I don't remember that."

"I do."

"I guess it wasn't as memorable for me."

He tilted his head and studied the woman before him. The one he had actually thought might be for him all those years ago. Which proved he was young and dumb at the time and only thinking with his dick. "No? Didn't give you anything worth rememberin'?"

"You mean like crabs?"

He blew out an irritated breath. "Didn't give you crabs."

"Then I have no idea what you're talking about," she answered in a snotty tone.

He raised his eyebrows at her lie. "No idea?"

She lifted her chin. "Nope."

"Found out recently you've had somethin' of mine for the last fourteen years."

Her mouth gaped open, and she stumbled back. Dawg reached out and snagged her wrist again to keep her from tumbling backward onto the pavement.

"Let me go!"

Dawg released her and held his hands up in surrender. "Just tryin' to help."

"How are you helping me by coming here *now*, after all these years, and saying stuff like that?"

"It's true, ain't it?"

She glanced toward the house, a worried look on her face. "No."

"Bullshit, Regan. I saw her."

"When?" she breathed.

"A few months ago at her school."

"Why would you go there?"

"To see if it was true. To make sure she's mine."

Regan slammed her hands on her hips. "So what if she is? She doesn't know you. I don't want her to know you."

His body went solid. "That's fuckin' clear."

"Even if she *was* yours, you have nothing to offer her. Just look at you." She waved a well-manicured hand up and down his body.

His nostrils flared as he sucked in an impatient breath. "Regan, is she mine?" He needed to hear it once and for all. The absolute truth.

"She's my husband Paul's."

Another fucking lie. "On paper or by blood?"

Regan grimaced.

Dawg shook his head at her reaction. "Gettin' a DNA test."

"No! I'll fight it."

He shrugged. "Try it. It's gonna happen."

"Why would you want to screw up her life? Paul has given us a good one. He's giving her all the opportunities you'd never be able to give her. With you, she'd be lucky to end up in a community college, *if* she didn't end up on the pole. With him she's got a shot at an Ivy League school."

"Because her life's a lie."

"It's a good lie. She doesn't have a clue that Paul isn't her father. She knows no different, Dawg."

"But I do."

"Don't be so damn selfish. This isn't just about you. This is about my daughter."

"Just confirmed she's my daughter, too."

"It doesn't matter. You are nothing to her, Dawg. *Nothing.* Get that through your thick head. The only thing you had going for you was that you were decent in bed. That's it. My first mistake was missing a couple days of my birth control and thinking I would still be covered. My second was thinking it'd be fun to have a couple of nights with a bad boy like you. But my biggest mistake was actually fucking you."

His hands clenched into fists and his jaw got tight.

Dawg had never hit a woman before and he wasn't about to start. But it was close. So fucking close. She was lucky she wasn't a man because her ass would be on the ground right about now, knocked the fuck out.

"You were a damn biker. Obviously, you still are. Why would you have wanted to be saddled with a baby back then?"

"Took my fuckin' choice away, Regan. Didn't gimme a chance to decide how to handle it."

"You'd better think long and hard about this, Dawg. Think about what you're going to do to Caitlin. Think about what kind of turmoil you're going to cause in her life. Why would you do this and be so selfish? Why would you come in now and interrupt her life?"

"Maybe 'cause I didn't know 'bout her, Regan. So don't accuse me of being selfish. You," he poked his finger in her direction, "kept my blood from me. Now, *that's* fuckin' selfish. Wanna know my daughter. Have every right to know her. Wouldn't be any turmoil if I'd known about her from the fuckin' beginnin'."

"One reason I didn't tell you because I wasn't sure what I was going to do. I considered having an abortion. Just because I didn't, doesn't mean I want to relive my mistake over and over for the rest of my life."

"You didn't tell me because you considered me that mistake. You've made that pretty fuckin' clear."

She tilted her head as she stared at him through her sunglasses that probably cost a small fortune. "Are you still running that strip club? If you are, DNA test or not, you don't have a chance in hell on getting visitation rights. No judge in their right mind will give you that. So think hard on that, Dawg. What kind of morals are you going to teach a fourteen-year-old girl when you have naked women dancing on a stage in front of a bunch of perverted men?"

He couldn't argue that last point. But there was nothing illegal about his club. The women were treated well, and it was their choice to work there. They weren't coerced one bit. So she could take her self-righteous morals and shove them up her ass.

He might not be Paul-type rich, but he did well. He could provide for his daughter, give her most of what she needed. Maybe not everything this Paul could, but she didn't need to be spoiled, she just needed her father. She just needed to know she was loved. And wanted.

Fuck.

"Now get out of here before she comes outside looking for me."

He glanced toward the house. He'd had no idea that Caitlin was inside all this time. His heart began to pound. "Wanna see her."

"You have no right to see her."

"Need to tell 'er 'bout me."

"No, I don't, Dawg. That's why there are courts. Good luck with that. I'm sure we can tie things up in the system until you run out of money." She moved away from him back to her driveway. "If you don't leave right now, I'm calling the police and then she can see you being arrested and hauled off in handcuffs. Something I'm sure you're used to."

His jaw tightened. "Ain't a jailbird."

"Oh, well, let me give you a gold star. I'm sure you're an upstanding citizen with a lot to contribute to society. Go you!" she cheered, then sneered, "Now get out of here. Any further communication can be done through our attorneys."

With that, she spun on her heel and hurried toward the house.

He fought the temptation to follow her, force his way into the house and see Caitlin. To talk to her. Hear her voice. Discover everything about her that's been kept from him.

But he didn't.

Because ending up in jail wouldn't help him. Wouldn't help Emma.

She had told him to remain civil.

He was going to remain fucking civil even if it killed him.

———

"Got a bead on 'em," Diesel's voice grumbled through Dawg's cell phone three days later.

Dawg blew out a relieved breath and scrubbed a hand over his beard. "Where? Brunei?"

"Yeah," D grunted. "Looks like they were plannin' on stayin' for a while. Rented a place. Bought a car. Changed their names."

Dawg turned his back toward the stage and stepped away from Cubby, covering his ear with his hand so he could hear the DAMC's enforcer better over the music. "Your guys there now?"

"Yeah. Hunter. Walker. Mercy headin' that direction."

Fuck. With Mercy on his way, shit was about to go down and Lily might be home soon. Dawg needed to get his shit together and get their future in order. Talk to Z. Talk to Emma once he figured out their plans to see if she was on board.

He hoped to hell she was.

"They got Lily yet?"

"Nope. Watchin'. Waitin'. Makin' sure they don't bolt somewhere else."

"She okay?"

"Yeah."

"Can I tell Emma?"

"Fuck no. Ain't tellin' her shit. Once the kid's back on the ground in PA, we'll tell 'er. Not a second before, got me?"

"She worries, D. Wanna tell her Lily's safe."

"Just gonna hafta worry for now. Don't want this fucked six ways to Sunday. Keepin' it on a need-to-know basis. Gonna do this the way my guys wanna do it. They're the ones puttin' their asses on the line."

"Understood," Dawg answered. He understood it, but he didn't like it. Emma needed some reassurance. He turned with his phone still up to his ear and immediately spotted *Ember* working a customer at the other end of the stage.

He didn't like keeping shit from her. Not about her own daughter. But he had to do what was best for Lily and for D's crew. D was right, they were putting their asses on the line. They didn't have to, but they wanted to since D confessed that they had decided to volunteer their time. D and the DAMC coffers were covering a lot of the travel expenses. Dawg would cover anything else needed.

This was a costly mission in more ways than one. But he wasn't giving the rat bastard who stole Emma's daughter more than a second of his thoughts. Not more than one fucking second.

He did Emma wrong. He did Lily wrong by ripping her away from her mother. A mother who loved and cared for her. He deprived both of them a year and a half of their lives together.

He was a selfish prick who needed to pay. However Mercy decided the fucker needed to pay, Dawg was okay with it.

Did that make him a cold-hearted bastard? Probably. But there were consequences to every action. And Emma's ex was going to find that out.

"You know shit's gonna change once she's back with her mother, right?" D's deep grumble came through the phone.

"For Lily?"

"For you, brother. Woman's got a seven-year-old. You got a strip club. Gotta make a plan. Ain't gonna be a fight on her end with the husband. That problem's bein' permanently solved. Don't know jack 'bout 'is family. They decide to fight 'er, she might lose. Some people get jacked 'bout women dancin' naked on a stage. Ain't gonna look good durin' a custody battle."

"Yeah. Gonna talk to Z as soon as you hang the fuck up."

Dawg heard a grunt on the other end of the phone and then his cell went dead.

He pulled the phone away and immediately texted Z. He needed a meeting with the prez and his VP.

Like yesterday.

After telling Emma he needed to go take care of business, he approached the private bar at church not an hour later where Hawk waited for him. The VP's eyes were serious as he tracked Dawg heading in his direction.

Hawk stepped from behind the bar and they clasped hands and bumped shoulders. "Brother," Hawk grunted.

"Brother," Dawg greeted back. His head twisted toward the end of the bar where Grizz had his ass settled in his regular seat and a half-empty pint glass already in front of him. "Mama Bear must be workin' in the kitchen if the old man's already in his seat."

"Yeah," Hawk said. "Can't pay that woman enough to keep my kitchen runnin' as smoothly as it does."

"Hear ya, brother."

Hawk ducked back behind the bar. "Jack?"

"Fuck yeah, will need it for this."

With a raised brow, Hawk pulled a bottle of JD off the shelf, cracking the top and lining up a few shot glasses along the bar. He filled two of them and handed one to Dawg, who downed it in one swallow and hissed away the burn.

"Fuck," he muttered, dragging a hand over his mouth.

Hawk blew out a breath. "I'd say that's a good way to start the day, but it's fuckin' two o'clock."

Dawg turned his head when he heard someone coming down the steps from the rooms upstairs. Crow, his black hair wet and loose around his shoulders, appeared, spotted them and headed over.

"Don't you gotta open up shop?" Dawg asked him.

"What time is it?" Crow asked, rubbing a hand over his dark, tired eyes. He waved a dismissing hand and shook his head at the full shot glass Hawk offered him.

"Fuckin' day's half over," Hawk grumbled.

"The fuck it is," Crow grumbled back. He headed toward the commercial coffeemaker tucked away in the corner and looked at the pot. "How long has this sludge been sittin' here on the burner?"

"The fuck if I know," Hawk answered. "Don't live here. You do."

Crow grimaced as he emptied the coffee out in the sink and started a fresh batch.

"Don't you got customers waitin' on you?" Hawk asked Crow.

"Fuck no. Got a large piece scheduled for later. Ain't doin' shit before that. An' that fucker who's scheduled don't roll outta bed until..." He glanced at the clock behind the bar. "'bout now. I'll still be there before him. What're you two here for?"

Crow's answer was the back door from the parking lot opening and Zak stepping inside. He spotted them and flipped his hand up over his shoulder in a greeting.

"Didn't bring the kid?" Crow called out as Z made his way across the common area.

"I look like his mother?" Z shouted back.

"No, thank fuck," Crow muttered as he moved closer to where Hawk and Dawg were standing, downing their second shot of whiskey. He sipped his coffee and sighed. "Now that shit's good. Just need one of your woman's cupcakes to go along with it. Can't be bakin' shit when she got a baby hangin' 'round her neck. Should be doin' daddy daycare."

Z hit the bar, clasped hands and bumped shoulders with all of them before accepting a shot of Jack. "Got my sled. Can't be stickin' the fuckin' baby seat on the back of that."

"Well, you could," Hawk said, then laughed.

"Yeah, well, he still needs Soph's tits. Kid's a greedy mother-fucker. Can't wait to get her tits back."

"Like you don't..." Crow started, shook his head and then smiled. "Never mind."

Z shot him a look. "Ain't goin' there."

Crow lifted a hand. "Yep, brother, you're right. Ain't goin' there."

Z glanced down the bar at Grizz and then back to Dawg. "Okay to talk here? Or we gotta move into the meetin' room?"

"Nah, it's okay. Ain't a secret. Just wanted to discuss some important shit with you an' the VP."

"Have to do with Emma?" Z asked, pinning his gaze on Dawg.

"Yeah, sorta. But it's more than that."

"Ah, shit. You fuckin' claimin' her?" the club's president asked, the surprise evident in his voice.

Dawg's head jerked back. Was he? He hadn't even thought that far ahead. In his mind, he'd already claimed her. Though, she wasn't his ol' lady officially, and he wasn't even sure that Emma would want that.

"Little early to be claimin' her," Hawk said, downed another double shot and barked out a "Fuck!" as he winced.

"Hell no, it ain't. Knew Soph was the one after the first night, Chicken Hawk. Can't tell me you weren't ready to claim Kiki after the first time she made you blow your load."

Hawk poured himself another double and smiled. "Was ready to claim 'er as soon as 'er hot fuckin' ass wearin' that tight skirt walked into the visitin' room at County. An' when she put on 'er glasses... *Fuck!* Was ready to bend 'er over the table an'... Yeah. Got your point." Hawk reached down and adjusted himself.

Dawg grinned and shook his head. "Ain't 'bout claimin' her... yet. Need to get shit settled. Askin' if we can patch in Moose before his year's up."

"What the fuck? Why?" Z asked. "Know he's a good one, but..."

"Yeah, he's pullin' his weight at Heaven's Angels," Dawg explained. "He's a fuckin' trustworthy prospect. Worth patchin' 'im."

"Agreed," Hawk said.

"'Kay, we'll patch 'im in. That it?" Z asked.

"Fuck no. Wish it was. Once he's patched in, thinkin' 'bout handin' over the club to 'im. Lettin' 'im take over my apartment, take over managin'—"

Z shouted, "Hold up! Back the fuck up, Dawg. What the fuck you sayin'? You buyin' out your membership? You givin' up your colors? For Emma?"

"Fuck no. Ain't ever leavin' this club. But need to get a place. Need to do somethin' else. She might have a fight on her hands when it comes to custody an' I don't wanna be the reason she loses her daughter. She already lost her for the past year an' a half. Got me?"

Zak stared at him for a moment. "You're handin' over the reins for Heaven's Angels? You've been the only one who's ever run it.

You make the MC a fuckload of scratch from that club. Moose gonna be able to fill your shoes?"

"Dunno. Think so. He's got a smart head on his shoulders. Ain't a squirrelly piece of shit like some of the others. Trust 'im. If you think he ain't right, then maybe Dex or Linc can take over."

Hawk shook his head, a frown covering his face. "Nope. Linc's managin' the bar for me. He's good at it. Want 'im to continue."

"Then what the fuck are *you* doin'?" Dawg asked.

"Managin' Linc," Hawk answered with a grin. "He's doin' the late shift so I can be with my woman. I'm takin' daylight when Kiki's workin'."

Yeah, Kiki had definitely taken the top spot with Hawk after she walked into his life. The bar was now in second place. The club's VP no longer worked long and late hours at The Iron Horse. He did what he had to do, then went home and did what he wanted to do. With his woman.

That was exactly what Dawg needed, too. He was getting older; he didn't need to be working until three in the morning anymore. He'd leave that to the younger members.

"What 'bout Dex?" Dawg asked.

"Dex ain't managin' the strip club. His dick will be in the girls more than he'll be managin' 'em. Got a good policy 'bout not doin' your girls. Needs to stay that way," Hawk stated.

True. Dex wouldn't be as concerned with a lot of the things Dawg was. He also could see Dex running the club into the ground. And Dawg didn't want to see all his hard work fall to shit. Then he'd have to kick Dex's ass.

And that probably wouldn't go over very well.

"So back to Moose. Best person in my opinion," Dawg said.

"Yeah, thinkin' that's true. But sure you wanna do this? Give up everythin' you worked hard for just for pussy?" Hawk asked.

Dawg's nostrils flared and his fingers curled into his palm. Hawk was fucking with him. He had to be. Because if Dawg had ever said the same thing about Kiki, not just now but in the beginning when the couple first crossed paths, Hawk would have pounded him into the ground without a second thought.

"Brother," Crow warned Hawk with a low voice and a shake to his head. "You two goin' at it in here's gonna break a lot of shit. Hope you're just fuckin' with 'im."

Hawk's face broke out in a grin, then he whacked Dawg on the back. "Know how serious you are 'bout her, Dawg Pound. Just messin' with ya. But still... ready to give all that up? Again, it's only been what? A couple of weeks?"

"Yeah. But I get what you're sayin'. Been runnin' the club for fifteen years. Don't know anything else."

"You'll need to do somethin'," Z said.

"Right. Been thinkin' 'bout that, too."

All eyes landed on him.

He continued since he had their attention. "Shit that went down with Pierce... The Committee didn't strip 'im of his colors for a couple reasons. One that I know of was the gun shop."

Hawk straightened up from leaning back on the bar. "Whataya sayin'?"

"Thought it might be a good idea for someone to slide in there an' learn the biz from the inside out. This would be a good excuse to do it. Our bylaws state I gotta work an' bring money into the club account. So no better place for me than the gun shop and range, right? Nothin' would be suspicious. But once I get a good handle on the business, we got the option to kick 'is ass the fuck down the road. Strip 'is colors, if need be."

Z looked thoughtful but nodded his head. "Might be a good idea. He's always bitchin' he don't got enough help. I can't help 'em 'cause of my felony charge. But you've gotta good brain for business an' a good excuse to move into a spot over there." He looked pensive for a moment. "Yeah, fuck it. Like that idea. Chicken Hawk?"

Hawk nodded, too. "Fuck yeah. Like it. D will love it. So will Jag an' maybe even Ace. Pretty sure Dex will vote yes on that motion, too."

"Gotta get a meetin' scheduled quick then, brothers. Gotta get Moose patched in ASAP. Hunter an' Walker got a bead on Lily. She should be comin' home soon. Need to get this shit movin'. Also need to find a place to live," Dawg announced.

"For you? Or for the three of you?" Hawk asked, a brow cocked.

"Hopin' it's the three of us," Dawg answered.

"Ace's farm?" Crow suggested.

"Maybe. Not sure if I wanna live out in the country."

"Not sure if Ace's got anythin' available, anyhow," Z answered. "'Specially with Annie an' Allie each takin' up a cabin. Diamond an' Slade shackin' up in another. I think he's got the rest rented."

"Like I said, not sure if I wanna move out into the boonies. Not sure what Emma wants, either. She don't know what I'm here talkin' about. I'm sure she'll want a say where her an' Lily settle. Got cash for a house, but have a feelin' it's gonna go to fightin' for Caitlin."

Zak's head spun toward him, his brows pinned together. "Who's Caitlin?"

"Dawg's daughter," Hawk answered.

"What?" Z turned wide eyes to Dawg.

Dawg frowned at Hawk. "Guess Kiki told you."

Hawk ran a hand over his short mohawk. "Yeah. Kiki don't keep shit from me."

Dawg grimaced. "Nothin' like attorney-client privilege."

Hawk gave him an answering frown, then growled, "If the club's payin' for it, then we're all the client. Got me?"

Unfortunately, the man had a good point. "Yeah."

"So Zeke ain't the first kid to be the fourth generation," Zak muttered, sounding a little disappointed.

"Fourth generation of the foundin' members, but not fourth in the club itself. Sorry, Z," Dawg said.

"How old is she?" Crow asked, leaning against the bar with his second cup of coffee.

"Fourteen."

"Shit," Z mumbled. "That's a helluva long time to keep a secret from us."

Hell, it was a long time for a secret to be kept from *him*. Dawg continued, "Wasn't holdin' out on you. Didn't know 'bout 'er until recently."

"An' she wants to have visitation with you?" Z asked.

"Don't know I'm her pop."

"What the fuck!" Z exclaimed. "That's some bullshit right there, brother."

"Yeah," Dawg agreed.

"Sure you wanna do that to her?" Hawk asked quietly.

The million-dollar question. Everybody asked it, so it made him wonder if pushing this was the right thing. His gut said it was, but everyone was making him question his motives.

"You sayin' it's better that I leave well enough alone?" Dawg asked.

Crow tilted his head and narrowed his dark eyes. "She blood?"

"Yeah." Though he couldn't be one hundred percent sure until they had the DNA results. And that might take a while since Kiki would have to file the paperwork and he was positive that Regan would fight it tooth and nail.

"Your blood. You claim her," Crow said firmly. He grabbed Dawg's shoulder and shook it, then he clapped him on the back. "Got me, brother?"

"Yeah, brother, got you."

Hawk shifted. "Not sure if I agree with that."

"Ain't your blood," Crow told him. "If it was, you'd think differently."

"Right," Hawk grunted, but still didn't look convinced. However, Dawg had known Hawk for what seemed like forever. And he knew that man would fight for his kid if he found out he had one out there somewhere. Most likely most of his brothers would. Family was serious shit to them.

"Speakin' of kids an' shit...You get to warn Linc?" Dawg asked Hawk.

"'Bout what?" Z asked.

"Guess you havin' Zeke stoked a fire inside your baby sister, Z," Dawg said.

"Yeah. And?"

"Kiki thought it'd be a good idea to warn Linc to be... cautious," Hawk answered.

"Of what?" Z asked, clearly confused.

Hawk rolled his eyes. "Of your fuckin' sister," he barked at Z.

Z's spine straightened and his blue eyes narrowed. "They fuckin'?"

Dawg shrugged. "Not that I know of. But you've seen 'em eyeballin' each other. Talkin' close."

"Here's the thing..." Hawk began. "What I'm gonna tell you don't go past here. Got me? It's early yet, but it's not goin' to help Jayde's baby fever or whatever Keeks fuckin' calls it."

Then the man just stopped talking. And a few seconds later, it seemed to hit them all at once.

Z groaned, "Fuck."

"Yeah," Hawk grunted.

The club's president slammed his hand on the bar. "Ivy was supposed to be next. Just lost a fuckin' Benjamin on that bet."

Hawk snorted. "Yeah, maybe Jag's gettin' it in the wrong hole or somethin'. Dunno. But Ivy ain't next."

"Shouldn't we be celebratin'?" Crow asked.

"Fuck yeah. But don't tell Keeks I told you. She's hornier than ever, so ain't gonna end up in the dog house 'cause of you fuckers runnin' your traps."

"Fuck. This club's gonna turn into a fuckin' daycare," Dawg muttered.

Crow slapped Dawg's back. "Ain't a bad thing, brother. Bringin' new life into this club, into this family. Ain't nothin' wrong with that. Ensures the DAMC will live on."

"That it will," Z said. "Pour us some shots, Chicken Hawk."

With a grin, Hawk filled all the shot glasses he had lined up earlier, then passed them out. As one they all raised them.

Crow lifted his face to the ceiling and yelled, "Here's to Hawk's new fledgling. Dawg an' Emma gettin' their girls back. An' Z knockin' up his ol' lady again."

Hawk and Dawg hooted and knocked back their shots while Z shouted, "No! Those are my tits. Want 'em back before another kid steals 'em from me."

Crow laughed and downed his whiskey.

Grizz surprised all of them by coming up and joining them. "You fuckers are makin' this ol' man proud. Gimme one of them shots, boy."

Hawk handed the older man one, and he swallowed the double with barely an eye twitch. Then he raised his shot glass over his head and shouted, "Down an' dirty..."

The rest of them roared out a "'til dead!" in answer.

Fuck yeah.

CHAPTER THIRTEEN

"Dawg, the paperwork's filed for Emma's divorce, her request for full custody, and for the PFA. Also for your paternity claim. Did you get to the lab I told you to go to?"

"Yeah." He had done it the second Kiki had told him he should.

"Good. As soon as the DNA test is ordered by the court, Caitlin's mother will have to get it done. She can lie to Caitlin about why it's being done, but as long as it's done, we're good. Then once we have the results and we have proof Caitlin's yours, I'll file for visitation. Just be aware that it may be supervised visitation at first, okay?"

He nodded his head even though he knew she couldn't see it. "Yeah, Keeks. Appreciate it."

"Are you having second thoughts about this at all?"

Was he?

When he didn't answer, Kiki continued, her gentle voice coming through the other end of the phone. "Look, you can always change your mind later, Dawg. Let's get the results first and then, if you're sure, we can go ahead with the rest. Sound good?"

"Yeah."

"As for Lily..."

"Gonna claim Emma," he blurted out before he could think better of it. Hell, he just told Hawk's ol' lady he was claiming Emma, and he hadn't even discussed it with the woman herself.

Fuck me.

Kiki hissed out a breath and her reaction made his gut twist.

"Here's the thing, Dawg... I know I probably shouldn't be the one suggesting this, since Hawk and I aren't married yet, and he told me you know about my... *condition*... but, honey, I really think you need to make it legal. Not just claim her as your ol' lady. Claiming her in the club is all well and good, but you need to continue on the path of getting Heaven's Angels off your hands, finding a decent place to live and showing both Emma and the courts that you're serious about making a family with her. Getting a place where you'll make a home. An actual wedding. Real life things." Before he could answer, she asked softly, "Does that scare you?"

It didn't. He had known Emma was going to change his life. Had he known how much? Fuck no. Did he care that his life was heading in this new direction at the speed of a runaway train?

"No. It don't, Keeks. Honestly, it surprises the shit outta me with how much I want all that. Besides Emma, Caitlin's all I can think about right now."

"It also will make it look good for you when it comes to asking the courts for visitation. Stable home. Wife. Stepdaughter. Do you catch my drift?"

"Yeah, Keeks, I do. But she ain't divorced." And she wasn't a widow... yet, from what he knew. Not yet, but soon. And he doubted Kiki would know what was going down or would even *want* to know.

"I know, but it's something you need to seriously consider once she is. All of this stuff will take time, but you need to get your ducks in a row. *Got me?*"

Her "got me" drew a smile from him. The woman was something else. Hawk was a lucky fucker, that was for damn sure.

"Got you, Keeks. When you tellin' everyone about Hawk Jr.?"

"Hawk Jr.?" she squeaked.

"Yeah. It's a good name for a 'lil badass biker."

"A biker?"

The woman was not only engaged to a badass biker but now was knocked up by him, too. So she shouldn't be surprised that any son of hers would end up as a Harley riding hellion.

"Yeah. Gonna be ridin' on the back of his daddy's sled as soon as he learns not to fall off."

"Dawg," she groaned.

"What?"

"You're making me rethink this whole having a kid thing."

"Think it's a little too late now."

"Fuck," she muttered into the phone.

Dawg laughed. "If it's a girl, name 'er Tweetie Bird."

"I'm hanging up now."

"Keeks, wait."

"What?"

"Seriously, you can't even imagine how much I appreciate the shit you're doin' for Em an' me. An' gotta say I'm fuckin' thrilled for you an' Hawk. He's gonna make a damn good dad."

"Yeah," she breathed. "Damn it, you're going to make me cry! These freaking hormones!"

"He loves you, Keeks. More than life itself."

"I know." She sniffled loudly.

"Want me an' Em to have what you an' he got."

"Shut up before I run out of tissues and have to use my sleeve!"

Dawg chuckled.

"Dawg..."

"Yeah?"

"You're a good man. Never doubt that, hear me?"

"Yeah," he mumbled before the phone went dead.

———

"Talked to Kiki. She's got everything filed."

Emma stared up at the large man who had pulled her away from the customer she'd been trying to talk into a lap dance with Cocoa. Luckily, Cocoa noticed Dawg dragging her away and slipped in next to the customer to get the sale.

Emma should be relieved at Dawg's news, but it made her stomach twist more than anything. This was only the beginning of what she expected to be a long, difficult fight. One she was not looking forward to at all.

Her husband's family had money. If they wanted to, they could drag out not only the divorce, but the custody agreement and certainly fight the restraining order.

"And what's going on with Diesel and his men locating her?"

Dawg hadn't said anything lately, and she didn't want to keep bugging, but he had told her several times already that Diesel's men were experts at finding people who didn't want to be found. So if anyone could find her husband and daughter, it would be them.

"Think they got a location. On their way to check it out."

Her heart raced with the anticipation of possibly getting her daughter back soon. "Is she okay?"

"Yeah, baby girl, she's okay. Have a feelin' she'll be home soon. 'Cause of that, need to have a talk."

Her stomach flipped. "What kind of talk?"

"'Bout us. What's gonna happen when Lily gets home. 'Cause she *is* comin' home, baby girl. No doubt."

He grabbed her hand and dragged her toward the back of the club. She followed as fast as her heels would allow. "Slow down! Where are we going?"

"Upstairs. Need quiet an' privacy."

This sounded serious. She wasn't sure if she liked the sound of this whole thing. "Is this a serious talk?"

He glanced over his shoulder at her. "Baby girl, stop askin' questions an' walk faster, will you?"

"But the club…"

"Moose got it handled."

"But—"

"No lip, woman."

Her mouth dropped open, then she snapped it shut. "Well, you're being awfully bossy."

"Yeah," he grunted.

Yeah.

If he was going to be bossy, then she was going to ask a million questions, which drove him nuts. "We couldn't talk in your office?"

"Fuckin' Em, the questions!"

Emma giggled. "You don't like all of my questions?"

"Fuckin' killin' me here."

Fighting back her smirk, she asked, "How am I *killin'* you?"

With a growl, Dawg picked her up and tossed her over his shoulder, making her squeal with laughter. He plowed through the back door of the club and up the stairs to his apartment, his shoulder knocking the air out her lungs with each determined step he took.

"Am I heavy?" she asked as soon as she got her breath back.

"Gonna give you a damn spankin'."

"And what reason do you have to spank me?"

With another growl he strode through the apartment and back to the bedroom to throw her on the bed, where she landed with a bounce, her hair falling over her face. She swept it away just in time to see him stripping off his cut and shirt, exposing his broad tattooed chest.

And that really got her in the gut. The man was beautiful. She'd seen him naked more times than she could count by now and he still made her heart flutter and her insides get warm when he took his clothes off.

Who would have thought some heavily tattooed biker who wore clunky silver jewelry and sported a beard would turn her on so much?

Not her.

But the man before her drove her crazy in a good way.

"Aren't we going to talk?"

"Got lots to talk 'bout. First gonna fuck."

His low, gravelly voice announcing they were "gonna fuck" made her pussy clench. "Why?"

He paused in unbuttoning his jeans. "Why?"

"Yes, why?"

"Emma," he growled.

"What?" she asked, then rolled her lips under to hide her amusement.

"Holy fuck. Never heard anyone ask so many fuckin' questions as you."

"Really?"

He snorted. Then he undid his boots, yanked them and his socks off, tossing them across the room. As soon as he shoved his jeans down, along with his boxers, he dove onto the bed, tackling her.

Emma lost her breath as his weight hit her, and she squealed as he shoved his bearded face into her neck and rubbed the wiry whiskers against her skin.

She giggled, digging her fingers into his hair and yanked his head back. "You're bad. We should be working."

"Don't think the manager's gonna care." He pushed one of the straps of her dress off her shoulder and down her arm, so he could latch his lips onto her hard, aching nipple. Rolling her head back, she gasped when the pull of his mouth drew a line of lightning straight from her breast directly to her pussy.

Lord, this man was good in bed. He knew exactly what to do to her to make her lose her mind. He was not a selfish lover at all. As his mouth tugged on one nipple, his fingers dug under her dress to find the other and when they did...

Her back arched, and she cried out.

"Like that?" he murmured against her damp skin.

"Oh, yes," she whimpered. "Love it."

He moved up and pressed his mouth to her ear, his warm

breath and his words made a shiver skitter down her spine. "More than you love me?"

"It's a close second, baby."

He took her mouth then, dragging his tongue over her lips, then dipping it inside, the tips of their tongues touching. She couldn't help but groan. He got her so wet, so ready, so quickly.

"Baby," she managed to get out.

"Yeah?"

"Is there a reason why you're doing this before we talk?"

"Yeah."

She waited for his explanation as he kissed down her neck and then scraped his teeth over her collar bone before working his way down and latching onto her nipple again, which made her forget what she just asked.

He tugged the dress farther down her body, kissing her skin as he went. Over her belly, her hips, his breath hot and damp, making her break out in goosebumps. Cupping her breasts, she thumbed her own nipples as Dawg finished sliding the dress down her legs and over her feet. He tossed it aside, then sat back on his heels, watching her touch herself, his green eyes dark, his nostrils flaring.

"Baby girl," he murmured, his eyelids heavy, his cock long and hard jutting away from his body. "Can't get enough of you."

"Same here."

"Want the beard?"

"Yes," she moaned, spreading her legs to give him access. Hell yes, she wanted the beard.

With a grin, he got into position and his mouth on her wasn't gentle, it was rough. The way she liked it. He sucked, and bit and flicked her clit, shoving two fingers inside her, curling them, driving her hips off the bed as he found the spot he liked to tease.

"Yes, baby, that's it," she encouraged him, her mind spinning out of control, her heart beating furiously.

"Taste so good, baby girl," he murmured against her mound, then ground his face harder against her. "Gonna taste like you the rest of the night."

What? "No!"

"Yep. Ain't gonna wash my face an' gonna go back downstairs knowin' that none of those fuckers will ever get to taste you. All mine, baby girl."

"Dawson, that's gross."

"No, it ain't. Wanna savor you the rest of the night."

Emma groaned and threw her head back onto the pillow. There was no way she was letting him go back downstairs like that. She'd be embarrassed the rest of the night, whether anyone else realized what was lurking in his beard or not. She'd know.

He moved back up her body and went nose to nose with her. "Wanna see how good you taste?"

"Not really, I—"

He kissed her anyway, letting her experience her own flavor. After she completely melted into the bed, he lifted his head. "So hot."

"What?" she asked then bit her bottom lip, playing innocent.

"You tastin' yourself."

"Hmm, we might have to try that with you."

He frowned. "Ain't gonna happen."

She forced herself to keep her expression serious. "Why? It's okay for me but not for you?"

"Right," he grunted.

She laughed. "Men!"

He shrugged. "Now time to get down to business."

"You mean our talk?" she teased.

"Got somethin' better to do first," he said as he settled between her parted thighs and pressed the head of his cock between her slick folds.

Yes, they did.

"Want me?" he asked, his eyelids heavy, his green eyes dark. The intensity in his look made a warmth spread through her.

He was pressing just enough to make her want more but not enough to satisfy her. He was being a total tease. "Yes. Do you want me?"

"Fuck yeah." He grunted as he thrusted forward, filling her, making her feel complete. "Nobody but you."

The man knew how to move his hips in a way that caused her neck to arch, her mouth to part with short bursts of breath and whimpers, to encourage her to wrap her legs around his hips and dig her heels into the backs of his thighs.

The man who looked so rough on the outside had such surprising finesse in bed.

They *fit*.

They weren't anything alike, but they fit together perfectly.

He grunted again as she raked her nails over his shoulders and down his back. Digging her fingers into the flesh of his ass, she encouraged him to move faster, harder. But he didn't.

He kept his pace slow and steady until she was squirming beneath him, crying out, cursing him, begging him to give it to her the way she loved it. No, the way she loved it with Dawg. No, with *Dawson*.

He dropped his head and snagged a nipple into his mouth, tugging on it, scraping it with his teeth.

Yes. That's how she liked it from him.

But it wasn't just the sex with him that did it for her.

He made her feel something she hadn't felt in a long time. Her heart had been ripped out of her chest when Lily had been taken. And now, it was almost full again. By not only the knowledge that her daughter would soon be home but also by this man.

She pushed all of that out of her head, so she could enjoy these moments with him. The mindless pleasure and the connection they shared.

"Em," he murmured, then licked her all the way from her nipple up to her neck, trailing his warm, wet tongue up her throat.

"Hmm?"

"Thinkin' too much," he grumbled against her now damp skin.

"Think so?"

"Know so."

"Then make it so I can't think of anything but you and what

you're doing." With that she slapped his ass so hard that he jerked in surprise.

He growled and increased his pace, pounding her until she could think of nothing but him and how her body reacted to him. He gently nipped the delicate skin behind her ear, then traced his tongue around the outer edge. "Love fuckin' you."

The feeling was mutual.

Every forceful thrust of his hips jolted her, but she wasn't going to tell him to let up. No...

"Give me all of you, Dawson."

"Givin' it."

"Not enough. I need more," she encouraged. "Give me everything."

He lifted his head, his expression serious. "Em, givin' you everythin' I have. It's all yours."

She dug her hands into his hair and yanked his head down, grabbing his lower lip with her teeth and tugging hard enough for him to feel it.

With a groan, he shuddered, his pace stuttering. He took her mouth forcefully, smothering her moan as he increased his rhythm once again.

He worked his hand down between them, finding her clit and pinching her hard, swallowing her cry. That was all it took...

Her core squeezed him tight and everything exploded around her, dragging him with her on that journey. He released her mouth and grunted loudly as he thrust hard once more, grinding his hips tightly against her. His cock twitched as he buried his face into her neck and came deep inside her. For a split moment, she imagined what it would be like not to be on birth control, to become pregnant, to carry this man's baby, to bear his children. To let him experience everything he missed by being shut out of his daughter's life.

He'd missed out on so much.

She lightly drew her fingers up his back, over his damp skin and the "colors" he wore on his skin. The tattoos that represented his unusual family, the people he belonged to, his brotherhood. Visible proof that he was an extremely loyal man.

When she finally caught her breath, she asked, "I know the tattoos on your back are there for a reason, but what about the rest? Do they all have meaning?" She stroked his hair, his weight on her a satisfying feeling.

He shifted slightly, relieving some of his bulk from her, but his cock remained inside her, still hard. He probably felt the same as her, not ready to break that intimate connection.

"A lot of 'em do, yeah," he murmured into her neck.

"I'm not sure I'd ever get a tattoo..." she admitted. "Did they hurt?"

"Some did. Depends where they're at," he said.

"I honestly don't understand it."

"Gettin' ink?"

"Yes," she answered.

"Don't like 'em?"

She considered that question for a moment. "You know, if someone would've asked me that before meeting you, I would've said no, I don't like them. But now that I've seen you naked, I can't say I hate them. It's you. It makes you who you are and I actually can't imagine you without them."

"Em..." he murmured.

Every time he simply said her name in that deep, grumbly voice of his, it set the butterflies afloat in her stomach. She'd never tire of him saying it. "Yeah?"

With a sigh, he slipped out of her, slid to her side and gathered her in his arms. "If you would've met me in another way other than what you did, would you've given me the time of day?"

Emma's breath hitched. She knew the answer, and he knew the answer, so she wasn't sure why he was asking it.

"Truth," he prodded.

"You know the answer, Dawson."

"Know this is fucked up an' ain't glad Lily was taken, but if she hadn't been, I'd never would've met you."

"Probably not."

"Sometimes fate's fucked up."

She turned her head to glance at him, but he wasn't looking at her. Instead, he was staring across the room, a thoughtful, faraway look on his face. She brushed her fingers down his cheek and over his beard, drawing his attention. "Yes, it is."

Was fate why they met? Were they destined to be together? Did she even believe in that kind of stuff?

She couldn't imagine what happened with Lily came about so that she'd meet the man lying next to her.

That didn't make any sense. Because if it was, the fates were twisted.

CHAPTER FOURTEEN

Dawg felt bad for what happened to Lily, but like he said, if it hadn't happened this woman never would have walked into his life, never would've given him a second look.

But it was more than that. Her calling him for an audition set things in motion he never would have expected.

"Gotta thank you, Em."

"For what?"

"If it wasn't' for you showin' up at my club, forcin' your way into my life 'cause you were so damned determined to get your girl back, I mighta never thought 'bout my own daughter. Mighta let it go. Fuckin' missed out on knowin' my own flesh an' blood."

"Dawson," she whispered. "We still don't know what's going to happen with that. Even if you prove she's your daughter, you might have a bigger fight on your hands than me. I don't want you to get your hopes up to only have them dashed because her mother can afford to fight long and hard over keeping you away from Caitlin."

"Can't keep her out of my life forever." He waited fourteen years, he could wait four more if he had to.

"Right. Once she's an adult, she can choose for herself, but still..."

"Em..."

"Yeah, baby?"

Her simply calling him "baby" made him happy. Something as simple as that. "That's why I need to talk to you. 'Bout us. 'Bout what's gonna happen from here on out. Need to make some decisions."

"What decisions?"

"Important ones." He rolled until he was over her once more, and he tried to keep the worry off his face. "Need to know how we stand."

"Dawson, I'm not even divorced, and Lily isn't even home yet."

"Will be soon," he said, his eyes sliding to the side as he thought about how she would never need that divorce. Then they pinned back on her. "It's because of Lily an' Caitlin we gotta have this talk now. Not later. Gotta know if you're in this all the way."

"You want us to continue," she murmured.

"Yeah. I do. Do you?"

Emma sucked in a deep breath and he knew why she hesitated. If it was just her, she'd probably have no problem with being with him. But it wasn't just her. Her decision would affect more than just the woman beneath him.

"Said you love me. Figured you weren't lyin'." For fuck's sake, he hoped she hadn't lied. Or even been mistaken. His chest got tight at that thought.

"No, I wasn't lying. I wouldn't lie about something like that."

"You weren't confused 'bout it, either, right?"

"No. You're an easy person to love," she admitted.

No, she was wrong. So fucking wrong.

"Think you got that backward, baby girl. Gonna lay my balls out on the table an' say, never been in love with anyone before. Never. So, I'd like you to stick, Em. Wanna make this work, make a family. You, me, Lily, an', hopefully, Caitlin, too." She opened her mouth to speak, but he raised a hand to let him finish. "Before you tell me that you can't raise your little girl above this club, I got it.

Believe me. Definitely decided to let the club go. Talked to Z an'
Hawk. Made some decisions to move forward with that."

Her blue eyes widened. "What?"

"Yeah, gonna move on to another DAMC business an' also find
a decent place to live."

"Dawson, I told you before, you can't give up everything
for us!"

He could, and he would if he needed to, but... "And like I told
you, ain't just for you, Em. Doin' it for Caitlin, too. Keeks
confirmed that my chances will be better to get visitation if I ain't
livin' above this club an' not managin' it, too."

"Are you *sure* you want to do that?"

"Yeah. Even if you decide not to stick, gonna do it no matter
what. You made me see how important my daughter should be to
me. An' if you do stick, you three girls will be my number one
priority. Got me?"

"Dawson." The way she let his name escape on a breath caused
his stomach to flip and not in a good way.

He shook his head. "No. Gonna do it no matter what, baby
girl." He braced himself because what he was about to say was the
hardest shit he'd said in a long time. "So don't feel like you're obligated to stick." *Fuck!* "You need to go, you go." *But don't fuckin' go.*
"Do what's best for you an' Lily, got me? I'll be okay either way."
*Probably would flay me open an' rip my fuckin' guts out, but, yeah, I'll be
okay. Eventually.*

She raised her eyebrows. "So you'd be perfectly fine with me
leaving?"

"Truth?"

"Of course," she insisted.

"Fuck no!" he shouted.

Emma laughed. "Didn't think so, but it sure sounded good and
it was almost convincing."

"Fuck, Em, don't want you to leave. Fuck no. Wanna marry
you, make you my ol' lady."

Her head jerked on the pillow at his words. "Dawson... like I said, I'm not even divorced yet."

"And like I said, you'll be free soon." *Sooner than you think.* "Just wanna hear you say yes. That you wanna be with me an' the rest will fall into place."

"Are you sure you want to help raise a seven-year-old?"

"Wouldn't offer if I didn't want that."

She covered her face with her hands. "Everything's happening so fast."

He grabbed her wrists and pulled her hands away. "Know it, baby girl. If it's too fast, we'll get you an' Lily settled somewhere that ain't here, an' I'll move into one of the rooms at church 'til you're ready."

Emma stared up into his face and he could see the mix of emotions rolling through her. "Dawson, I need to find a teaching job, and I might not be able to find one in this area. And now that I gave up my apartment... It... it opens up opportunities for me to move where there's work. It might not be feasible to stay in Shadow Valley. Or, hell, even in the Pittsburgh area. I can't not work. I can't put you in that position that you'd have to support me and even Lily. That's not fair to you."

"Baby girl..."

"No, I've never not worked, Dawson. Lily's seven. She'll be in school. She doesn't need me to stay home. I..."

"Lily might not be your only kid..."

Her mouth gaped open. "This is too much. I can't... You're talking marriage and moving in together and helping raise my daughter... Having a baby with you! It's too much to wrap my head around. I'm sorry. I need time... We've known each other for only a little more than three weeks now. Why—"

"Why," he repeated. He grabbed her hand and pressed it to his chest over his heart. "Why? 'Cause I know here, it's the right thing to do, Em. This is right. There was a reason you walked into my life. For both of us."

"You're sacrificing so much..."

"Ain't a sacrifice. Wouldn't do shit if I didn't wanna."

"These are huge decisions for both of us..."

"An' that's tellin' you how fuckin' serious I am."

"The cursing, Dawson..."

What? "Fuck," his eyes widened. "Oh shit, sorry. Gotta learn to quit cursin' in front of the girls, right?"

Emma chuckled as she grinned and shook her head. "Yes, that would be a good idea. Can you do it?"

Fuck. Could he? "Don't know. Hard habit to break. Will do my best though."

"You can say fudge instead of fuck."

The fuck if he was going to say fudge instead of fuck. Especially around the brothers. He'd just try not to let it slip. Too often, anyhow.

"So, what're you sayin'?"

"I..."

He was pushing her, and he needed to stop. Otherwise, she might give him an outright no. And that couldn't happen. He needed to give her space and time. Lily would need to adjust back to being with her mother before some stranger was living with her. Especially one like him.

He needed a better plan, one she could agree with more easily.

"Listen, gonna give it time. I'll take a room at church. We'll set you up somewhere for six months. I'll get to know Lily slowly. We'll get all the legal shit squared away. Then, when six months are up, you're with me. We'll get a place big enough for all of us. When a teachin' job comes up, it comes up. No worries. Got me?"

He grimaced at allowing the last part to slip out. He was being bossy and now was not the time for that. Now was a time for asking, not telling, even though that went against his grain.

All the breath left him when she answered softly, "Got you."

He stared at her. Did she just say...

Did she just agree?

Was she sticking?

Holy fuck.

Holy fuck.

HOLY FUCK!

He dropped his head and kissed her, taking her mouth hard. With relief, she gave the kiss the same fervor he did. His heart was racing, his mind spinning at everything those two words meant. Everything that those two words would change in his life.

For the better.

They could do this, he and Em. The two of them. There was nothing he wanted more. Well, except...

"Wanna fudge you, baby girl. Once more before we go back downstairs."

He smiled at her peal of laughter. Laughter that quickly dissipated into groans, moans and whispered confessions of how much they needed and wanted each other.

———

As Dawg carried a box up the steps to Emma's temporary place, an extended stay hotel that she said was bigger than her former apartment, his phone vibrated in his back pocket.

He walked through the open door as Rooster was heading back to the truck to get another box. They had left most of her stuff in storage since this place was not only furnished, but, he reminded himself again, was only temporary. Six months. That's all he had to wait.

Six months felt like an eternity but he needed to find the patience to deal with it. Until Lily was home, Emma would spend her nights with him, but once Lily was back on American soil, Emma would be staying in her own place, in her own bed, and he'd be in his. And that fucking sucked.

And he would lose his hostess. Moose was being patched in within the week and the prospect was already on notice that he'd be taking over the reins of Heaven's Angels. He had also been warned he better not fuck it up.

Not just by Dawg, but by every one of the brothers sitting on the Executive Committee. Z was also planning a little visit to Shadow Valley Gun Shop to let Pierce know he would soon have an assistant manager in the DAMC owned business.

Dawg would have a hard time swallowing the idea of reporting to Pierce and if the former DAMC president had any sense, he'd just teach Dawg the basic ins and outs of the business and then let Dawg do his thing. But the way Pierce was, Dawg doubted that's how it would roll.

Again, Dawg would need patience. Resettling his life was going to take time.

He went into the bedroom to set the box on the bed and watched Emma unpacking some of her clothes and organizing them into a dresser.

"Should help you unpack your clothes, baby girl, an' make a pile to burn."

She glanced up from what she was doing. "Why?"

"That shit you wore that first day... That shit's gotta go in a burn barrel."

Her eyes crinkled at the corners. "You didn't like it?"

"Fuck no."

"Fudge," she corrected him.

"Fuckin' fudge no."

She bit her bottom lip, shook her head and continued to pull clothes out of the box.

Fuck! Her and that tasty bottom lip. "Too bad the prospects are comin' in an' outta here, I'd fudge you on the bed, so we can christen it."

"Mmm. I like fudge," she said playfully.

"Me, too. Never had a sweet tooth before."

Her laughter filled the small room, which made him want to throw her on the bed anyway, prospects or not, and take her right then and there. The room had a door and a lock...

To hell with the bed, taking her against the wall would work, too. Or on the kitchen counter, or over the back of the couch. Any of those spots would work just fine.

His ass vibrated again. Between that and hearing Jester cursing out in the living room, he sighed. He wasn't going to get pussy any time soon.

He pulled the phone from his back pocket and hit the power button. Two texts from Diesel. Short and to the point in typical D style.

Church. Now.

Bring your woman.

Fuck.

There were only two things that Dawg could think why they were being summoned. Either Z talked to Pierce and there were issues, or it had to do with Lily.

Since D wanted Em there, he figured it was the second reason.

"Em."

She lifted her head. "Yeah?"

"Gotta go to church."

"Okay, I'll finish up here—"

"No," he said with a shake of his head. "You, too."

Her eyes widened. "Why? What's going on?"

"Dunno. Gonna go find out. Gonna leave the prospects here to finish an' then have 'em drop your key off at the club. Yeah?"

"But—"

"Ain't no buts. D wants us there, gotta be there. Got me?"

She sighed. "Yeah, baby, I got you." Then suddenly her spine straightened. "Maybe it's about Lily!"

The excitement in her voice made him hope that it was and that it was only good news.

She grabbed his cut and tugged. "Oh my God, we have to go. Like now!"

Damn. "Got it, baby girl. We're goin'. Grab your brain bucket. Takin' my sled."

She rushed out of the bedroom to wherever she had put the

helmet he bought her. He figured since she was sticking around she needed one of her very own. He'd get Lily one eventually, as well.

"Come on, Daw... Dawg! Let's go!" he heard her yell from the other room. He snorted, shook his head and followed her out.

CHAPTER FIFTEEN

As Dawg escorted Emma into church with a hand to the small of her back, his eyes immediately landed on the large man standing next to the club's private bar with his ol' lady.

And it wasn't just Jewel that accompanied him. It was Ivy and, even more surprising, Diamond.

What the fuck was going on?

As they approached the bar with the huge DAMC logo hand carved out of wood above it, Jewel greeted, "Hey, Emma!"

"Hi," Emma answered back with a smile. She hadn't wiped that smile off her face since she got the idea in her head that this meet was about Lily.

Dawg's gaze slid to Diesel and, of course, D's expression didn't give him shit. His face might as well had been chiseled in stone.

Jewel came around the bar to give Emma a quick hug, then turned toward Diamond. "This is my sister, Diamond. She's also Slade's ol' lady. You haven't met them yet. They've been busy setting up a new business for the DAMC." She gave her sister a wicked smile. "And other stuff..."

Diamond approached with a laugh and enveloped Emma in her arms, giving her a hug, too. "Welcome to the sisterhood."

Dawg was pleased as hell that the DAMC women were so welcoming and being friendly and open. Emma would eventually fit in perfectly with them. And it would be nice to have the women help her out with Lily when needed, like being available as babysitters for when he and Em would need some private time.

There wasn't one DAMC woman he wouldn't trust. And he was sure that wasn't the norm in most MC's since women could be catty bitches. He'd seen it first-hand just how brutal they could be at Heaven's Angels. He'd broken up cat fights before over stupid shit. Like a fucking tube of lipstick. Any dancer that continued to cause problems found her ass outside looking in.

"Glad you've decided to stick around," Ivy said, giving Emma a wide smile. "We can't wait to meet Lily."

Jewel and Diamond murmured their agreement.

Dawg let his gaze roll over the redhead wondering why Jag hadn't knocked her up yet. "Know you fucked up the betting pool," he told Ivy.

She smirked. "Wasn't me." She waved a hand toward Jewel. "Jewelee fucked it all up."

"It wasn't me!" Jewel exclaimed. She jerked a thumb toward D. "I can't help that he's a beast in bed."

"What the fuck," D muttered. "Was on birth control!"

"Yeah, but all the sex you demand gave me a UTI, and I had to go on antibiotics which screwed up—"

Diesel slammed his hand on the bar, making the women jump. "Ain't here to talk 'bout your insides."

Ivy dropped her head and turned her face away, but it was hard to miss her body shaking with laughter.

Diamond smiled, announcing loudly, "Your Ass-holiness has spoken!"

"Diamond, shut the fuck up," D grumbled with a frown.

She saluted him and rolled her lips under, her blue eyes twinkling.

"Well, D, you called us all here for a reason, so get to it," Ivy said.

"You mean, you don't know, either?" Dawg asked her, surprised.

Before Ivy could answer, D spoke up. "Wanted 'em here for your woman."

Dawg's stomach sank, and he glanced at Emma who had suddenly paled. He moved next to her and threw an arm around her shoulders, pulling her into his side. She automatically put an arm around his waist and tucked her hand inside his cut, planting it on his gut. When she lifted worried eyes up to him, he gave her a reassuring squeeze.

"Well, baby, now you got them both worried. Will you spill what's going on and stop leaving us hanging?" Jewel asked her man, the impatience thick in her voice.

So, Jewel didn't know either. *Fuck.*

"Maybe she should sit down on one of the couches," D suggested but his words were quickly drowned by all three of the DAMC women screaming, "No!"

"No one's sitting on those couches," Diamond said, shuddering.

"They need to be burned," Ivy agreed.

"Whatever," D muttered. "Got bad news." At Emma's gasp, D lifted his hand. "Lily's all right. But there was a bad car accident." D's dark eyes met his. Dawg knew what was coming next... "Husband didn't make it. My guys are in the country an' was 'bout to make contact when they heard. Not thinkin' the girlfriend's goin' to fight my men takin' custody of her an' escortin' her back to the States, but need your permission anyhow, just in case."

D's gaze dropped from Dawg to Emma as he waited for her answer.

The whole time D was talking, Emma had become stiff. Now, she still stood frozen in place, clinging to him. He adjusted his hold on her to make sure she didn't drop to the floor.

The women's worried eyes were also glued to his woman. Then it hit Dawg why they were there... In case she needed support while dealing with the news. D must have thought the women could help.

It was hard to imagine that the man would care enough to think that through. But sometimes he surprised them all.

Dawg also realized D had purposely blown quickly through the explanation and wondered when it would hit Emma that her estranged husband was dead.

Though, it didn't take long for D's words to sink in...

"Oh my God, he's *dead?*" Emma whispered in a shaky voice.

The DAMC women watched her carefully, as if ready to step in if they were needed. Dawg never loved them more than at that moment.

Emma's shiny blue eyes landed on Diesel. "You said he's *dead?*"

"Yeah," D grunted. "Lily ain't hurt. Wasn't in the car. Was with the girlfriend."

"I..."

"You okay, baby girl?" Dawg pressed a kiss to the top of her head and gave her a reassuring squeeze. "Painful shit, I know, but you gotta give D's crew permission to take Lily from the girlfriend an' bring 'er home. Got me?"

Dawg couldn't imagine the girlfriend would resist. There would be no reason for the woman to want to keep Lily, especially now that the girl's father was dead.

Em looked up at him, tears brimming in her eyes but not falling. Not yet. Her brain was still processing the information. "I... I want to go. I have a passport. I can fly to wherever they are and get her."

"No," Diesel said firmly with a shake of his head.

"But—"

"My crew's there. Gonna get her home ASAP, got me? No reason to delay 'er return so you fly all those fuckin' hours to be there. She'll be safe with 'em."

She glanced up at Dawg again, worry in her red-rimmed eyes.

"Yeah, baby girl, she'll be safe. Promise." He had enough confidence in D's men to make her that guarantee.

She pressed shaky fingers to her lips. "Oh my God, she must be upset."

D's eyes flicked to Dawg's, but he spoke to Emma. "Don't know 'bout the crash. Just that she's comin' home to you. Gonna leave that discussion to her mother. Got me?"

After a long pause, Emma whispered, "Yes."

She pulled away from Dawg and walked across the room with one hand on her hip and the other pressed to her forehead, leaving a cushion of space between her and the rest of them.

Ivy gave Dawg a questioning look, and he answered her with a slight shake of his head. Emma might need the space to help her process. If she broke down, he'd let them go over and comfort her.

Emma turned on her heel and headed back in Dawg's direction, the tears finally spilling over. "Oh Lord, I *hated* him for doing what he did... but I didn't wish him dead!"

"Shit happens," Diesel grumbled. "Ain't your fault that the asshole don't know how to drive in a foreign country."

"But—"

"Ain't your fault," D repeated, cutting Emma off. "Get over it."

Jewel let out a hiss. "Baby..."

D's dark eyes landed on his ol' lady, his face an angry mask. "Bastard stole her kid. Cheated on 'er. Took the kid to another country with no plans on ever bringin' her back. Fucker don't deserve a drop of fuckin' sympathy." He turned his attention to Emma and raised an eyebrow. "Don't deserve one fuckin' tear either. Didn't give a shit 'bout your feelin's. Didn't give a shit 'bout your daughter's, either. Don't you fuckin' give a shit 'bout 'im. Give 'im the same damn respect he gave you, got me?"

Emma's gaping mouth snapped shut and she wiped a hand across her eyes, sweeping away any stray tears. Dawg could see her visibly brace herself, pull her emotions together, and give the club enforcer a sharp nod in answer.

Dawg agreed with everything D said, but Diesel could be a little cold on the delivery, even though it was truth that Emma needed to hear.

Emma shouldn't shed one more fucking tear over her husband since he probably never shed one over her loss. And he probably didn't care that she had shed bucket loads once her daughter was taken.

"What about the death certificate?" Dawg asked carefully, knowing once Emma had that, things were going to get a lot easier for her and Lily.

"Walker said the Embassy was notified, so that'll be taken care of. Will make sure Kiki gets copies for the legal shit."

"When will she be here?" Emma asked, moving back to Dawg and gripping onto his cut so tightly Dawg noticed her knuckles becoming white. He wrapped his fingers around the back of her neck and gave it a squeeze.

"Friday."

Emma's eyes widened. "What time? Where?"

"Will let you know when. Will have 'em bring 'er straight to the warehouse."

"I'd rather be at the airport waiting!"

"No," D grunted.

"But it's my daughter!"

"An' it's my mission," D barked. "Gonna do it my way, got me?"

Emma sucked in a breath, probably to give D hell, but Dawg squeezed her neck again, so she nodded instead. "Yes, okay. Sorry. I..."

"Nothin' to be sorry 'bout, Em," Dawg assured her in a low, comforting voice. "Know you're anxious. D knows you are, too. Right, D?"

Diesel grunted.

"He definitely knows," Jewel spoke up. "He probably felt the same way when the fucking Warriors snatched me."

"You have no clue," Diamond muttered.

"He was a mental case," Ivy agreed.

D slammed his hand on the bar again. He opened his mouth to probably bellow and deny everything the women just said, but he snapped his mouth shut, shook his head and headed toward the door with a pissed-off look on his face.

As he passed Dawg, he grumbled, "Will let you know."

Dawg nodded. "Thanks."

D grunted again and quickly ate up the real estate to the exit.

"Emma," Jewel began as she came around the bar, heading in the direction of her ol' man. "We're all here if you need *anything*. It could be the smallest, most stupid thing ever, but if you need it, need us, we'll help. I promise you that. We're all here for you and Lily. We all do for each other. And you're one of us now."

"What Jewelee's saying is one hundred percent true, Emma. Don't hesitate to ask any one of us for anything. And not just the three of us. Kiki, Sophie, Jayde, Bella and even Kelsea. Any of us. We love Dawg, he's family. And even though this MC is made up of men, they might not say it out loud, but us women are just as important. We're the glue," Diamond said.

"What the fuck," Diesel muttered from across the room.

"He knows it's true," Jewel added with a smile. "He'll just never admit it."

"Whatever, woman. Let's go!" D bellowed.

Jewel snorted. "He's really a loveable teddy bear."

D pushed outside with a grumble and once Jewel followed him out, he slammed the door shut.

Ivy and Diamond looked at each other and burst out laughing.

"Somebody's going to get one of her favorite 'lessons,'" Diamond snickered.

"All right, I've got to get back to the pawn shop," Ivy announced.

"Hold up," Dawg said, lifting a palm. "Gotta know, Ivy, should I be putting a Benjamin down on you as next up?"

Ivy's gaze landed pointedly on Diamond and then on Emma. "I don't know. Should you?" She wiggled her eyebrows.

"Are you two at least tryin'?"

Ivy's face fell flat at his question.

Oh fuck. He just stuck his boot in his fucking mouth.

"I gotta go," she mumbled as she pushed past him and Emma to rush out of the door.

"Stay here," he ordered Emma, then followed Ivy out into the early afternoon heat, making sure the back door was secure behind him. He caught up with her before she got into her Dodge.

"Hey," he grabbed her arm and swung her to face him.

Damn. She was crying.

"Ivy," he murmured. "Sorry. I fucked up. Was just teasin'."

Ivy swiped at her face. "I know."

He opened his arms and Ivy melted against him, shoving her damp face into his chest. "Didn't mean to upset you."

"It's not your fault."

"Wanna talk 'bout it?"

A muffled, "No," came from between the flaps of his cut. She sniffled, then said, "We've been trying. Believe me. Jag didn't buy a four-bedroom house for nothing. Yeah, we wanted an art studio for him to do his drawings, but we didn't need a house that big for only that. I'm not sure why I'm not getting pregnant. Doctor said there's nothing wrong with me or Jag. But I don't want to disappoint him since he wants kids. Hell, I want kids with him."

"Ain't gonna disappoint him. He loves you, baby. So fuckin' much. He wanted you forever. Fought for you. Even if you two never have any babies, he'd love you 'til the day you die. Even after that. He'll haunt your ass."

Ivy did a combination sniffle-snort. "I know, but I want to give him this. He loves Zeke. He's thrilled for D. And I know we're not supposed to know yet, but Hawk and Kiki... It's hard to watch everyone around getting knocked up but not us."

Dawg brushed a tear off her cheek. "You've got time, baby. Just enjoy the process."

Ivy pulled back and looked up at him, red nose and red eyes to match her red hair. "I'm happy for you, Dawg. I'm glad you finally have someone. Emma's great, and, even though she's not from our world, I think she's perfect for you."

Dawg pressed his face into Ivy's hair and nodded. "Love 'er, Ivy. Know it's crazy. Fell fast an' hard. Never loved a woman before. But she smacked me right between the eyes."

She patted his chest then curled her fingers into his T-shirt.

"All you guys go down hard. But you only do it when you find the right one. Going down fast and hard just means Emma's the right one."

"Yeah," he grunted.

"Heard what you're doing. Giving up everything for her."

He grimaced. "Not everything an' not just for her..."

"Yeah, I know. Word's out about your daughter."

"Figured it wouldn't take long."

"Everybody loves you, Dawg. Seriously. Everybody's rooting for you, too. If anyone will make it happen, it's Kiki. She loves this club like she was born into it. She'll fight long and hard for you. For your daughter."

"Know it, Ivy. Diamond was right. You women are the glue to this club. D will deny it, though he knows it's true. I won't. Caitlin's mother may not like me bein' in an MC, but I want Caitlin to be 'round all of you women. Know why? 'Cause you're all strong, capable women who have backbone an' determination. You take shit from us an' then turn 'round an' hand us our fuckin' asses on a plate. You teach us to respect women. We might be hard on you all an' bossy but it's 'cause we care an' wanna protect you. You're ours. All of you. An' you know we'd lay down our fuckin' lives for any of you."

Ivy pulled back in his arms and reached to cup his face. "Emma's a lucky woman."

Dawg smiled. "I'm the lucky one."

Ivy smiled back. "That, too."

"Stop stressin' 'bout babies. They'll come when the time's right."

She sighed, brushing her long hair out of her face. "I hope so."

"Know so." He released her and she moved to her car.

With her hand on the door handle, she said over her shoulder. "Can't wait to meet your daughter." Then she got into her Charger and the car roared to life.

As Dawg watched her drive away, he whispered, "Me, neither."

CHAPTER SIXTEEN

Emma shoved open the passenger door to Dawg's truck, slammed it, and ran to the back door of Diesel's warehouse. She bounced up and down on her toes as she waited for Dawg to put his Chevy in park and shut off the ignition.

"Hurry!" she yelled across the parking lot. Why was the man taking so long? And why was he spending precious moments to turn his cut right side out? She didn't understand the whole wearing the vest inside out while in a vehicle, or "cage" as he called it, right side out when not.

While she was sad that last night was the last time for a long while she'd spend with him in his bed, she was super excited to finally see her daughter. To not only see and talk to her, but hold her, make sure she was really home. That she was real.

If he didn't hurry up she was going in without him and would scream her head off in the immense building until she found Lily.

"Dawson!" she screamed, wringing her hands together, her heart beating a mile a minute.

He lumbered across the parking lot, a smile on his face. "I get you're excited, baby girl. But here you need to call me Dawg."

Right. *Right.* A conversation they've had a million times, she needed to remember to call him Dawg in front of his buddies. Or brothers. Or anyone, really.

"Got it! Dawg, hurry the hell up!"

He chuckled and when he got to her, he reached out and grabbed her shoulder, turning her toward him. "Hang on. Got somethin' to say first."

Now? "What?"

"Happy as hell that you're gettin' your girl back. Anythin' you need, I got you, got me?"

She stopped bouncing and stared up at him. "Got you."

"Love you. Here for you, no matter what, got me?"

She nodded, biting her bottom lip, trying to keep the tears at bay. She sucked in a shaky breath.

He cupped her face and brushed a thumb over her cheek. "No cryin'. Gotta stay strong for Lily. Might be a little confusin' for her. Lots of fuckin' shit went down."

"Cursing, please," she reminded him.

"Right." He shook his head, his eyes crinkling at the corners. "Lots of fudgy stuff went down."

She shot him a smile. "God, I love you, Dawson," she whispered. And that was so true.

"Know it. Will always do my best for you. Promise. Got me?"

This man. "Yes. I got you." In a flash, she grabbed his hair, yanked his head down and planted a kiss on his lips. Before he could deepen it, she pulled away in her excitement. "Now let's get Lily!"

He chuckled and grabbed the door handle, yanking it open and escorting her through.

They moved down a long, dark corridor and made a right at the end into another hallway, heading toward what she assumed was Diesel's office. Dawg kept a hand on her arm, preventing her from sprinting forward.

Not that she had any idea where she was going. She grabbed his arm and yanked hard. "Come on! Walk faster."

He just shook his head and kept his steady pace, but when he stopped in front of an open door, she rushed past him and stopped dead.

Jewel was sitting on the floor, her legs spread open, Lily settled between them leaning back against the woman as Emma's daughter did something on what looked like a tablet. From the noises coming from it, it sounded like a game.

Emma lost her breath at seeing her daughter for the first time in over a year and a half. She had grown, her hair was longer, and it had been dyed a dark brown. Her hair was no longer the light blonde she'd been born with.

Her knees wobbled as she reached out to grab the door jamb for support. She couldn't breathe. She couldn't move. She was frozen in place.

Besides her hair color and her being a bit bigger in size, she looked healthy and fascinated by whatever game Jewel had her distracted with.

Dawg bumped her from behind with his chest, making her let go of the door jamb and step inside the room.

Lily looked up, blinked, and blinked again. Then a look of recognition crossed her face. "Momma!" she yelled, jumping to her feet and running over.

Overwhelmed, Emma didn't know what to do. She wanted to cry, scream with relief and hug her daughter all at once.

So that's what she did. She dropped to her knees and scooped her daughter into her arms and squeezed her tight. Lily's arms wrapped around her neck and she shoved her face into Emma's hair. Emma laughed with joy, while hot tears streamed down her face, and all she could do was murmur Lily's name over and over.

After a few moments, Emma felt a hand on top of her head, and she glanced up through a blur of tears to see Dawg standing over them, a crooked smile on his face, his nostrils flaring. He gave her a quick nod, then moved across the room to where she realized two other men stood. One being Diesel, the other she didn't recognize.

She shoved her face back into Lily's hair and whispered, "I've missed you so much, lady bug. I was so sad not to see your pretty face every day."

"Me, too, Momma!"

"You've grown so much..."

"I know. I'm seven now!" she exclaimed, lifting her hands and showing Emma seven fingers.

"Yes, you are. I'm so sorry I missed your birthday. I hope you got lots of cake and presents!"

Lily nodded, a smile on her face, then her smile turned upside down. "Momma?"

Emma sniffled. "Yeah, lady bug?"

"Daddy said you were gone forever."

Emma closed her eyes and waited for the sharp sting to pass and the bitterness that bubbled up to settle. "Did he? He must have been mistaken."

"You're not going to go away again, right?"

Emma's heart skipped a beat at her daughter's question. "I promise to never leave you." And she hoped to never break that promise, but even with her husband dying in a car crash, she had no idea what his family was capable of.

She was sure they helped finance Todd and his girlfriend leaving the country with Lily. Why they would? She'd never know. And she didn't care, she just knew she'd fight them to the ends of the earth. They were never getting Lily.

Never.

Her daughter was finally home with her and that's where she was staying. With her.

And eventually with Dawson.

She needed to at least introduce them. Then they could take Lily back to their temporary home and get her settled in.

She had a feeling she wouldn't get any sleep tonight. She might just camp out in Lily's room and watch her sleep all night.

She held her hand out to the man who helped make this all happen. "Lily, I have someone important for you to meet."

D awg stared at Emma's outstretched hand. He'd stepped away from the two of them because he was struggling not to break down like a fucking pussy in front of D, Mercy and Jewel.

But watching Emma and Lily had made his chest tight and his eyes sting. He had tightened his jaw and his fists to ward off any runaway emotions, which was working to a point, but he really needed to take a page from both Mercy and D's book. They stood watching the reunion without even a slight change of expression.

Jewel, on the other hand, was bawling her eyes out, still sitting on the floor. Sobbing uncontrollably, like someone had run over her dog. But he didn't blame her, if he could get away with it, he'd be down there joining her.

He steeled himself and moved closer to his woman and his future stepdaughter.

Emma pushed to her feet, holding Lily's hand. She raised her other hand toward Dawg. "This is Dawson."

Dawg grimaced at her use of his real name. His eyes flicked over to D, but like normal, his face was like granite. Not even a smirk. Though, Dawg was sure he'd hear about it later. Not everyone could have a cool name like Diesel from birth. Lucky fucker.

His gaze dropped back down to the little girl pinned to Emma's side. Sky-blue eyes stared back up at him.

"Honey, you look just like your momma." He brushed what was obviously dyed hair off her forehead, leaned over and placed a kiss on it. "Just like your momma," he mumbled again.

If Lily had blonde hair, she'd look exactly like Emma. Which meant when she became a teen, he'd be threatening the hormone crazy teenage boys who were interested in her. She wouldn't be allowed to date until she was at least twenty-one. Twenty-five. Hell, thirty.

"Did the guys treat you good?" he asked her.

Lily nodded shyly.

"Your momma's so happy that you're finally home. She missed you like crazy."

"I love my momma."

So do I.

"We've got a new place that we're going to stay in for a little while. It has a pool. But after that little while, we're going to get a place that has a big backyard. Is that okay?" Emma asked her.

"Can we get a dog?"

Emma's eyes met Dawg's.

He smiled. Lily had no idea she was already getting one. Spelled a little differently but still...

"We'll see about that," Emma answered her daughter.

"Can we go swimming now?" Lily asked, pulling on her mother's hand.

"When we get back, yes. We'll stop and get you a bathing suit and some clothes on the way home. Then after that, later tonight, we need to have a long talk, lady bug. Okay?"

"Yeah, Momma. Is Daddy and Gloria waiting at home?"

Dawg watched as Emma's face twisted, but she quickly hid her thoughts and took a deep breath. "No, lady bug. It's just going to be you and me at our new home."

"Is Daddy going to visit?"

"We'll talk about that later after your swim. Sound good?"

"Yes! Let's go swimming!"

The resilience of kids amazed him.

Emma swiped a hand over her red eyes and glanced over at Dawg, who said, "Take her outside to the truck. Gotta talk to D. Can you find your way back out?"

Emma nodded. "Yes. I think so. Come on, lady bug, Dawson has to talk to the men who helped you."

Dawg grimaced again at Em's use of his real name. He just needed to give up and accept it.

Like saying fudge instead of fuck. Shoot instead of shit.

He sighed.

Fucking shit was going to change. That was for damn sure.

"Say goodbye to the guys, Lily," Em encouraged her.

"Bye!" she yelled, waving at Mercy and D.

"Bye, Lily. You were a real trooper," Mercy answered.

D grunted his goodbye, then looked at Jewel who was still a mess on the floor. "Woman, go with 'em."

"Why? I—"

"Got important shit to talk 'bout." He tilted his head toward the door and cocked an eyebrow.

"Men shit?" she asked with a frown.

"Yeah."

"Fsst," Jewel answered, swiping a hand in his direction, then headed out the door.

"Shut it," D barked.

Jewel slammed the door shut, but not until thrusting her hand back into the room and giving D the middle finger.

Dawg chuckled. Jewel didn't take any shit from anyone, especially her ol' man.

"Fuckin' woman drives me crazy," D grumbled.

What the man wouldn't admit to is how much he loved Jewel. And how she had him wrapped around her little finger. She had tamed the savage beast.

"Don't know how she puts up with your ass," Mercy told him, shaking his head, a smirk pulling up one side of his mouth.

"I give good dick," D muttered, grabbing his crotch and jerking it.

Mercy snorted. He turned his grey eyes to Dawg. "So... Dawson, huh?"

"Keep tellin' 'er not to call me that, but she don't listen," Dawg answered with a shrug.

"Need to teach 'er a lesson, then," D answered, moving around to behind his desk and settling into his chair with a grunt.

"Yeah, all those 'lessons' you teach Jewelee knocked 'er up."

Diesel lifted his heavy shoulders and let them drop. "She's mouthy."

"You wouldn't want 'er any other way," Dawg told him.

"That's the truth," Mercy mumbled.

Diesel scowled.

"Gotta thank you for gettin' Lily home safe," Dawg started. "Thanks for goin' above an' beyond, too."

"Wasn't nothin'," Mercy answered with a shrug. "Easy mission."

"Easy?" Dawg asked with a frown. Did D's men think nothing about killing a man? No regrets?

"Yeah. Got the news from Hunter an' Walker as soon as I landed in Brunei that her husband was takin' care of."

"They didn't wait for you?" Dawg asked Mercy, surprised.

Mercy shook his head. "Didn't have to. Man fuckin' crashed his rental car. Fucker's tire blew out, hit a guide rail, car flipped over that an' down an embankment. No seatbelt, major head trauma. Problem solved. Couldn't have been more convenient."

Right. Pretty fucking convenient. Dawg glanced at D to see if he believed that story.

Of course, D had no expression at all, like normal.

"Wanted to make the fucker suffer like he made that poor woman, but never got the chance. Fuckin' sucks."

Dawg eyeballed the man with the scarred face. He certainly could be a scary fucker and he wondered if the man even had a conscience. Maybe with all that he'd seen during his stint with the Special Forces that had chipped away at his humanity.

"Had a little problem with the girlfriend, Gloria, though. Thought she had the right to keep Lily. We told her differently. Convinced her it was in Lily's best interest, as well as hers, to let the girl go home to her mother. She might be a little loco, but finally got through to her and decided to hand over Lily without a fight."

"Lily see anything that Emma needs to be worried 'bout?" Dawg asked carefully.

"Nope. She was outside playin' when we had our little discussion with Gloria. Lily didn't hear or see shit. Gloria then went out, got her, introduced us as friends of her father, then off we went. No shit, all shine."

"Good," Dawg said, relieved. Lily had been through enough with the kidnapping, she didn't need to witness any "coercive" discussions.

Mercy nodded his head, pushed off the wall he was leaning against and said, "Done here. Gettin' outta here, boss."

"Right," D grunted. "Bonus in it for you guys. Got me?"

Mercy flipped a hand over his shoulder in acknowledgement and when he passed Dawg, he whacked him on the back. "The bonus was seein' Emma an' her daughter reunited. Worth more than money."

"Got your six, dude. Anytime," Dawg said. "Walker an' Hunter, too."

"Will tell 'em. Never know when we might need extra hands. 'Specially when it comes to those squirrelly Warriors."

"Still workin' on that?" Dawg asked, surprised. "Figured something was goin' on behind the scenes since we haven't heard a peep from those fuckers since they grabbed Slade."

"The roaches are still scurryin' but been doin' some pest control," Mercy began.

Mercy started to say something else, but D made a noise from behind his desk and have his man a pointed look. "Get gone, Mercy."

Ah, Diesel was keeping whatever was going on with the Warriors under wraps. Dawg could understand that.

Mercy's gaze landed on D then he gave his boss a nod. "Got you." He headed out of the office.

Once the door closed behind the man, Dawg turned to D.

"Got your woman, got her daughter back. Now what?"

"Gettin' Keeks to get my daughter back."

D nodded. "Hear ya on that. Moose ready to take over Heaven's Angels?"

"Workin' on it. Just a little more shit I gotta go over with 'im an' he'll be good."

"Pierce didn't resist the idea of you helpin' 'im out at the gun shop. The reasons didn't make 'im suspicious."

Dawg nodded. "Good. Gonna look for a house to rent and move my shit out of the apartment above the club. In the meantime, I'll crash at church." He considered the big man behind the desk. "You're gonna need a house, too. Can't be livin' over the pawn shop when your kid comes. It's not big enough for a family."

"Big enough. Just havin' the one kid."

Dawg grinned. "Sure 'bout that?"

"Yep."

"Sure you don't want a place with a fenced yard an' shit?"

D made a disgusted face. "Fuck no."

Dawg bit back his laugh. "Okay." He gave D a chin lift. "Gonna take Lily an' Em home. Sure she's anxious to get Lily settled."

"Then fuckin' get gone."

Dawg smirked. "Thanks, brother. For everything."

D grunted. "Get gone. Go take care of your woman."

"Plan on it."

That was for damn sure.

EPILOGUE

Dawg sat at the table watching Emma move around the kitchen making breakfast.

Lily sat in his lap with the excuse that she was helping him with his homework.

Yeah, his fucking fudgy homework.

Emma thought it would be a good idea for him to get his GED. There was no reason for him to get it, other than it *sort of* being a good influence on the girls. Education was important his wife said.

Dawg didn't need an education. He had life experience, and he was helping Pierce take the gun shop and range to the next level. Dawg's goal was for it to bring more money into the club coffers than ever before. Pierce was a lazy fucker, and the books showed that.

Since Dawg took over as assistant manager, the cash flow looked so much fucking better. *Assistant manager.*

What-fucking-ever.

Hopefully, a change was coming. Sooner than later.

Though he loved the challenge of turning the gun shop around, he hated Pierce more each day. He had to step in several times when the man got handsy with female customers. He was a lawsuit waiting to happen.

Jag wanted to be the one to carve the colors off Pierce's back, but Dawg would help him. No fucking doubt. Though, for some reason Diesel was in no rush to oust the older member. He seemed to be the most resistant on stripping the man's colors.

He wouldn't say why, but there was something D knew that the rest of them didn't. So he'd have to trust D for now.

But Dawg's patience with Pierce was running thin.

Really thin.

"Are you going to answer that?" Lily asked him, tugging on his beard. He dropped his gaze to the blonde haired, blue-eyed miniature of Emma.

His heart swelled for a moment, then it hit him what girl said. "What?"

"Your phone! Looks like Aunt Kiki is calling!" she exclaimed.

Dawg's gaze landed on his cell which vibrated again. She was right. Kiki's name was coming up on the caller ID.

He snagged it and swiped to answer, lifting it to his ear. "Hey, Keeks, what's up?" Out of the corner of his eye, he noticed Emma freeze where she stood and turn to face him.

"Got good news."

"Hawk Jr. coming?" he teased. Kiki seemed ready to pop any day now.

"No! And I wouldn't be calling *you* if I was in labor!"

"Ow. That wounded me."

"You'll get over it. It's better than that."

"Better than hatchin' Tweetie Bird?" he asked with a smirk.

"Fuck," she muttered, though he could hear her muffling her laughter on purpose. "Good Lord, I pity Emma if you two ever have a kid. You are forbidden to name it."

"We'll see."

"Do you want to hear the news?"

"F..." He glanced down at Lily in his lap. "Fudge yeah. Hit me."

Lily whacked him on the arm and laughed.

Dawg pulled the phone away from his ear. "Didn't mean you, lady bug."

Lily shrugged and gave him a big smile.

Putting the phone back to his ear, he said, "Go."

"Visitation was approved!" she shouted into the phone.

"What?" he asked in shock.

"Yes! Approved! And better yet, not supervised."

"What?"

"Yes!" Kiki yelled into the phone as if she couldn't believe it, either.

"So what does that mean?"

"It means you get to visit with your daughter. You'll get to know her. She'll get to know you. For a couple hours at first. Then, eventually, if everything goes well, she'll be able to stay overnight with you and Em. That's if Caitlin wants to. She's old enough to decide that for herself. And the judge wants her to be comfortable."

"What?"

"Dawg!"

"What?"

"Stop saying 'what!'"

"Holy... *fudge*."

"I know! This is freaking exciting!"

His hand went automatically to his heart. It was beating a mile a minute. "When?"

"A schedule will be made up. I'm getting together with a mediator and their attorney to sit down and work something out. Are you okay with that?"

"Hell yeah. Soon, though, right?"

"Yes. Very soon. Like within the week."

"So... she knows 'bout me now?"

"Yes."

"Was..." He hesitated. "Was she okay with it?"

Kiki got silent on the other end of the phone. A pain shot through Dawg's chest. His daughter didn't want to see him. Didn't want to meet her real father.

They fucking did all of this for nothing.

There was no way he'd force her to get to know him. He didn't want her to be miserable and hate him for the rest of her life.

No fucking way.

He never should've let Kiki start the process. It had been a big mistake.

"Dawg..."

"Yeah?"

"She does want to meet you. I think she's confused, maybe even a bit scared, which is only to be expected. But she's almost fifteen. She's old enough to process it. Lily took to you like a fish in water because that's how easy you are to love. Caitlin will be the same way. She'll meet you and love you, just like Lily. Like Emma."

Dawg pressed a hand to his eyes and dropped his head back, fighting back the burn in his eyes. "She ain't the only one scared," he murmured.

"It might be rough in the beginning. But, Dawg, it's going to be worth it. I'm not sure what they told her about why you were never in her life from the beginning. I'm not sure you should talk about that right away. Maybe down the road. You don't want to turn her against her mother, even though Regan was in the wrong."

Dawg nodded even though Kiki couldn't see it. As he processed what she was saying, he finally grunted, "Yeah. Got you."

"Good. Hanging up now so you can tell Emma the good news."

Dawg's gaze met his wife's across the kitchen. "Think she figured it out."

"Good. Give her my love."

"Take care of that kid. See you soon." The phone went dead in his hand and he placed it on the table.

"Am I going to meet my sister?" Lily asked, staring up at him with wide blue eyes.

"Yeah, lady bug. Eventually. Maybe not at first, 'kay?"

"But I want to play dolls with her."

Emma rushed over to them. "Lily, why don't you go take Oscar out back and throw the ball for him?"

Lily hopped off Dawg's lap and screamed for the dog that was only five feet away, asleep on the floor.

Emma frowned. "No need to scream. He's right there, Lily."

"I know but he was sleeping!"

"Well, he's not now," Emma answered with exasperation.

"That was the point," Lily told her mother with a huff.

Emma sighed as she watched Lily take the American Bulldog that they had adopted from the shelter a few weeks ago out the back door to the fenced yard.

Then she climbed into Dawg's lap, taking Lily's former spot. Dawg wrapped his arms around his ol' lady and she did the same, looping her arms around his neck.

"Good news," she murmured, pressing a kiss to his lips.

"Yeah."

"I know you're worried," she said, running soothing fingers through his beard.

"Yeah."

"Baby, it's going to be all right."

"Yeah."

Emma frowned. "Take it slow. Let her set the pace."

"Right."

"Dawson," Emma whispered.

He dropped his gaze to hers. "Yeah?"

"She's going to love you."

"Ain't nothin' like her mom and stepdad."

"Exactly. That's why she'll love you. You're one hundred percent genuine. She'll see that and appreciate it."

"Sure?"

"Fudge yeah," Emma answered with a smile.

"Love you, baby girl."

"Love you, too, *Dawg*."

He shook his head. "Just for that, need to give you one of D's 'lessons.'"

"Can't wait." She pressed her mouth to his ear. "Tonight after Lily goes to bed."

Dawg reached between them to adjust his now hard dick. "How soon's that?"

Emma laughed. "Since it's only breakfast time, hours from now."

"Fuck," he muttered. "Maybe she'll take a nap."

"She's almost eight. I doubt she'll want to take a nap."

"Fuck. Maybe one of the women will wanna watch her for a few hours."

Emma laughed. "A few hours? Since when do you need a few hours?"

"Damn, woman. That's harsh."

She pressed a kiss to his cheek and ran her hand through his beard again. "But true."

"Then we'll do it a few times."

"I'm okay with that," she whispered.

"Didn't know you had a choice," he said, keeping his face serious.

"Hmm. Bossy."

He lifted his left hand and wiggled his ring finger which now sported a titanium wedding band in front of her face. "Remember our vows 'bout you obeyin'?"

"I had my fingers crossed behind my back."

"Someone needs a spankin'," he announced quietly.

"Yes, someone does," she breathed, brushing a hand over his hard dick.

"Keep teasin' me an' gonna lock the back door an' take you right here on the table."

"You wouldn't do that."

"Try me."

With a laugh, Emma took his mouth and kissed him hard. He groaned and tangled his tongue with hers. He wouldn't ever get enough of this woman.

And once things were on the right track with Caitlin, he was going to talk with Em about them trying to have their own kid. One that was a piece of both of them.

After their breathing became ragged, and Dawg's dick couldn't get any harder, Emma broke the kiss and pressed her forehead against his, whispering "Everything's going to be all right, baby."

"Know it. Got you. Got Lily. Gonna get Caitlin."

"And we all have you. We're the lucky ones."

No. She had that wrong. No one was luckier than him.

No one.

———

D awg couldn't stop bouncing his leg. He tried. It was simply impossible. He sat at the table in the diner, waiting. He had been a half hour early, and he was ready to climb the fucking walls.

He was glad none of his brothers were there to witness what a basket case he was acting.

He thought about having this initial meeting under the pavilion in the courtyard at church. But Emma talked him out of it. She said it would be better to find a neutral location.

One where no one would be interrupting.

And he wasn't sure how he'd act if one of the hang-arounds or prospect even remotely eyeballed Caitlin. He'd hate to be hauled off for murder before he even got to know his teenaged daughter.

His heart stopped when the diner's front door opened and Hawk came through the door. Hawk was so fucking big he couldn't see if his daughter was behind him. But Hawk didn't approach the booth where Dawg sat, he stepped to the side instead and gave him a chin lift.

Dawg returned it and noticed a very pregnant Kiki leading Caitlin over to him.

When she reached the table, the club's attorney gave him a wink. He jumped to his feet and yanked on his cut to straighten it.

"Caitlin, this is your... father," Kiki introduced him in a gentle tone.

"Cait," his daughter said to Kiki. Then she faced Dawg. "I go by Cait."

"Hi, Cait," Dawg greeted, suddenly unable to see her clearly because something was in his eyes. But he knew she had his green eyes and dark blonde hair. And she was tall for an almost fifteen-year-old. She was a spitting image of him, though much prettier and way more feminine. He rubbed roughly at his eyes. Now was no time to break the fuck down.

"I look just like you," she stated with a curious tilt to her head.

His heart swelled. "Yeah."

"What's with the vest?" she asked, jerking her chin up and eyeballing his cut.

He liked how outgoing she was. Unafraid to ask questions. "Represents family," Dawg answered.

She nodded as if she understood. Even though he was sure she didn't. But she would. Eventually.

"We're going to go," Kiki said softly, with one hand to her huge belly. "Hawk and I will be waiting outside to take you back home when you're done, Cait. Okay? Whenever you're ready."

Caitlin nodded without looking at Kiki since she was too busy staring at Dawg. He shuffled his feet, wanting to ask her to sit down. But he froze when she asked, "What should I call you?"

He took a deep breath, then said, "My name's Dawg. But would love it if you called me Dad."

Turn the page to read the first chapter of Down & Dirty: Dex, book 8 of the Dirty Angels MC series

DOWN & DIRTY: DEX SNEAK PEEK

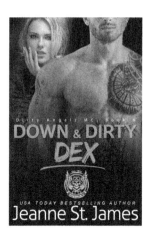

Turn the page for a sneak peek of the next book in the Down & Dirty: Dirty Angels MC series.

DOWN & DIRTY: DEX SNEAK PEEK

Chapter One

Dex had a fucking half chub. He grimaced because needed to adjust it, but if his sister caught him doing so, she would give him shit. He glanced over his shoulder through the large picture window into the pawn shop's office where Ivy sat working in front of a computer.

Fucking hell.

Then his neck twisted to once again stare at the woman who was wandering around Shadow Valley Pawn pretending to check out the items that were for sale.

She was faking it and he wanted to know why.

Maybe she was just trying to pass the time. Maybe she was sent here from that asshole rival MC, the Shadow Warriors, to case the joint to wreak future havoc.

They haven't heard from those outlaw nomads in a while, so it was about time for them to show their bastard faces.

But no matter why the woman was here, Dex couldn't ignore the fact that the woman was fucking dick-hardening hot.

Smoking hot.

Tall. Leggy. And tits that made his mouth water.

Fuck.

Now his half chub was a full-blown hard-on.

Fuck it. He reached down and yanked it to a more comfortable position. Fuck Ivy. She could bitch all she wanted.

Maybe she hadn't noticed.

Now that he wasn't hurting so much, he leaned back against the counter behind the glass display case and crossed his arms over his chest as he continued to check the "customer" out.

Her hair was like a strawberry blonde. He was pretty sure that's what chicks called it. Not as red as his sister Ivy's and not as light blonde as Emma's, Dawg's ol' lady. An in-between.

He could imagine the woman on her knees in front of him, his dick in her mouth, his fingers wrapped tightly in her hair and her head bobbing up and down.

Fuck yeah.

His dick twitched and his balls pulled tight as he wondered if the carpet matched the drapes.

He never wanted to lick a carpet as badly as he did that moment.

He needed to see her eye color. He wanted to imagine what those peepers would look like when she tipped them up towards him as he blew his load in her mouth.

He groaned. Then groaned again when she ran her fingers over a marble sculpture that reminded him of some ancient dildo.

Yeah, that's it.

When she circled the base of the sculpture with her fingers, a soft whimper escaped him before he could stop it.

Fuck. He was going commando today and his dick was making a mess in his jeans. He shifted. Then shifted again as the denim scraped the sensitive head.

He would have to go back into the storage area, lock himself in a closet and relieve the load in his balls.

He checked over his shoulder once more to make sure Ivy was

doing whatever she does. Her head was down and she was busy, typing away on the keyboard.

His gaze shot back to the *sex-on-a-stick* who was now running her thumb over the crown of the...

It was a fucking sculpture!

Why the fuck did Ace accept that pawn? No one in their right mind was going to pay a grand for a marble thing that looked too much like a dick.

Maybe this chick would. She seemed fascinated by it.

He pushed off the counter, adjusted himself one more time and strode over to where she stood fondling the...

"Hey," his voice cracked. He cleared his throat and dropped his voice an octave. "Hey, you need any help?"

She glanced up from running her finger up and down the smooth veiny marble and pinned him in place with...

He couldn't tell what color her eyes were. They were blue but not a typical blue. Like a greyish blue, sky blue, slate blue, whatever. He had no fucking clue since they seemed to keep changing the longer he stared at her.

"What are they?" he asked as if in a trance.

"What?" she asked softly.

"Your eyes. What color are they?"

She raised her brows and tilted her head to study his face. "Do you ask all of your customers that?"

Just the ones that make my dick hard. "Yeah, it's a requirement."

"Like a credit check?"

"Somethin' like that."

Her lips twitched and she shrugged. "They're blue."

Simple enough. Those blue eyes meet his and he pictured himself pumping his cum down her throat.

She jerked her head toward his now throbbing dick. "You always sport wood when you talk to your customers, too?"

Dex smiled, but kept his hand from creeping down to touch what she was looking at. "Depends who the customer is."

"You know that's sexual harassment, right?"

He frowned. "What is?"

"Undressing me with your eyes the moment I walked in the door, staring at my tits, standing this close to me with a hard-on."

"Well, maybe you shouldn't jerk off a marble dick."

Her gaze bounced to the sculpture and she removed her hand. "Is that what it is?"

"Dunno. Don't care. Just know I'd like to be in its place."

She clicked her tongue. "I guess you didn't hear what I just said."

"Nope." He grinned. "Haven't touched you yet. When I do, you can warn me again about my bad behavior."

"Or misbehavior."

Dex shrugged. "Just want to let you know, I like what I see."

"So the marble sculpture turned you on?" Her eyes crinkled at the corners.

"You touchin' it did."

"No filter, huh?"

"Whataya mean?"

"You just say whatever's in your head."

"Yep. Pretty much."

She laughed and shook her head.

Damn, that laugh didn't help the little problem in his jeans. Fuck that, his *big* problem.

"I guess you work here?"

"Yeah."

She jerked her chin at his cut. "Is that a uniform all the employees wear?"

"Some of us." At least Ace and Dex wore the Dirty Angels MC colors. Ivy didn't wear her ol' man's cut. And Ace had a couple part-timers who worked in the pawn shop, but they weren't a part of their club. "Ain't a uniform. It's a cut."

"I know what it is," she answered.

Dex pursed his lips and let his gaze from her from top to toe. Sexual harassment be damned. Did the Warriors send her in?

She wore jeans that hugged her thighs and hips, brown high-heeled boots that came to her knees, and a tight long sleeved-top that... *yeah*, emphasized her rack. A brown leather coat was tossed over her arm.

"Don't look like a biker chick," he murmured.

"What does a biker chick look like?"

Good fucking question.

The buzzer went off, indicating the front door to the shop had opened, and Ace stepped inside. His eyes immediately landed on them and Dex's uncle shook his head.

As he passed, he gave Dex a pointed look. Ace didn't like Dex flirting with the customers. He'd warned him time and time again not to turn into Pierce, the former DAMC president who was a total dick and liked to take advantage of women by...

Sexually harassing them.

Fuck.

He shuffled his feet, hoping Ace didn't spot his hard-on, and cleared his throat again. He was supposed to be helping customers and making sales.

"So... you wanna buy that... thing?" He cocked a brow toward the sculpture.

"For a thousand bucks? I could buy a Rabbit cheaper."

"What?"

"I said no."

That wasn't what she said. But he had no idea what a rabbit was, besides the kind that hopped. But maybe he should find out.

Later. When he was alone.

"So if you don't want it, what are you here for? What are you lookin' for?"

"My father."

The guy was handsome... sort of. In a bit of a rough biker way. But he wasn't bad. He didn't have a beer gut. Yet. And he didn't have a long beard. Yet. Unlike the older man that had just entered and walked through the pawn shop in worn jeans, heavy biker boots and wearing a similar cut as this one.

Brooke's gaze went over to where the man stood behind the counter. Could he be him? Her father?

"Who's your father?"

Her attention was drawn back to the man before her. Colorful tattoos spilled from his forearms, where his long-sleeved thermal shirt was pushed up past his elbows, down to his wrists. He sported a small gold hoop in one ear and a couple fingers were encircled by clunky brass-colored rings. A wide band of leather wrapped around his left wrist. So typical of a biker. "Trying to figure that out."

He had good teeth, though, and he looked clean. Well, except for his leather vest. The patches were dirty. But then it wasn't like he could throw his cut into the washing machine. A white rectangular patch over his right chest said "Secretary."

"Why would you come here, though? Gotta have a reason."

Brooke moved behind the biker to read the back of his cut. She reached out and brushed her fingers over the top rocker of his colors. "Because of that."

He twisted his head. "What?"

"What your patches say."

He spun around to face her. "Fuckin' speak English."

She shrugged. "Okay. Like I said, I'm looking for my father."

His dark brows furrowed. "And what does that have to do with the DAMC?"

"I pretty sure he's a member. Or was. At least when I was conceived. Not sure if he still is."

Brooke watched a look cross his face. It held a mixture of disbelief and surprise. Her gaze dropped to his name patch. *Dex.*

She wondered what that name meant. Surely all bikers had a nickname. "Dex."

"Yeah," he grunted then turned to yell across the shop to the older biker behind the counter. "Ace, you gotta 'nother kid you don't know about?"

The older biker's eyes widened, then narrowed as they landed on Brooke.

"What the fuck you talkin' 'bout?" this "Ace" grumbled as he rounded the long glass display counter and headed in their direction.

"A kid. Think you knocked up a bitch an' didn't know?"

Brooke sighed. She should take offense at this Dex calling her mother a bitch. Hell, she should take offense at the way he fucked her with his eyes.

Ace was pulling on his long salt and pepper beard as he approached and eyeballed her up and down. Almost as if he was trying to see if she looked familiar. She did look like her mother, at least before the cancer turned her into nothing but a shell.

Ace's voice was gruff and worn like his cut. "How old are you?"

Some women would also take offense at that question. But she was here for a specific reason, so it would be smart for her to answer. "Thirty."

Ace snorted and ran a hand over his brow as if he was wiping off sweat. "Ain't mine. Janice had me neutered after Diesel came outta her like a wreckin' ball."

Brooke should feel relieved that this biker wasn't her father. But she wasn't. Disappointment crept in before she could knock it away. Because that meant she had to keep looking.

"Also, haven't fucked anyone other than Janice since Hawk was conceived on the back of my sled. Knew right then it was true love." He shot her a wide grin and then leaned closer like he was about to tell her a secret. "Tight pussy over a Harley. Yeah. Nothin' better than that."

Dex whacked Ace on the arm. "True, brother. Maybe a good head job's a close second." Then his eyes landed on her lips.

Brooke tipped her head down to hide the roll of her eyes. She needed to keep them on the topic at hand.

"I'm sorry. I just know he's a biker and might own a business in Shadow Valley. I asked around town and there seems to be a few businesses owned by bikers. So I'm stopping at them all. This happened to be the first one on my list."

"Well, the only bikers working in this shop are me and Dex here. An' this boy might be a horny fucker but I doubt he knocked anyone up when he was two."

"Are you two related?"

"Uncle. An' club brothers," Ace stated and then tilted his head. "Sure your pop was an Angel?"

"Pretty sure."

"How come you're only lookin' for 'im now?"

"My mom passed away a couple months ago and when I was going through her things I found out my father wasn't really my father. Or at least he wasn't my biological father."

Ace regarded her for a long moment. "Gotta name?'

Brooke shook her head. "Nope. Just found some things hidden away in the attic. Some had to do with your MC. Newspaper clippings. Other stuff. All dated about the time I was born."

"You think she hung around the club thirty years ago?" Ace asked her.

Brooke shrugged. "I don't know. I'm not sure how involved she was with this biker. Might have been just a one-night stand since she *was* married when she got pregnant with me. Whatever happened, she never talked about it. Never told me the truth. I always just assumed my father was... my father. His name was even on my birth certificate."

Dex shifted next to her. "So why do you think he ain't your father?"

She regarded him for a moment. "I found it curious that I never looked like him. I never even looked like my brother or sister, either. I just didn't fit in." Though she looked like her mother, she looked nothing like her father while her younger siblings did. Brooke had always wondered about that, but never got a good answer. So she let it go. Until she began to wonder again as she cleaned her mother's house out and came across a few things that made her question who her real father was.

"Did you ask your pop?" Ace asked her, hands on his hips.

She shook her head. "No, he died when I was a teenager."

"Damn. Lost both your mom and pop. Sorry to hear that," Ace mumbled. "But still don't understand why you'd think your biological father was an Angel. Just a few mementos or whatever don't indicate shit. I've been a member of this club forever. Hell, I was born into it. My pop was a founding member. So I know everyone who's come an' gone an' has worn our colors. Had to be a brother who was around my age or older. Unless..."

"Unless?"

Ace shrugged his broad shoulders. "Unless it was a hang-around or a prospect who didn't pan out. Ain't too many members left from back then. Rocky and Doc's in prison. As for the rest, quit a few of 'em got taken out when shit began to get hot and heavy with the Shadow Warriors."

"Grizz," Dex mentioned.

"Who's Grizz?" Brooke asked.

"One of the oldest members," Dex answered. "At least not in prison," he added quickly. He glanced at Ace. "Could it be Grizz?"

"Fuck. Don't even say that out loud. Momma Bear would have his balls on a spit an' be servin' 'em up at The Iron Horse lickity split."

"Is The Iron Horse one of the club's businesses?" Brooke asked. She didn't remember if that one was on her list.

"Yeah," Dex answered.

"Who runs that?"

Ace snorted. "My son, Hawk. He definitely ain't your father, either."

"If it ain't Grizz, then who?" Dex asked. "One of the members the Warriors killed?"

Ace pulled at his beard slowly and frowned. "Could be."

"How 'bout Rocky?"

"Dunno, boy. He's old enough to be." Ace regarded Brooke. "Question is, if you find 'im, then what?"

That was a damn good question. She hadn't thought that far

ahead. She figured she needed to find out who he was and if he was still breathing, then...

Then depending who it was...

"If it ain't you an' it ain't Grizz. Might be Rocky."

"Could be anyone, Dex. An' she don't even got any solid proof. Not even a fuckin' name."

"Maybe she could talk to D. Maybe his crew can help 'er out."

Ace scowled at Dex. "For what?"

"To help her figure out who 'er pop is. What the fuck, Ace?"

"Why do you fuckin' care, boy? Why do you wanna bring more drama into this damn club? Ain't we got enough? You just wanna stick your dick in 'er an' think she'll give you a little grateful pussy if you help 'er. Keep your nose outta it. For all we know her pop could be the same as yours since that deadbeat took off, leaving your fuckin' mother with three little ones."

"Ace."

"No." He threw up his hands. "Don't be stickin' your dick in 'er 'til you know she ain't your sister. For fuck's sake! That's all we fuckin' need." He stalked away grumbling.

"Um," Brooke started, feeling heat crawl up her neck.

"Yeah," Dex muttered. He raked his fingers through his short dark hair. His dark brown eyes landed on her. "Sorry 'bout that. Kinda killed my fuckin' boner, too."

Brooke's gaze automatically dropped to where his hand landed and then she closed her eyes and cursed herself for doing just that. But Ace was right, they could be siblings. She shuddered as she thought back on how Dex was staring at her earlier.

A knuckle grazed her cheek and she opened her eyes. "Ace is wrong. You ain't my sister. My pop was no longer an Angel when your mom got knocked up. He got on his sled, took off and never came back."

"Are you sure?"

"Yeah, babe. 'Cause that woulda sucked."

"Why?"

"'Cause I'm gonna buy you a fuckin' beer."

"I don't drink beer."

"Whiskey, then."

"We could still have a whiskey together even if we were related."

"Yeah, but couldn't do the rest of the stuff I have planned."

Her eyebrows shot up her forehead. "Oh?"

"Oh, fuck yeah," he whispered.

"Dex!" Ace yelled across the shop. "Leave 'er alone an' get the fuck back to work. She needs to get gone."

Dex's lips twisted in a frown. "I'm guessin' you ain't from around here."

Brooke shook her head.

"Where you stayin'?"

"I..." Why the hell was she even going to answer his question? "Nowhere, yet."

"Need a place to crash?"

"Are you offering?" she asked in disbelief.

"Gotta room above church. Bed's too small. Was hopin' you had a motel room or somethin'."

Or somethin'.

"Church," she repeated. She knew that didn't mean what it should. She had done some research on MC's before hopping in her car and heading to Shadow Valley. But she couldn't remember what church meant in biker speak.

"Yeah. Was gonna move into the apartment upstairs, but D's a stubborn fuck an' thinks he'll be raisin' his kid up there. Jewelee's havin' a shit fit about it."

She shook her head, lost on who he was talking about.

"Don't matter. You end up being a part of the DAMC family, you'll meet 'em all eventually. This club's like a big dysfunctional family."

Her plan wasn't to join the MC. Her plan was to find her father. Ask some questions. Take care of business and go the hell home. She wasn't here to settle in with a bunch of bikers like they were long-lost family.

"How about if I just meet you somewhere?" She quickly added, "For that whiskey." She certainly wasn't meeting him for anything else. But she wouldn't mind getting together with him and asking more questions, maybe meeting more of the club members. Try to figure out who her father really was.

Or is.

And why she should even care. She hadn't figured that out yet.

She had loved the father who raised her, whether he was blood or not. But when she dug through that shoebox and found info in it to make her wonder who she really was, something had pulled at her.

Curiosity.

It wasn't like she needed a relationship with her biological father. But she just wanted to know who he was. She was thirty. She didn't need any type of "daddy."

And especially not the type that stood in front of her.

Wanting to buy her a whiskey.

Learn more about *Down & Dirty: Dex* here:
http://www.jeannestjames.com/down-dirty-dex

IN THE SHADOWS SECURITY SERIES

COMING SOON!

Want to read more about Diesel's "Shadows?"

Keep an eye out in 2019 for the spin-off series starring the hard-core former special ops crew of
In the Shadows Security:

Mercy
Brick
Walker
Steel
Hunter
Ryder

And learn how they earned their call names.
More information coming soon!
www.jeannestjames.com

IF YOU ENJOYED THIS BOOK

Thank you for reading Down & Dirty: Dawg. If you enjoyed Dawg and Emma's story, please consider leaving a review at your favorite retailer and/or Goodreads to let other readers know. Reviews are always appreciated and just a few words can help an independent author like me tremendously!

Want to read a sample of my work? Download a sampler book here: BookHip.com/MTQQKK

BEAR'S FAMILY TREE

BEAR Jamison
DAMC Founder
Murdered 1986

MITCH Jamison
Blue Avengers MC
b. 1967

ROCKY Jamison
DAMC
b. 1964

ZAK Jamison
DAMC (Former President)
b. 1985

AXEL Jamison
Blue Avengers MC
b.1987

JAYDE Jamison
b. 1993

JEWEL Jamison
b. 1989

DIAMOND Jamison
b. 1988

JAG Jamison
DAMC (Road Captain)
b. 1987

DOC'S FAMILY TREE

DOC Dougherty	ACE Dougherty	DIESEL Dougherty
DAMC Founder	DAMC (Treasurer)	DAMC (Enforcer)
b. 1943	b. 1963	b. 1985

DOC Dougherty
DAMC Founder
b. 1943

ACE Dougherty
DAMC (Treasurer)
b. 1963

DIESEL Dougherty
DAMC (Enforcer)
b. 1985

HAWK Dougherty
DAMC (Vice President)
b. 1987

DEX McBride
DAMC (Secretary)
b 1986

ALLIE McBride
b. 1968

IVY McBride
b. 1988

ISABELLA McBride
b. 1987

ANNIE Dougherty
b. 1971

Kelsea Dougherty
b. 1991

ALSO BY JEANNE ST. JAMES

Made Maleen: A Modern Twist on a Fairy Tale

Damaged

Rip Cord: The Complete Trilogy

Brothers in Blue Series:

(Can be read as standalones)

Brothers in Blue: Max

Brothers in Blue: Marc

Brothers in Blue: Matt

Teddy: A Brothers in Blue Novelette

The Dare Ménage Series:

(Can be read as standalones)

Double Dare

Daring Proposal

Dare to Be Three

A Daring Desire

Dare to Surrender

The Obsessed Novellas:

(All the novellas in this series are standalones)

Forever Him

Only Him

Needing Him

Loving Her

<u>Temping Him</u>

<u>Down & Dirty: Dirty Angels MC Series:</u>

(Can be read as standalones)

<u>Down & Dirty: Zak</u>

<u>Down & Dirty: Jag</u>

<u>Down & Dirty: Hawk</u>

<u>Down & Dirty: Diesel</u>

<u>Down & Dirty: Axel</u>

<u>Down & Dirty: Slade</u>

<u>Down & Dirty: Dawg</u>

<u>Down & Dirty: Dex</u>

<u>Down & Dirty: Linc</u>

<u>Down & Dirty: Crow</u>

You can find information on all of Jeanne's books here:

<u>http://www.jeannestjames.com/</u>

AUDIO BOOKS BY JEANNE ST. JAMES

The following books are available in audio!
Damaged
Down & Dirty: Zak (Dirty Angels MC, bk 1)
Forever Him (An Obsessed Novella)
Rip Cord: The Complete Trilogy

Coming soon:
Down & Dirty: Jag (Dirty Angels MC, bk 2)
Double Dare (The Dare Menage Series, bk 1)

ABOUT THE AUTHOR

JEANNE ST. JAMES is a USA Today bestselling erotic romance author who loves an alpha male (or two). She was only thirteen when she started writing and her first paid published piece was an erotic story in Playgirl magazine. Her first erotic romance novel, Banged Up, was published in 2009. She is happily owned by farting French bulldogs. She writes M/F, M/M, and M/M/F ménages.

Want to read a sample of her work? Download a sampler book here: BookHip.com/MTQQKK

To keep up with her busy release schedule check her website at www.jeannestjames.com or sign up for her newsletter: http://www.jeannestjames.com/newslettersignup

www.jeannestjames.com
jeanne@jeannestjames.com

Blog: http://jeannestjames.blogspot.com
Newsletter: http://www.jeannestjames.com/newslettersignup
Jeanne's Down & Dirty Book Crew:
https://www.facebook.com/groups/JeannesReviewCrew/

facebook.com/JeanneStJamesAuthor

twitter.com/JeanneStJames

amazon.com/author/jeannestjames

instagram.com/JeanneStJames

bookbub.com/authors/jeanne-st-james

goodreads.com/JeanneStJames

pinterest.com/JeanneStJames

Get a FREE Erotic Romance Sampler Book

This book contains the first chapter of a variety of my books. This will give you a taste of the type of books I write and if you enjoy the first chapter, I hope you'll be interested in reading the rest of the book.

Each book I list in the sampler will include the description of the book, the genre, and the first chapter, along with links to find out more. I hope you find a book you will enjoy curling up with!

Get it here: BookHip.com/MTQQKK

Made in the USA
Coppell, TX
03 August 2021